SEER OF STRANDS

SEER OF STRANDS

BOOK THREE OF THE TRIANID

ANNE MOLLOVA

ROSE LEAF PRESS

Seer of Strands

Published by Rose Leaf Press, LLC
502 W 7th St, Ste 100
Erie, PA 16502
anne@annemollova.com

ebook: 979-8-9857603-8-5; paperback: 979-8-9857603-7-8;
hardcover: 979-8-9857603-6-1

Printed and bound by IngramSpark.
Australia: Ingram Content Group AU Pty Ltd, Melbourne, Victoria. US:
Lightning Source LLC, La Vergne, Tennessee / Allentown, Pennsylvania /
Jackson, Tennessee, United States. UK: Lightning Source UK Ltd, Milton
Keynes, United Kingdom. Europe: Lightning Source UK Ltd, with facilities
in Germany, France, and Spain.

The authorized representative in the European Economic Area is Lightning
Source France, 1 Av. Johannes Gutenberg, 78310 Maurepas, France.
compliance@lightningsource.fr

This book was manufactured using paper and ink products in accordance
with commercial standards.

This is a work of fiction. Names, characters, events, and incidents are the
products of the author's imagination. Any resemblance to actual persons,
living or dead, or actual events is purely coincidental.

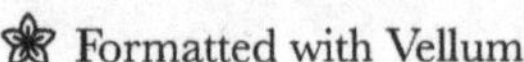 Formatted with Vellum

ALSO BY ANNE MOLLOVA

Keeper of Scales

Slayer of Monsters

DÚRAMAIR

Hammel⊙

SEARING PLAIN

MOOR of MOIN

ROYAL WOOD

Castle Dúr

Monstar Abbey

CRANN

SHEANEN

DRAGON TERRITORIES

⊙ Doclann

MOUNTAINS of GEAL

Tiragel ⊙

Dunmaer ⊙

BRANN DALA

Tirann ⊙

Norsan Oasis

Lunalar Oasis

SANDAMAR

EASTERN SEA

N
W   E
S

EASTERN KINGDOMS

LYNDROS

Maelstrom

Dragon's Head

THE ISLAND

Sea Serpent Territory

SEER OF STRANDS

I

THE WEAVING

For Lirianna, journeys always began with a sleepless night.

It had always been so, whether it was a trip to the seaside with her family, leaving home for Monstar Abbey, or traveling to Castle Dúr to prepare for war. And tonight was no exception. The midnight silence between the thick, stone walls of Monstar lay heavily upon Lirianna as she turned over to face the dark window. She'd blown out the candle what seemed like hours ago, but sleep was no closer than when the bell had tolled evening services at sunset. She sighed in defeat —it would be an exhausting ride tomorrow.

Suddenly she frowned, squinting into the blackness beyond her windowpane. A glow was coming from one window of the tower Lirianna could see from her room—the window belonging to the Seer's workroom.

Lirianna sat up, her eyes trained on the greenish glow. She was sure she hadn't left a lamp burning, and it was the wrong color for candlelight, anyway. Could Mother Brenwyn be awake at this hour? Perhaps … but the abbess hadn't woven in months, and besides, Lirianna had thought she had the only key.

She briefly entertained the idea of an intruder in her workroom, but that was unlikely. It would be hard enough to get to Monstar without being seen, let alone enter the abbey and its most highly secured room.

There was only one other possibility. One other person who'd gained entrance without her knowledge before.

Faer Dinnán.

Lirianna slid out of bed and pulled a shawl around her shoulders, feet burrowing into her slippers as her heartbeat quickened. Something told her it was best not to attract attention to her movements, so she took no candle but stole quietly into the shadowy corridor. She made her way carefully through the abbey, leaving the dormitories behind and winding through the passages and stairways that led to the weaving rooms.

She paused when she reached her workroom, wondering briefly if it had been foolish to come alone. What if she'd been mistaken, and it wasn't Faer Dinnán after all on the other side of the door? The looms in the weaving room stood in silent rows as Lirianna gripped the cold iron of the door handle. She took a breath and pushed.

The door didn't budge.

Lirianna let out her breath, a hint of relief easing the tension in her chest. The door was still locked. That had to be a good sign, right? The door was the only way in, so surely no human could have entered. It must be Faer Dinnán, unless it was some other supernatural being. Lirianna pushed the thought away with a shudder. It was hard to discount anything after the events of the past year, but it was also all too easy to let the mind run away with things.

Lirianna's fingers fumbled in her pocket until they closed around the key to the workroom door. She slid it into the lock and turned it, wincing at the *thunk* of the turning bolt in the silence. She swung open the door, hoping she didn't look as nervous as she felt, and stepped within.

Faer Dinnán stood by the windows, his face serious and serene, his glow of green and gold throwing a soft light over the room. "Seer of Strands," he said by way of greeting.

Lirianna exhaled, half relieved, half exasperated and pushed the door closed behind her. "You could have told me you wanted to meet," she said, turning to face the faerie king. "It's creepy just showing up in the middle of the night like this."

"My apologies," Faer Dinnán said. "I thought it best to keep our activities private."

Lirianna stepped forward into the moonlight spilling over the floor. "And what activities would those be?" She hoped her voice didn't sound too wary.

Faer Dinnán joined her in the center of the room, shadows shifting across his timeless face. "Do you recall the promise you made in the spring?"

Lirianna's stomach squirmed uncomfortably. *Promise* was a strong word, but she didn't want to start an argument until she had a better idea of what the faerie king had in mind. She chose her words carefully. "I agreed to help you fix things between Alyen and Aaron."

If Faer Dinnán took any offense at the implication that the trouble between the other two members of the Trianid had been caused by him, he didn't show it. Instead, he merely nodded. "Exactly. The time has come for us to act. I've come to ask you to play your part."

Lirianna's brow crinkled. "What … now?"

"You leave tomorrow for Tiragel, do you not?"

"Yes."

"Then it must be tonight. What I'm asking you to do cannot be done away from Monstar."

Lirianna narrowed her eyes. "What is it, exactly, that you want me to do?"

Faer Dinnán's voice was soft, alluring. "I wish you to do what you were born to do, Seer. I wish you to weave."

Lirianna felt a shiver pass through her and she tried to keep her voice steady. "How will looking into the future help? Do you want me to see if Alyen and Aaron reconcile? Search for the thing that will bring them back together?"

"Not exactly," said Faer Dinnán, his eyes boring into her own. "I wish you to ensure that the thing which will bring them back together comes to pass."

Lirianna stepped backward, her mind recoiling from the faerie king's words, the fear she'd carried since their last meeting realized. "You want me to tamper with Destiny," she breathed.

"Tamper?" Faer Dinnán asked mildly. "Or fulfill?"

Lirianna shook her head. "I can't. The Seer can only observe, never interfere. I'd be breaking our highest law. It would compromise the Trianid."

"The Trianid is already compromised," Faer Dinnán said. "And besides, what of your gift? You know there is unexplored magic within you, do you not?"

Lirianna looked away, her face troubled. When she gave no reply, Faer Dinnán spoke again, his voice soft but earnest.

"Your magic is a gift, Seer, and Béathan does not bestow her gifts at random. What if you are meant to use your light to restore that which darkness has torn apart?"

Lirianna hesitated. She knew she should reject the idea. She shouldn't even consider it. Faer Dinnán's words—logical as they may seem—were nothing more than faerie mind tricks. Tricks that had already caused enough trouble.

And yet …

She was tempted. As much as she hated to admit it and despite the guilt clawing at her stomach, she couldn't deny that deep inside, she yearned to reach for the magic she sensed running in her veins. Magic that could change things. Magic that could make a difference. Magic that made her feel powerful. Unique. *Whole.*

Lirianna's eyes drifted to her loom standing silently in the strange but beautiful mix of moon and faerie light. Once she'd looked on her weaving space with a sense of peace and purpose. Now the sight of it instilled uncertainty and confusion—perhaps even fear. But that was a change that had occurred in her. The loom was the same as it had always been: sturdy, simple, and even now … inviting.

Lirianna wet her lips and without moving her gaze away from her weaving said, "I don't know how to fix Alyen and Aaron. I wouldn't even know what to ask for. I don't really know how this—my—magic works."

"And does this make you happy? Are you content to leave a part of yourself in the shadows?" asked Faer Dinnán, his voice mildly curious, as if unaware of the impact his words would have. Perhaps he was.

Lirianna swallowed against the ache in her chest that rose to her throat. She walked over to her loom, her hand running across the frame's polished wood, the taut strings of the warp, the soft wool of the weft.

No. No, she was not content. Nor happy. And the guilt of it pulled at her heart with a weight like a stone.

Lirianna sat at the loom, her feet automatically finding their spots on the treadles. Faer Dinnán joined her, standing at the edge of the moonlight that illuminated her workspace. She fingered the shuttles of dyed wool, lined neatly on a table beside her, waiting to see which color her visions would dictate for her weaving.

"I can't promise anything," she said, her voice hoarse. "I can reach out for the strands of the Balance, and I can make my wishes known, but that's all. That's all I've ever done before."

"Then we shall hope that is enough," Faer Dinnán replied, a hint of eagerness in his voice.

Lirianna pressed down on a treadle, and the warp shifted to attention with a *clack*. She looked up at Faer Dinnán's shadowed face and whispered, "Are you sure this is the right thing to do?"

The faerie king's face was unreadable. "Would doing nothing be better?"

Lirianna shut her eyes, biting down on her lip, indecision making her feel that she was being torn apart from the inside out. Once more, she heard the faerie king's voice whisper in the darkness.

"Come now, Lirianna. Don't you want to know who you are?"

Lirianna drew one shuddering breath, knowing that if she

let herself think too much about what she knew she'd already decided to do, she'd lose her nerve. *Béathan help me,* she pleaded silently, then relaxed her gaze and opened her mind to the space beyond and the threads that wove together in the tapestry of the world.

Slowly, the workroom began to fade. Her hand reached automatically for a shuttle, her feet taking up the rhythm of the treadles while her other arm pulled the beater forward and back. As she settled into the predictable pattern of weaving, her surroundings faded ever faster until Monstar, Faer Dinnán, and the moonlight disappeared altogether, and she found herself in the misty realm of Destiny, staring ahead at the strands of the Balance that floated in the air like the many tentacles of some great sea creature floating adrift in an endless ocean of fate.

She paused to take a few breaths, comforted by the familiarity of the weaving and the timelessness the Balance always exuded. Then, feeling more grounded, she turned her thoughts to Alyen and Aaron.

Show me the Trianid. Show me my friends, the Keeper and the Slayer. Show me their present and their future together.

At once, one strand shimmered in the mist, floating closer as if in invitation. Lirianna's hand reached out and grasped it, even as the same hand reached for a new shuttle as she wove at Monstar, and the world suddenly reformed around her.

She saw Alyen, alone in the Keeper's cottage, sadness dripping from the rafters like rain. The vision shifted, and she saw Aaron, alone in the Southlands—perhaps Brann Dala by the looks of the canyons. His face was grim, his posture slumped in a way that made Lirianna's brow furrow with concern. Again the scene shifted and now the three of them were together, standing in the courtyard of Monstar. They all looked older, but instead of the joviality that had marked their previous gatherings, now they looked strained and tense, a chill sweeping over the courtyard like an icy wind. Lirianna watched as her future self tried to bridge the frosty gap between her fellow Trianid members, but succeeded only in increasing the awkward unease that permeated the vision. Aaron and Alyen barely acknowledged each other. No one smiled.

The vision shifted once more, and now Lirianna was watching herself, much older, with streaks of white mingling with the red of her hair. She was alone in her weaving room, fingering her hearing stone. Without knowing how, young Lirianna knew that the hearing stone was the only way older Lirianna had spoken with Alyen and Aaron in years. Loneliness, a grieving for the connection the Trianid used to share so naturally, was etched across her every feature. It was clear that the Trianid was not only strained—it had broken entirely.

Lirianna, unused to seeing herself in visions, felt her chest constrict. It was worse than she'd feared. It seemed that not only was the rift between Alyen and Aaron destined to remain, but that the Trianid itself wouldn't be able to weather the storm of their shattered bond.

What do I do now? she thought, her hands and feet still working over her loom. *What did I do before?*

Her mind raked through memories of the previous times her magic had unintentionally leaked into her weaving, searching for the common thread that had triggered an alteration of fate. The first time, she'd been worrying about Aaron and Alyen as she wove, wishing something would happen to assure Aaron that not all hope for his love was lost. And the second time—she shuddered to think of it again—she had been overcome with horror and grief over the destined death of her youngest brother, Seamus. She hadn't even been capable of coherent thought—she'd just hurled everything within her at the vision, willing it to change, to disappear, to never come to pass.

So perhaps that's it, then, Lirianna thought. *Some combination of strong emotion with a desire to change the inevitable?*

It seemed too simple; it felt somehow incomplete. The magic in her stirred as if eager to be used, yet she couldn't shake the thought that she was still missing something.

But she had no other ideas, and something told her she wouldn't be able to figure it out tonight. So she turned her focus back to the vision. Snippets of each scene kept flashing in succession before her gaze, and with each image of loneliness and ruin, Lirianna's unease grew. Rather than steadying herself, she allowed the discomfort to grow, larger and more desperate with each pass of her shuttle through the warp. Her face twisted as the agony of the Trianid's shared future spread through her and, when finally she felt close to losing all control, she gathered the roiling chaos within her and pushed it forcefully outward into the vision.

It was an inelegant attempt. The magic slammed out of her, colliding with the tapestry of the Balance, sending a shudder through the vision that suddenly shattered into pieces around her. Desperate to regain control and ensure the magic did what she'd intended for it to do, she sent her thoughts chasing after her magic, out into whatever remained of the crumbling vision world.

May these visions never come to pass! May Destiny bring Alyen and

Aaron together again. Let them find a way to heal and reunite. May their love be restored—and the Trianid as well.

A tremble passed through the vision world, a sudden, oppressive fog obscuring everything. Lirianna gasped as her eyes flew open, sweat running in rivulets down the sides of her face. Panting for air, she struggled to reorient herself to her surroundings: her workroom, the moonlight, her loom comfortingly solid before her. As her breathing slowed, her gaze trailed down to her weaving and her eyes grew wide as they took in the sight before her.

Her hands were resting still upon the woven cloth, shimmering with a radiance brighter than anything else in the room, brighter even than the moon hanging in the dark sky beyond her window. From her fingers, streams of blue and gold light flowed into her weaving, making its pattern glow with an unearthly gleam.

Lirianna's first instinct was to snatch her hands away from the weaving, but Faer Dinnán's voice stopped her. "Wait, Lirianna. Let your magic complete its work."

With some effort, Lirianna willed her hands to remain still. She watched in silence as the glow of her magic slowly faded, the last tendrils of light seeping into the threads of her weaving. When, finally, the last of the glow had evaporated, and the room was illuminated once more by moon and faerie light alone, Lirianna and Faer Dinnán both leaned forward to see the image Lirianna's weaving had produced.

It was a harp. Simple and elegant, against a background of black wool.

Lirianna's brow furrowed, her stomach twisting with anxiety. What did a harp have to do with anything she'd seen in her vision? Had she done it wrong? Perhaps she'd somehow projected her forthcoming journey to Tiragel into her magic, and the weaving was nothing more than a reflection of her anticipation of hearing the bards play while she was there.

But if her magic *had* worked in a way she hadn't intended … which parts of Destiny had she changed?

Lirianna looked up into Faer Dinnán's face, her face twisted with worry. "Why a harp?" she asked, her voice sounding small in the darkness.

The faerie king's eyes gleamed, but his words were few. "We shall have to see."

Lirianna sniffed, her gaze returning to her weaving. She pulled her hands away, fingers trembling, and clasped them tightly in her lap.

"Are you well, Seer?" Faer Dinnán's voice held a hint of concern.

Lirianna shook her head. "I'm not sure. I don't know if this was the most wonderful thing I've ever done … or the most terrible."

The faerie king studied her face for a moment before answering. "Can it be both?"

Lirianna looked up, incredulous, but was suddenly hit by a wave of exhaustion. Abandoning any thought of a retort, she rose shakily to her feet. "I'd like to return to my room now. Are we finished here?"

"Of course," Faer Dinnán said, surprising Lirianna by offering her a supporting arm as she crossed the room to the door. She sensed him hesitate as she reached for the handle and looked up to meet his gaze.

"Thank you, Lirianna," he said softly, sincerity written across his face. "I'm aware that this night was not easy for you. Truly, I owe you a debt of gratitude."

Lirianna smiled weakly, too tired to register the full implications of having the faerie king indebted to her. "I just hope it works."

"As do I. Rest well, Seer." Faer Dinnán's grip on her arm tightened for a moment, and Lirianna felt a warmth spread through her that both returned some of her strength and sent a wave of sleepiness throughout her body. She sighed in relief.

"Thank you. Good night."

She left the faerie king at the door and made her way back to her room, where she sank gratefully into her bed. She was asleep in moments, Faer Dinnán's magic granting her deep and dreamless slumber.

And throughout Dúramair, the threads of the Balance quivered with the shifting of Destiny.

2
QUIET

The Keeper's cottage was quiet.

The hallowed forest quiet of sheltering trees.

The blissful quiet of a simple life in a simple place.

The still quiet of solitude after too much time among too many others.

It was the kind of quiet Alyen craved after everything that had happened—the kind she'd surrendered to and often wished to remain in forever.

It had been three months, or thereabouts. Three months since she'd ridden south from Illya with Nah'dar and Brother Hugh at her side. They'd planned on riding straight to Castle Dúr, but the closer their destination loomed, the less at ease Alyen had felt.

It was instinct more than any real intention that made her insist on a detour to the Keeper's cottage the day before they were due to arrive at the castle, and once she entered the clearing with the stable, the gardens, and the small dwelling that was her own, she knew her part of the journey was over. Ignoring the objections of her companions, she'd written a lengthy letter, recounting the journey to Castle Illya and the events that had led to the healing of the darkling swarm. She was generous with details, as she knew her parents would wish, and took care to ensure she'd included everything that had transpired since her departure from Castle Dúr in the spring.

That is, *almost* everything.

She said nothing about the night she and Aaron had spent together in the Keeper's cottage. And when it came time to write of the morning after and the choice she'd made to have Aaron's memories altered by Faer Dinnán, she found she couldn't force her hand to write the words. So, she omitted it, pushing away the sensation that felt suspiciously like shame rising in her chest. Her parents were concerned only with how she'd rid the kingdom of darklings, after all. There was no need to muddy the waters with personal matters.

She'd sent her companions on to Castle Dúr with the letter, and once they'd vanished from sight through the trees, she'd sunk gratefully into the waiting arms of solitude.

Of course, she wasn't completely alone, even if she didn't count the elementals that were always with her. She made weekly trips to the market for food. It was only an hour's ride away, and the scenery along the path was pleasant. Occasionally, someone would show up at her cottage seeking relief from one ailment or another. It felt good to do her healing work in small, simple ways that lifted pain or discomfort, and Alyen welcomed the chance to use her magic in a way that would gain her trust rather than fear. Still, she always breathed a sigh of relief when her visitor had gone and she was left to the quiet once again.

She didn't know how long she planned to stay. Days turned into weeks and weeks to months as spring slid into the warm haze of summer. Much of Alyen's time was spent tending her gardens, gathering and drying herbs, taking stock of her inventory of medicines, and replenishing her stores as needed. Some days she simply walked through the woods, letting the stillness of the trees wash over her weary soul, emptying her mind of everything other than the forest and the elementals around her.

Eventually, she directed some of her efforts toward making the cottage feel like home. She began by giving the place a thorough cleaning—the first time she'd ever thoroughly cleaned anything herself in her life. She found the task surprisingly therapeutic, and by the time she'd finished and added a few of her own touches to the decor, she no longer felt like a guest in someone else's space.

More importantly, the Keeper's cottage became the place she lived—not just the place she and Aaron had had their best and worst days. The table became the place she ate and worked—not only the place they'd sipped tea together, knowing what the night would bring, or the scene of their argument and Alyen's subsequent betrayal. The bed, likewise, became the place she slept. A place she found peace and rest —not merely the place she'd spent one perfect night with Aaron before their world had crumbled. Gradually, as she filled the cottage day by day with her own life, the ache of what had been, and the emptiness of what now might never be, grew smaller.

Yet no matter how comfortable the cottage became, she

couldn't escape the memories entirely, and she found herself spending much of her time in the workroom. True, it was still the place she'd discovered the Keeper's book and learned of the darkling reversal she thought would doom Aaron, but at least Aaron himself had never been there. It was the closest thing to an escape she had.

The Keeper's book had been waiting for her, just as she'd left it. She spent hours poring over its ancient pages, sometimes late into the night. Besides being fascinating reading, Alyen was eager to learn all she could from the collected wisdom of past Keepers—particularly as her own training had been cut tragically short. When she discovered that the last few entries were written by Rowenna herself, Alyen read and re-read the words, fingering the pages fondly as if they could somehow bring her closer to the memory of her mentor.

She knew she should probably write her own entries. She should write about her melding magic and the new way she'd discovered to heal darklings. Just because no one had had melding magic before didn't mean no one would again. But she couldn't bring herself to write about it. Not yet. It was still too raw—all of it. So, she turned her mind away from her thoughts, back to the welcome quiet. And if some days she confused the quiet with loneliness, then she needed only to remember that quiet was easy. Quiet was healing. Quiet was safe.

It was yet another quiet, sunny morning, and Alyen was just clearing away the remnants of her breakfast, when she heard a familiar sound that made her breath draw sharply inward.

"Ooooooooooooh, the Keeper's cottage should be here,
A derry derry dally,
Unless it's somewhere else quite near,
Perhaps it's in the valley!"

Brother Hugh.

At first, Alyen's heart leapt joyfully at the prospect of seeing her friend again, but almost immediately it plummeted straight into her stomach, and her brows drew together in a frown. If Brother Hugh was here, she doubted it was simply for a social visit. He'd come to take her back. Back to the castle, back to the Trianid, back to life beyond her cottage and garden and herbs. And she didn't want to go.

Half-panicked, she thought absurdly of hiding somewhere until he left, but before she could take any kind of action, she heard Brother Hugh's triumphant crow from the clearing. Evidently, he'd found the cottage, and she'd have to speak with him.

Sighing, Alyen smoothed her skirts and approached the door, pausing to collect herself before opening it. She swung open the door, revealing the former monk already on her doorstep, one fist raised to knock. He gave a startled hop backward, then his eyes crinkled with delight and he flung his arms wide.

"Alyen, my dear! How absolutely splendid to see you. I knew I could find your cottage. Nah'dar had his doubts, but I assured him I have an excellent sense of direction. And here I am!"

"Brother Hugh," Alyen said with genuine if tentative fondness as she returned her friend's embrace. "It's good to see you. Please, come in."

Brother Hugh entered the cottage and peered around appreciatively. "Well, this really is lovely, isn't it? You've kept it up beautifully—much better than my old hermitage, if I do say so myself. My dear … it suits you."

He beamed at Alyen and her nerves settled somewhat under the glow of his approval. Perhaps he was just visiting, after all? She returned his smile.

"Can I offer you some tea, Brother Hugh? I have biscuits as well. They're a couple days old, but they should still be soft enough—"

"Oh no, thank you, my dear." Brother Hugh waved the biscuit basket away. "I'm here on castle business, after all, and we really should be leaving soon."

Alyen swallowed and set the biscuits back on the table, her stomach clenching. "What do you mean?"

Brother Hugh's gaze was sympathetic, though he couldn't quite hide the note of pride in his voice. "The king and queen have sent me with a delivery for you." He reached into his tunic and withdrew a letter, the sigil of Castle Dúr imprinted in the wax of the seal.

Wordlessly, Alyen took the letter, broke the seal with a trembling finger, and read.

Dearest Alyen,

We hope this letter finds you well and that your time in the Keeper's cottage has proved rejuvenating. After reading your report, we can only express pride and awe at what you accomplished at Illya. Truly, Dúramair owes you a great debt of gratitude. We hope that you will join us soon at Castle Dúr, at which time we will bestow upon you every honor, as is your right.

Before that happy time, however, there is one matter that must be addressed: the health of the Trianid. Detailed as your letter was, it would seem that your account is incomplete. Nothing you wrote explains why you and Aaron didn't travel back together, why neither of you returned to the castle, or why both of you have spent the last few months separated, avoiding your duties as Keeper and Slayer. We will not pry into your reasons—your personal life is yours to share or not as you wish, and certainly a respite was in order for you both. But as rulers of a people who have suffered greatly over the past year —people who need the Trianid now more than ever—we see that action is needed to restore the kingdom to Balance.

As king and queen of Dúramair, we must command you to travel to Brann Dala, where Aaron will be for the phoenix burning. You are tasked with restoring your relationship with him and returning the Trianid to its full capacity.

As your parents, we know it's not fair. You've already saved our kingdom twice, and we hope we never need to ask more of you. We are here for you in every way we can be, and our love goes with you. But our people need their Trianid. They need you.

Alyen shook her head, unshed tears burning behind her closed eyes. "I have already done enough for Dúramair," she whispered through clenched teeth.

Brother Hugh nodded at the bitter words. "Indeed, you have, my dear. But, as it's a royal order, perhaps we should be on our way?"

Alyen opened her eyes, incredulous. "What, this instant? Surely, they can't expect me to just pick up and leave today. I'm in the middle of … things."

"Oh?" Brother Hugh looked sincerely interested as he peered around the room. "What sort of things?"

"Well, you know. *Things,*" Alyen said, trying not to sound

flustered as she began pacing about, fidgeting aimlessly with teacups and the biscuit basket. "There's the garden that needs tending and medicines to make before winter."

Brother Hugh eyed the shelves, all stocked to bursting with jars of creams, salves, and herbs, but said nothing.

"And I've been cleaning out the cottage," Alyen added, her voice rising in pitch as she realized too late that the cottage looked inconveniently pristine.

Brother Hugh hummed in a noncommittal way as he watched Alyen pointlessly rearrange teas on their shelf.

"Besides," Alyen said around the growing tightness in her throat, "I'd have to plan and pack … There's lots to get in order, so I can't leave today even if—"

She was cut off as Brother Hugh stepped in front of her, taking her two hands in his and gently forcing her to stop her reorganizing. Slowly, she lifted her gaze to his, and the kindness shining from his blue eyes made tears spring suddenly into her own.

"I don't want to leave," she pleaded in a whisper.

Brother Hugh nodded. "I know. Leaving is hard. It always is."

Alyen shook her head. "But I'm not ready to go back. I don't think I can."

"Well, if you can't go back, my dear, then you must go forward. What you must not do is to become stuck where you are. Take it from someone who knows."

Alyen sniffed and looked back into the former monk's gentle face. "I don't know how."

Brother Hugh's mouth stretched in an understanding smile. "My dear, you once helped me out of my own cottage in the woods. Will you let me do the same for you?"

His eyebrows lifted in invitation, and at once, the tears Alyen hadn't been able to shed all summer came flooding out.

Brother Hugh's arms folded around her and held her as she wept. She wept for the battles. She wept for her mistakes. She wept for the weight of the world she'd borne on her shoulders not once but twice in as many years. She wept for the people she'd lost and the way life had been before. And she wept for Aaron, whom she'd lost in an entirely different way, but which was somehow even more devastating than when she'd thought him dead.

Throughout her weeping, Brother Hugh held her, patting her back and making consoling noises that Alyen couldn't really hear through her tears, but comforted her, anyway. When, at last, her sobs began to subside, he pulled back, produced a thankfully clean handkerchief from inside his tunic, and waited while Alyen mopped her face.

When she emerged, red and blotchy but somehow lighter than she'd felt in months, he smiled and said, "Now, then. Why don't you pack your bag while I make tea?"

One hour later, bag packed, cottage tidied, tea drunk and cleared, Alyen found herself closing the door to the Keeper's cottage. Her heart twisted as she led her horse, Lusa, out of the clearing and down the path. Suddenly she wanted nothing more than to turn back, shut herself in her workroom, and refuse to leave—royal command or not. But as they approached the edge of the wood, Alyen saw another figure standing at silent attention. Her heart caught in her throat as she recognized Nah'dar, waiting for his sanahara to emerge from the trees.

Alyen stopped in front of him and looked up into his stoic face. "Hello, Nah'dar."

Nah'dar remained motionless, and Alyen was momentarily confused by his air of formality and lack of greeting. Then he spoke, his voice soft, but firm.

"Alyen of Dúr. You are the firstborn heir to the throne of Dúramair. You are Keeper of Scales in the kingdom's Trianid. You are the savior of the faerie king and sanahara to the First Assassin of the Bahari. You have nobly fought many battles and achieved many victories. Alyen of Dúr. It will not do to make yourself small."

For a moment, Alyen looked into the dark sincerity of Nah'dar's eyes, then on sudden impulse, wrapped her arms around him in a tight embrace. She felt the warrior stiffen at her touch, then slowly relax as one hand came to rest between her shoulder blades. Alyen smiled into the black fabric of his clothing, then pulled back, her expression serious once more.

"Thank you," she said, looking at both her companions. "Thank you for coming for me."

Nah'dar said nothing, but Brother Hugh readily filled the silence with his chatter.

"Well, it's really quite a nice ride between your cottage and the castle, isn't it? A ride we should probably be starting if we're to keep to schedule, wouldn't you say?"

And without further ado, the three mounted their horses and set their sights toward the Moor of Moin.

3

THE HALL OF BARDS

Lirianna woke in her bed—her childhood bed—with Tiragel's sun streaming through her window. Never one to lounge after waking, this morning she allowed herself a moment before rising to soak in the warmth, the muffled farm sounds drifting in from outside, and the smell of bread wafting from the kitchen. Mother Brenwyn had been right to insist on the visit. Lirianna hadn't realized how much she'd craved the simple comforts of home.

She rose and dressed, noting that excitement was already tingling through her body. Feeling slightly abashed at having slept later than she ever would have before Monstar, she left the tiny room she'd once shared with her two older sisters to find her mother in the kitchen.

Lirianna's mother had the same red hair as Lirianna, pulled back and barely contained as always, but now with streaks of white running through it at the temples. This morning she was up to her elbows in flour, kneading what looked to be twenty loaves of bread with more already in the oven, but she still paused to give her daughter a warm smile and a peck on the cheek.

"I'm sorry. I didn't realize you had so much to do," Lirianna apologized. "I should have been up to help you."

"Oh, pish." Her mother dismissed the comment. "It's only bread for the Gathering feast and it's almost done. I've saved you breakfast. Did you sleep well?"

Lirianna grinned as she took up the offered plate of eggs and ham and settled at the table. "Very well, without Margit and Alys kicking me."

"Well, with both of them married off, the room is yours."

"What about the boys? Some of them could move into that room."

Her mother shrugged. "I think they like piling in together. Besides, Rob's been out of the house for at least five years now, and if I'm reading the signs right, Sean will be out soon with a new bride as well. That'll leave just the three youngest … My children are growing up too quickly." Her mother smiled, then turned her attention back to the bread. "You should eat and go on into town. We'll see you there tonight for the Gathering."

Lirianna shoved the last of her eggs in her mouth, belatedly realizing how quickly she'd eaten. "Are you sure? I'm happy to stay here and help. I can go in with you later."

"No, go and enjoy yourself," her mother insisted. "I'll be done shortly, and I know you'll want to see Master Oram and your friends before things get too busy. Besides," she came around the table, dusting her hands off on her apron, and wrapping her arms around Lirianna's shoulders, "after these last couple of years, no one deserves a day off more than you."

Lirianna let out a grateful sigh, savoring the warmth of her mother's closeness for a moment before she broke away and cleared her dishes. "You're right," she said over her shoulder. "It'll be good to see the school again, and Master Oram, and Tris … and Tom! I'll have to find Tom first."

"Oh, about Tom …" her mother said, a frown suddenly appearing on her face. "We didn't tell you with so much going on—"

"Mama!"

A boy no more than four raced into the kitchen, muddy hands outstretched to show his mother his latest discovery. Lirianna couldn't see what her youngest sibling was cradling in his hands, but it must have been alive because her mother shrieked and steered him briskly back toward the door, away from the table and the loaves of festival bread.

Lirianna's good mood faltered for a moment as she watched her mother wet a cloth in the well and scour Seamus's tiny hands, scolding him thoroughly for whatever he'd brought into the house. She hadn't told her mother about her weaving at Monstar—the one that had burned to ash and saved Seamus's life. Even now, as the memory rose in her mind, Lirianna felt the guilt and the fear of what she'd done rise with it. *But how could it have been wrong?* she thought, watching her brother grimace as their mother scrubbed dirt from his face. *Surely it's better that Seamus is here, alive, and my family saved from unbearable grief?* They were the same unanswerable questions that had haunted her for months and that Faer Dinnán's recent visit had only made worse. They were questions she'd come to Tiragel to escape.

Lirianna tore her gaze away with a shake of her head, determined to return to the levity of the morning. She ducked into her room to grab a shawl, banishing the thoughts to the back of her mind. Today was the Gathering. A day for music and celebration with people she loved. She wouldn't spend it brooding over things she didn't understand and could do nothing about.

"Goodbye, Mother. Goodbye, Seamus," she called as she crossed their yard, eager to be on her way. "I'll see you tonight."

"Have a wonderful day," her mother replied, sending her daughter off with a wave before returning to her son and her bread.

Lirianna strode briskly down the familiar road to town and breathed in the smell of summer grass in the warm Tiragel sun. She let a smile return to her lips as any remaining thoughts of broken Trianids, faerie kings, and morally questionable weavings evaporated with the last tendrils of morning mist. With the beauty of home surrounding her and the excitement of the Gathering ahead, she felt for the first time in a long time that—at least for today—nothing could possibly go wrong.

The Hall of Bards stood as it always had: a great stone room with vaulted ceilings designed specifically to let sound ring and linger in the air as it only could in the home of Dúramair's barding guild. Lirianna walked slowly down the center aisle, her footsteps echoing off the stone walls as her fingers trailed over the benches decorated with summer blooms in anticipation of the evening's festivities. She was surprised the hall was empty, given how many preparations must still be underway. But she was glad to have the space to herself, if only for a moment. Like so many things in her life, this space, once so familiar, still looked exactly as she remembered it—yet everything felt different.

"Lirianna," a soft but resonant voice intoned. "My protégée returns."

Lirianna spun around to find the source of the voice, and her eyes landed on her former teacher, Oram, Master of Harp and First Bard of the guild. With her heart in her throat, she crossed the room quickly to where he'd entered from his adjoining study. She grasped his hand in hers, taking in the familiar lines of his face and his milky gaze.

"Master Oram. How did you know it was me?"

The Master of Harp chuckled. "After how many years I listened to you coming and going from these walls?" He shook his head. "Those are footsteps I'll never forget."

Lirianna smiled and squeezed her former teacher's fingers. "It's good to be here again."

"And it's good to have you back."

The old bard lowered himself slowly onto a bench with a grunt. He propped up his staff and patted the seat next to him, which Lirianna took.

"The hall is beautiful," she commented. "It looks like everything's in order for tonight."

"Not at all," the master grinned. "Half the apprentices have been beside themselves with nerves for weeks, and three have already been to the healers this morning after losing their breakfasts. We shall see how they fare at the Gathering tonight

—few of them were blessed with your natural confidence for the stage."

Lirianna winced. "I'm sorry. I know you never approved of me leaving."

The master waved a hand. "Approved. It was never my place to approve or not. I admit, it was a blow to lose the harper I hoped would succeed me, but there will be other musicians. Not like you, of course." He chuckled again. "But others. No, in truth, I was only concerned about your happiness. How goes it with the weaving?"

"Well," Lirianna said almost too quickly, wishing the word didn't feel like a lie. She tried to ignore the way her stomach clenched with guilt and cleared her throat. "With Ylvain defeated and the storms gone, I think things will be peaceful for a while."

"Hmm." Master Oram nodded and said no more, but Lirianna couldn't help feeling that there was a hint of skepticism in the bard's expression. Her insides squirmed; despite the Master's lack of sight, she'd often felt that he could see straight through her—perhaps even better than Mother Brenwyn.

"It's true," the Master continued. "Ylvain and the storms have both passed, and yet ..."

"What is it?" Lirianna asked with a concern that mirrored the worry lines she suddenly noticed on her teacher's face.

Master Oram sighed. "Such times leave a mark. Our people's hearts are weary, their souls battered by things they could not foresee or control. It is the duty of the bards, as well you know, to tend to the soul of our kingdom in such times, yet ..." He shook his head. "I don't think we possess the music that Dúramair needs."

"What do you mean?"

The master shrugged. "In the past, when hard times fell upon Dúramair, we relied on the old ballads. Reminders of prophecies that would one day be fulfilled. Tales of courage and the promise of deliverance—usually by the Second Slayer. Now these things have all come to pass, yet our hearts are made weary by the events that were to be our salvation. We have no music for such a time. The old ballads don't work anymore, but we have nothing to take their place."

Lirianna's brow furrowed. "Is there no one to write new music? Surely some of the older bards ..."

Master Oram smiled, hearing the distress in Lirianna's voice, and patted her hand. "The old bards are trained in old traditions, but that will be a problem for me to figure out. It needn't worry you. You've already done your part in the saving of Dúramair. You may leave the repertoire crisis to me."

Lirianna sighed inwardly, trying to ignore the second stab of guilt that twisted in her chest. She'd loved writing songs at one time ... but she'd left that behind. The master was right. It wasn't for her to fix—but his words still rested heavy in her heart.

"You must be looking forward to the Gathering, though," she ventured, hoping to lighten her teacher's mood. "Every bard in Dúramair is here to perform. And I'm sure you've prepared a spectacular evening."

Master Oram's eyes crinkled. "Well, the Gathering happens only once every decade. One must go 'all out' as it were." One of his eyebrows quirked upward. "Of course, I would be happier if my best student were also performing tonight. But I suppose your duties haven't left you time for harping …?"

"They have!" The words burst out before she'd had time to think them over, and Master Oram's eyebrow rose higher. Lirianna flushed. "I mean, not as much as before. But I've tried to keep up my skills when I can."

Master Oram reached over and took Lirianna's hand. "Play something for us tonight, Lirianna."

Lirianna's chest ached at the words, but she shook her head. "No, really. I shouldn't. I haven't practiced nearly enough. Not for the Gathering. And I'm not a bard—nor even a student."

"I'm aware," the master said, his tone dry, then soft once more. "Will you do it for me? As a favor to an old man who once loved to hear you play?"

Lirianna swallowed against the lump that rose in her throat. "I …"

The Master of Harp leaned closer. "I might insist," he whispered.

This made Lirianna smile, and the master's chuckle joined her own. "All right," she agreed. "I'll play something. But only one song. And I'll have to borrow a harp."

"You may use mine," Master Oram said, patting her hand as he released it, and Lirianna's breath hitched at the honor. "It's in my study. You may practice as much as you like."

The master took up his staff and pulled himself laboriously to his feet. "Now, I must see to the apprentices. I'm sure a number of them have fainted over the last hour. I shall see you tonight."

Lirianna watched as her former teacher shuffled toward

the door, a sudden thought springing to her mind. "Master? Will Tom be playing tonight?"

Master Oram paused, then turned slowly to face her, a line etched between his brows. "Tom? Didn't you know? Tom is no longer an apprentice here."

The words left Lirianna stunned. "What? Why not? What happened?"

The old man shrugged, his face unreadable. "No one knows. One day he was here, the next he was gone."

"When—when did this happen?"

The master paused before answering, his voice soft. "Not long after you left."

The words settled in the air, and Lirianna could think of no response. Her heart felt as though someone were dragging it down into her stomach—a sensation she didn't know how to untangle or interpret.

Without another word, Master Oram turned back to the door, the tapping of his staff on the stone floor echoing pristinely through the vaulted hall.

4
THE GATHERING

Though Master Oram's news of Tom's disappearance left her unsettled, Lirianna had little time to dwell on it. Not if she was going to perform that night and for the Gathering, no less. All the best bards in Dúramair would be there, not to mention the entire barding school and all of Tiragel to boot. And she hadn't performed in years.

But she knew that the quiver in her stomach wasn't so much nerves as excitement. She'd left barding willingly, sure of her decision to take up the Seer's mantle, and hadn't once regretted it. She still had her harp, after all, and she often played for herself at Monstar. But she hadn't realized how much she'd missed performing. Now, the prospect of playing once more in the Hall of Bards had her insides jumping with eager anticipation, her mind swirling through ballads, airs, and dances, trying to decide which would be the best to play for the occasion.

She wanted it to be good.

She wanted everyone to remember that she had been good.

Just for tonight, she wanted everyone to know that she could have been a bard.

Lirianna spent most of the day in Master Oram's study, her fingers dancing over the strings of his beautiful harp. Allowing her to play for the Gathering was a privilege in itself —letting her do it on his own harp was the deepest of honors. She needed to make sure her performance didn't disappoint, so she immersed herself completely in her music as she hadn't done since leaving for Monstar, barely noticing how the hours slipped away.

Eventually, though, her stomach began to protest too loudly to ignore. Lirianna glanced out the window, surprised to see that the sun hung lower in the sky than she'd realized. She should rest, she thought. Rest and eat. It wouldn't do to over-practice and spoil her performance with exhaustion.

She rose from the chair, flexing her limbs, stiff from sitting so long. She left the study quietly and glanced around the hall. It was still empty, so it couldn't be that late, but the sounds of talking, laughter, and instruments being tuned were coming from outside. It must be nearly time for the feast.

The courtyard in front of the hall had been transformed in the time Lirianna had been in the master's study. Long tables covered with cloths dyed in the barding guild's colors of purple and copper sat in rows with summer blooms scattered down their centers. To one side, more tables groaned under the weight of the feast—enough to feed the several hundred people who had come for the Gathering, not to mention the locals. Lirianna smiled as she looked to the other end of the courtyard, where a group of the school's youngest apprentices

—children not older than six or seven—were preparing to play for the feasters. They clutched their tiny instruments, looking both excited and nervous at the prospect of playing for such a momentous occasion.

People were starting to gather, and Lirianna descended the steps to the courtyard, scanning the growing crowd for familiar faces. After exchanging polite greetings with several people she knew from Tiragel, her eyes landed on one of the apprentice bards she'd most hoped to see.

"Tris!"

The face of Lirianna's childhood friend split into a smile, and she squealed in delight as Lirianna ran up and clasped her tightly.

"You came!" Tris exclaimed. "I wondered if you would, but I didn't know if I should expect you. When did you get here?"

"Just yesterday, or I would have come to see you sooner. It's so good to see you, Tris!"

Her friend punched her playfully on the arm. "I've missed you. You need to come back more often. It's not the same without you."

"So I hear," Lirianna said, the frown line reappearing on her forehead. "What happened to Tom? I just found out that he left."

Tris shrugged, her face more serious. "No one really knows. A few weeks after you left, he just disappeared. Sends his mother letters every few months, so we know he's all right somewhere, but no one's sure exactly where he is or what he's doing."

"And no one knows why he left?"

Tris shook her head. "He never said. Not to me, at least. I

know we three were close, but things just weren't the same after you left."

Lirianna frowned, her face troubled. "People keep saying that. It's like they're saying it's my fault."

"Of course it's not your fault," Tris scoffed. "You certainly can't be held responsible for Tom's choices." But Lirianna couldn't help noticing that her friend didn't quite meet her eyes as she said it. She decided to change the subject.

"I want to hear everything. All the news from the school, everything about all the apprentices … Have you eaten?"

Tris shook her head, so they made their way to the tables of food, Lirianna allowing her friend's chatter to distract her mind from both thoughts of Tom and her impending performance.

A joyful hour passed, the courtyard filled with the sounds of clinking glasses, happy voices, and the music-making of young musicians. As the feast progressed, the sun slowly sank in the sky, and once the light sent slanting stripes of orange light and shadow across the tables, the tone of the voices changed to a buzz of anticipation.

The time for the Gathering had come.

What food was left was cleared away quickly. Plates and platters and glasses were deposited into barrels for later washing, and people started moving toward the Hall of Bards.

"We'd better go in and find seats before they're all gone," Lirianna remarked, draining the last of her cup.

"You go ahead," said Tris. "They have seats reserved for performers near the front. See if you can find us two together, and I'll clear our plates."

Lirianna nodded her thanks and joined the trickle of

people heading for the doors. She had just reached the top of the steps when she heard it.

"Lirianna?"

Lirianna spun around at the sound of the familiar voice. She froze.

It was Tom.

The first thought that crossed her mind was that his hair was longer. Perhaps an absurd thing to settle on after not seeing him for at least two years—but then she realized it wasn't just the hair. His skin was sun-bronzed in a way it never had been before, and he looked older, taller, with limbs now defined by ropey muscles that certainly didn't belong to a bard's apprentice. But it was his face that gave Lirianna pause. His gray eyes still rested beneath brows that rose in greeting. But there was no hint of the open smile she remembered. Instead, there was something guarded, something distant in his expression that she'd never seen on her friend's features.

"Tom," she breathed.

Tom jogged up the stairs to join her at the hall entrance, his gait also different than she remembered, his steps strangely rolling. They faced each other in distinctly uncomfortable silence. It was odd standing across from someone she'd once talked and laughed with so easily, yet who, for no good reason, now seemed like a stranger. Tom seemed to share the sentiment, one hand reaching up to scratch the back of his head as he stood before her, both at a loss for words.

"Um ... how are you?" he finally asked.

"I'm well," Lirianna replied, her words stilted as she struggled to gain her bearings. "How—where have you been? Master Oram said you left."

Tom nodded, not quite meeting her gaze. "Just here and there. Traveling mostly."

"But you loved music. You were going to be a bard."

"Yes, well … I guess life took us both on a different route."

An awkward pause ensued, and Tom cleared his throat. "You're looking well, though. Abbey life must suit you, then?"

There was an edge to his voice Lirianna didn't know how to interpret, so she made a noncommittal noise. "It's nice to be back. It feels good to be a harper again, even if it's just for the day."

A look of wary confusion flickered over Tom's features. "Wait, are you—you're not playing tonight, are you? For the Gathering?"

Lirianna shrugged one shoulder, unable to keep the corners of her mouth from twitching upward. "Just one piece. Master Oram asked if I would. Insisted really. You know how he can be."

"Aha," Tom said in a distracted manner. "Do you know what you're playing?"

Lirianna nodded and leaned forward, grinning. "I was thinking I'd play 'The Lady's Lace.'"

At once Tom drew back, a frown line appearing between his brows. "'The Lady's Lace?' Are you sure that's wise?"

"Why wouldn't it be?" Lirianna asked, taken aback at her friend's reaction.

"Well … It's a really difficult piece, and you've been away for a long time. You should go easy on yourself. Pick something simpler—one of the airs, maybe?"

Lirianna bristled. "Twelve-year-olds play the airs, Tom, and it's not as if I can't play anymore. I've kept it up at Monstar."

Tom's voice was suddenly agitated. "Right, well, good luck then. I'll see you inside."

Looking distinctly perturbed, Tom turned and retreated down the steps, leaving Lirianna unsure whether she felt insulted, confused, or just terribly sad.

"Was that Tom?" It was Tris, watching Tom's back as she joined Lirianna on the steps.

Lirianna nodded, at a loss for words that would capture the strange way their friend seemed to have changed.

Tris huffed. "Well, that's lovely. Shows up after disappearing for two years and doesn't even say hello to me. What did he say?"

"Nothing. Only that he didn't like my choice of repertoire for tonight."

Tris snorted and waved a dismissive hand. "Don't listen to him. What does he know? You're going to sound amazing. Let's go find seats." With that, Tris linked her arm with Lirianna's and steered her away from the entrance into the Hall of Bards.

The hall filled quickly, and there was an excited note to the chatter as people milled around, finding seats and shouting greetings across the room. Despite the size of the hall, soon all the seats were taken, and the latecomers had no choice but to find a place to stand or crouch against the wall.

Lirianna and Tris found seats near the front, close to the place where all the bards and their apprentices sat with their instruments. She felt a thrill looking down the line of musicians. Many she recognized from the last Gathering ten years before, and all the very best bards in Dúramair were present. The bards looked relaxed and eager, talking congenially among themselves; the apprentices, on the other hand, looked nervous, many of them fidgeting or running their fingers over their instruments, attempting to sneak in one more silent rehearsal before their moment of truth arrived.

Lirianna felt a sudden quiver of her own nerves. If she was honest, Tom wasn't wrong. It had been a long time since she'd performed, and even though she'd kept her musical abilities up as she'd said, performing was an entirely different skill that she'd had little chance to practice since leaving the school.

She pushed the thoughts firmly out of her mind, knowing that doubt would compromise her more than any lack of performing could. She drew in a few deep, calming breaths and resolved not to think about Tom anymore, not until the concert was over. This was her night to be a musician, a harper, a bard, and she wouldn't let anyone distract her from it.

The crowd settled rapidly, yet it seemed an eternity. Lirianna had no idea when Master Oram would call her to play, but her limbs were starting to tingle with nerves, and she wished the concert would start. All around the hall, candles and sconces were lit until the entire room was bathed in a golden glow. At last, Master Oram rose and walked to the center of the stage where his harp stood ready. The audience hushed immediately.

"Good evening, friends, musicians, bards, and apprentices. Welcome to the sixty-seventh Gathering of our guild in celebration of our craft and our service to the people of Dúramair. Whether it is your first Gathering or your tenth, whether you are performing or listening, I wish you all an evening of inspiration, of beauty, and of transformation as you enjoy the best that the barding guild has to offer."

Without further comment, Master Oram sat at his harp and began to play.

The concert was, indeed, magnificent. Master Oram played one of Dúramair's oldest and most beloved ballads that had half the audience dabbing at their eyes before he had finished. He was followed by the apprentices, all of whom managed to survive their performances with only minor mishaps. Tris sang well, accompanied by a few of the other apprentices in their year, and Lirianna joined in with the applause as her friend returned to her seat.

Tris had been the last of the apprentices, and Lirianna readied herself, certain that Master Oram would call her to the stage next, before the bards of the guild performed. But to her surprise, it was Beran, Bard of Doclann, that Master Oram announced, and Lirianna's stomach twisted with a mix of confusion, nerves, and disappointment.

Tris glanced at Lirianna as they applauded Beran's entrance to the stage. "When is he going to call you?" she hissed. Lirianna could only shrug. Perhaps Master Oram had forgotten her?

It certainly seemed as though that were the case as the evening progressed, each bard rising to perform after another. The music was spellbinding, and Lirianna found herself wishing more than once that she was better able to enjoy it without having to battle the jitters in her stomach and limbs.

When the last bard had performed and it seemed there was no one left, Master Oram rose once more to address the crowd in the hall. The sun had set long ago; everyone sat in the glow of firelight while nothing but darkness could be seen from the windows.

"My friends," began Master Oram. "We have been blessed tonight by the music that has filled these walls, and by your presence here, sharing it with us. Each of our bards and apprentices has performed beautifully, reminding us of our history, our traditions, and the art that connects our past to our future." As he spoke the word *future*, Master Oram turned toward the performers' seats. Lirianna suddenly felt as if the master's sightless eyes were looking straight at her. Her breath hitched, and Tris squeezed her hand.

"We are further blessed this evening," continued Master Oram, "by the presence of one of our former apprentices who studied with me as a harper for several years. Many of you will remember her, though if you haven't been back since the last Gathering, you will have seen her only as a small child. In my many years of teaching, I have rarely seen a student with such talent and finesse. It was my hope that she would one day lead this guild, but Destiny had other plans, and she was called instead to serve in Dúramair's Trianid. Nevertheless, she remains a gifted musician, and we are honored to hear her perform for us once more tonight. My friends, for the final performance of our sixty-seventh Gathering, I welcome to our stage Dúramair's Seer of Strands, Lirianna of Tiragel."

Lirianna's face burned as applause broke out, mixed with murmurs of recognition and interest. She rose, barely registering Tris's call of "good luck," and walked up the steps to the stage in a state of half-shock. Closing the Gathering was a slot usually reserved for one of the most revered and experienced bards. She'd never dreamed Master Oram would give it to her.

Master Oram took her hands and drew her close to

whisper in her ear, "Breathe deeply, find your heart, and you will enchant us all."

Lirianna smiled and closed her eyes momentarily. It was what he'd always said to her before she played, and the familiar words seemed to settle her as if they held magic themselves. She squeezed the master's hands in reply, and the old bard returned to his seat as the applause died away.

Lirianna crossed over to Master Oram's harp and settled onto the stool behind it. She took her time as she'd been taught, adjusting her garments and her posture, breathing deeply as she drew the instrument back against her shoulder. She rested her fingers against the strings, sinking into the silence that waited to be filled. In the stillness, she found the drum of her heart beating in rhythm with the flow of her breath. Then, when the silence and the stillness could wait no longer, her fingers began to move.

Lirianna forgot about the hall, the bards, the people watching. She forgot about Tom and Master Oram, and the creeping regret she hadn't expected to feel as she'd tasted once more the life she'd left. She forgot about Aaron and Alyen, the Trianid, her weaving, and the confused tangle of morals in which Faer Dinnán and her magic seemed to have ensnared her. Her fingers danced over the strings with ease despite the difficulty of the tune she'd chosen. With a lurch of joy, she realized that she'd found the place that all bards sought when they performed, but few could truly reach, and even fewer with any regularity. A place of complete focus and peace, where a bard no longer played, but simply partook in the music that was happening through them, effortless and whole.

Little by little, the hall seemed to fade away around her. She let herself sink even deeper into the sacred space, feeling almost as she did when she wove: dreamlike, but vibrant and completely present in the creation of the moment. She was blissfully and wholly alone, yet some part of her still felt the presence of those watching and knew that her music was connecting them to her, bringing delight, peace, and perhaps healing the secret parts of them all.

'The Lady's Lace' had been the right pick. Lirianna could feel it as her mind slowly returned to her surroundings, preparing for the end of her performance. When her fingers struck the final notes, silence spread around her once more, this time laced with a stunned awe. Then, the hall erupted with noise.

Joy and relief flooded Lirianna's body. She had performed well, and she knew it. Realizing her eyes were closed, she opened them, her gaze falling on her fingers that still hovered near the strings of the harp on her shoulder. Shock, followed by fear, hit her like a blow, her mind slamming fully into the present.

Her fingertips were glowing.

It was faint, but unmistakable. The same glow that happened when she wove with the magic that changed things. Instinctively, she snatched her hands away from the harp, balling her fingers into fists to hide the shimmer. It was only then, wondering if anyone else had noticed, that she realized how thunderous was the applause ringing in the hall. Lirianna swallowed, still not quite grounded in reality, and let the master's harp tilt away from her shoulder. As she guided the instrument down gently, she glanced once more at her fingers, hidden from the audience by the soundbox, and breathed a sigh of relief. The glowing was gone.

Lirianna stood to acknowledge the applause that showed

no signs of waning, a smile pulling at her mouth despite her moment of alarm. Placing one hand over her heart, she bowed her head, savoring this one night of living the life she could have had, the one she'd left without realizing how much she would miss it. As her head lifted, Lirianna's eyes scanned the assembly and landed on one face—the only face that didn't seem to have enjoyed her performance.

Tom stood in the back of the hall, arms crossed over his chest, his face a dark scowl. For a fleeting moment, Lirianna felt a stab of hurt and anger, but looked away before it could show on her face. She had no idea what had happened to her apparently *former* friend, but if that's how he felt, she'd leave him to it. Clearly she'd played well—the reaction of the crowd proved as much. And if he was going to be sour about it, she wasn't going to let it spoil her night.

"You were brilliant," Tris spoke in her ear as Lirianna rejoined her friend at the bottom of the stage. She barely had time to reply before several of the other apprentices from her year descended on her, followed by the bards, and what seemed to be half of Tiragel. For more than an hour, Lirianna stood in the hall, speaking with everyone, clasping hands, smiling at compliments, and exchanging bits of news or memories until her voice was hoarse.

At long last, the hall had mostly emptied, and the only people left were Tris, Master Oram, and her parents.

"You were wonderful, my dear," her mother said with an embrace that Lirianna returned, grateful to be among those who wouldn't mind seeing how tired she suddenly felt.

"Indeed," said Master Oram, a quiet smile resting on his features. "That was a performance to be remembered.

Though I do think you may have frightened away anyone else from attempting 'The Lady's Lace' for a long time to come."

Lirianna smiled. "My apologies, in that case. And thank you for lending me your instrument. It was an honor to play it."

"It was you who honored us, Lirianna," Master Oram said, patting her arm. "And now it is late, and I must take my old bones to bed."

"Bed sounds wonderful," Lirianna said with feeling.

"Oh, why don't you come stay in my room for the night?" Tris suggested, a plea in her voice. "It'll be just like old times, and you won't have to travel all the way back home tonight."

Lirianna looked to her parents. "You may as well," her father said. "The rest of us are sleeping at your aunt's, and it'll be crowded. I'm sure she won't mind if you stay here."

Final goodnights were said, Lirianna's parents left, and Master Oram made his way out, his wooden staff clicking on the stone floor as he followed his familiar path to his rooms.

At last, only Lirianna and Tris were left.

"Come on," Tris said, linking her arm in Lirianna's. "We can get an extra blanket and some pillows before—"

"Lirianna?"

The girls turned to see Tom hovering near one of the side entrances to the hall.

"Tom," Lirianna said, unsure if she wanted her tone to sound happy or cold.

Tom nodded in Tris's direction. "Tris, it's good to see you. You sang well."

Tris gave a snort, apparently still put off that he hadn't greeted her earlier.

Tom looked back at Lirianna, a strange look in his eyes that she didn't know how to interpret. "Lirianna, can I see you outside for a minute?"

"Now?" Lirianna asked. "We were just on our way to bed …"

"I know. You must be tired. Both of you," he said, acknowledging Tris once more. "But it won't take long. There's just … there's something I really need to say to you. Alone." He managed to look apologetic.

Lirianna looked to Tris and her friend rolled her eyes. "All right. I'll get the blankets and meet you back at my room."

"Thanks, Tris," Lirianna said. "I'll be there soon."

Lirianna and Tom watched their friend leave, the silence awkward. When Tris had gone, not bothering to say good-night to Tom, Lirianna turned back to her friend, her mind a mix of curiosity, confusion, and an angry hurt.

Tom seemed agitated again. "Let's … let's go out here. Get some fresh air." He gestured to the doorway behind him.

Lirianna shrugged and followed him out. She'd made the gesture seem casual, but she knew where he was taking her, and the thought sent a thrill down her spine. The doorway led to a small corridor that ran around the back of the stage, leading to another door to the outside right where the center of the stage would be. It was a doorway often used in performances so musicians and actors could access the stage without having to walk through the audience, but the area was seldom occupied when the hall was empty, and it was secluded from the rest of the school.

Lirianna's breath hitched as memories rose in her mind. This wasn't the first time she'd followed Tom out these doors. Was Tom remembering the same thing?

Stepping through the exit, Lirianna inhaled deeply. The cool night air was welcome after the heat inside from so many people and hundreds of candles. It must have been near midnight, perhaps even later, the darkness deep enough to make the spray of stars stretching across the sky look like diamonds in the moonlight. Tom stopped and turned to face her, the look on his face making her heart twist. She still couldn't figure out what was going on with him, and for some reason, she felt apprehensive about what he was about to say. She decided to set a light tone before he could start.

"So," she said, raising one eyebrow in what she hoped was a playful manner. "Still think 'The Lady's Lace' was a bad choice?"

Tom shook his head, and Lirianna frowned inwardly. Why did he look so sad?

"No," he said. "It was the perfect pick. Your playing—it was ..." He shook his head again, looking down at his feet. Even through the lingering joy of her performance, Lirianna could sense that something was wrong.

"Tom? What is it?"

Tom looked up at her, his face blank, but his eyes miserable. "It was perfect," he said. Then added softly, "I wish it hadn't been so perfect."

His eyes flicked to something behind her, and on instinct, alarm rose in her throat. She tried to turn to see what Tom was looking at, but suddenly two thick arms encircled her from behind, one gripping her waist, the other clamping over her mouth and nose. Lirianna tried to scream, but the sound was stifled by a cloth her assailant pressed against her face. Her nose filled with a scent that was sweet and sickly, and suddenly the world was spinning, dimming, points of light exploding in her vision. She struggled weakly against her captor, but her body hung heavy and lethargic. Darkness descended on her, and the last thing she saw was Tom's expressionless face, gray eyes resting on hers, before everything went black.

5

THE BELLADONNA

First, there was only darkness. Then rocking. For one fleeting moment, Lirianna was comforted by the swaying beneath her. But it lasted only a second before what had felt like gentle swaying turned into a violent roiling in her stomach. Her eyes flew open, and she had barely enough time to hurl herself onto her side before her stomach heaved and emptied itself into a surprisingly convenient metal bucket.

Lirianna retched and gagged, registering dimly that the bucket was being held in front of her by a hand—a hand that looked infuriatingly familiar. As the heaving subsided, she managed to throw a glare upward, confirming that the hand did, indeed, belong to Tom.

"*You*—what did you do?" she gasped out before her stomach lurched again, and her face was forced to retreat back into the bucket. This time, despite the retching, she struggled to a sitting position, snatching the bucket away from Tom and clutching it in front of her.

When her stomach felt like it was going to be stable for at least a few minutes, she ventured to take in her surroundings. With a jolt of shock that almost sent her back into the bucket, she realized that she was sitting on a rough cot in a small cell, closed in by heavy iron bars. Beyond her cage, the wooden walls of what was distinctly a ship surrounded her, confirmed by the incessant rocking of the vessel on the waves.

She was a prisoner at sea.

Her gaze fell back to Tom. As she'd relieved him of bucket duty, he was now busying himself with a kettle and a mug of what appeared to be tea—not that she'd trust anything he gave her to drink if he'd just done what she thought he'd done.

But how could he have? He'd been her closest friend, in some ways even closer than Tris. Perhaps she'd misunderstood. He was here in the cage with her—could he have been captured as well?

Then her eyes fell on the single piece of jewelry her friend wore. An earring he hadn't been wearing when she'd seen him at the Gathering. A gold ring etched with symbols that identified the wearer's ship and captain.

An earring that marked Tom as a pirate.

Fury and betrayal rose in Lirianna like a storm. Her eyes narrowed as they homed in on Tom's kneeling form. "That's new." Acid dripped from her voice as she glared at the ring in Tom's ear. "I suppose it didn't match your garments for the Gathering?"

Tom didn't look up or respond to the jab, which only incensed Lirianna more.

"Piracy?" she hissed. "Really, Tom? That's what you decided to do with your life?"

This time, Tom answered, though his eyes remained focused on the tea preparations. "Not all of us have such attractive options to choose from as you, Lirianna."

It was the perfect answer to justify a fight, and Lirianna unleashed her fury without hesitation.

"What are you talking about? We were training together! What happened to being a bard?"

"I was never as good as you, and pipers don't become legendary bards."

"That's a load of sheep's dung, Tom, and you know it. You never cared about being legendary, you just loved the music. And you were good! You could have easily found a post anywhere in Dúramair, even at Castle Dúr. You would have been a respected minstrel—"

"I didn't want a minstrel post."

"Why ever not? It's what we were training for!"

"It just wouldn't have worked for me."

"Oh, and this does? Being a pirate? Kidnapping people? People who used to be your *friends?*"

A muscle in Tom's jaw twitched. "I didn't know I would be taking *you.*"

"Oh, well, that makes it so much better," Lirianna spat, her eyes flashing. "I can't believe you would just throw your life away like this."

"It seemed like the best option at the time," Tom replied through clenched teeth, his fingers trembling slightly as they continued to fidget unnecessarily with Lirianna's tea.

Lirianna could hear the strain in her friend's voice—could

see him fighting to remain calm—but she was far beyond caring.

"You expect me to believe *this* was your best option? Saints, Tom, even if you didn't want a minstrel post, you still could have stayed in Tiragel with different work. You could have settled down, gotten married, started a family—"

Tom's eyes finally snapped up to Lirianna's, and it was clear she'd struck a nerve. She felt herself recoil at the heat in his gaze; *she* had always been the fiery one next to Tom's steady affability. Lirianna tensed, expecting him to shout, but his voice remained tightly, if barely, controlled.

"No, Lirianna. I could not do any of those things."

"Why not?" she asked, determined not to be cowed by the intensity of his glare.

Finally, Tom's voice rose, ringing against the walls of the ship. "Because the girl I wanted to do all those things with left to become a *nun*."

Silence filled the space around his words as they hung in the air between them. Lirianna felt as though she'd been punched in the stomach. For the first time in her life, she found herself truly speechless, pinned in place under Tom's furious stare.

Eventually she realized her mouth was hanging open, and she closed it, swallowing. After a moment, she said in a low voice, "I left to be the Trianid's Seer of Strands, Tom, not just a nun."

Tom's eyes lowered back to the tea, bitterness etching his features. "Didn't make much difference from where I stood."

He thrust the mug toward Lirianna, sloshing it over his hand in his anger, but he didn't flinch. "Here. Drink this. It'll stop the vomiting."

Lirianna reached out automatically and took the steaming mug. She watched in shocked silence as Tom gathered up the tea and kettle, his movements sharp and angry. Without another word, he left Lirianna's cell, the lock clanking harshly into place as he twisted the key.

He threw her one last glance filled with emotions she'd never seen on his face, and in that moment Lirianna realized she no longer knew Tom of Tiragel. That the boy she'd once spent her days with was no more, and this new, unknown, and possibly dangerous person had taken his place.

And that, perhaps, the transformation was her fault.

Tom left, his footsteps heavy on the wooden stairs as he stomped his way above deck, and Lirianna was left with nothing but a roiling stomach, a messy tin bucket, and a mug of tea that sloshed with each rock of the ship on the waves.

Lirianna refused to drink the tea. Though she drifted in and out of a miserable doze for what must have been the remainder of the night and most of the next day, the retching continued, never allowing her more than a few minutes of rest before her stomach would start heaving again. By the time she heard Tom's boots descending back down the stairs, she felt exhausted, limp, and unwilling to even attempt rising from her cot.

Tom stopped at the bars of her cell, looking at her abandoned mug with a frown. "You didn't drink the tea."

"Can you blame me?" Lirianna mumbled, then winced as her stomach clenched.

"It would have stopped the sickness," Tom said, a note of

distress in his voice. "The stuff that knocked you out causes heaving that lasts a while unless you take the antidote. I thought you'd be better by now."

"Well, I'm not," Lirianna responded through gritted teeth. With considerable effort, she pushed herself up to a sitting position, one hand clamping down on the top of her head as the world spun. "So, you kidnapped *and* poisoned me. How long is this supposed to last?"

"About a day."

"And what time is it now?"

"Just after sunset. Shouldn't be much longer. You'll feel better soon."

Lirianna bit off her scathing reply. She had no energy to argue, and it was slowly dawning on her that she should probably reserve what energy she could for figuring out her situation and making an escape plan. She eyed Tom, wondering how much he would tell her and how much of it she could trust. "Where am I?"

Tom stuffed his hands into his pockets, looking uncomfortable. "You're on the *Belladonna*."

"A pirate ship?"

Tom nodded.

"I assume you took me down the river to the coast?"

Tom nodded again.

"Are we still docked?"

"No."

There would be no escape, then. Not yet, at least.

"Why did you take me?"

Tom shifted, avoiding her eyes. "The captain will explain everything to you. He's just waiting for the sickness to pass."

"How considerate."

Worry crossed over Tom's features on hearing the spite in Lirianna's voice, and he gripped the bars of her cage, leaning closer and lowering his voice. "Listen. When you meet the captain, don't argue. Don't fight, don't say anything disrespectful. In fact, don't say much at all if you can help it. The captain ... he's not a kind man."

"Oh, really?" Lirianna's voice dripped with derision. "The pirate lord who poisoned and kidnapped me isn't kind? How shocking."

"I'm serious, Lirianna," Tom said, his voice sharp. "You don't want to tangle with him."

"Then why are you working for him?"

"Honestly, it was kind of an accident."

"An *accident?*" Lirianna said, incredulous. "How do you become a pirate by accident? Seriously, Tom, what happened to you?"

Tom pushed back from Lirianna's cell and raked his hands through his hair. He looked at her a moment, then dropped his arms, defeated. "When you left ... I didn't take it well." He was avoiding her gaze again, chewing on his lip as if he'd rather not remember what he was about to say. "I tried to keep things going like normal at the school, but ... my heart just wasn't in it anymore. A few weeks after you'd gone, I went down to the tavern and had too much ale—a lot too much ale—and to be honest, I don't remember much of what happened that night. But when I woke up the next morning, I was here on the *Belladonna* with this ring in my ear and ..." He shrugged and looked back at her.

Lirianna studied him for a moment. "So, why don't you just leave?"

Tom shook his head. "It's not that easy. Pirates take a

blood oath to their captain. He basically owns me for ten years, and he'd come after me if I tried to leave. And besides, it's not like I have anything else to go back to."

"Tom …" Lirianna shook her head, pity and exasperation warring within her. "We kissed behind the hall *once*. And we were so young. How could you think—"

"Don't," Tom said, holding up a hand, his face bitter. "Just don't. I already know you never felt the way I did. But you asked what happened, and now you know."

Lirianna made no reply, and after a silent moment, Tom looked away and shook his head. His voice was flat when he spoke. "Your stomach should calm down soon, and the captain will want to see you. I'll be back for you then."

He turned without another word and retreated back up the stairs.

Lirianna let out a long breath, collecting her thoughts. Her stomach did seem to be settling, and her mind was clearing enough to start sensing prickles of fear as the reality of her situation sank in. If she was in the middle of the ocean, there wasn't much she could do to carry out her escape, but she wasn't completely helpless either. She did have one resource that no one on the ship—not even Tom—knew about.

Glancing toward the stairs to make sure no one was coming, she reached beneath the neck of her dress and pulled out her hearing stone. She unclasped it quickly and balled it up in her fist. She'd keep it in one of her inner pockets from now on—somewhere none of the pirates would find it. But before she stashed it away, she closed her eyes and sent her thoughts out across the water, calling for the two people she trusted most in the world.

6

THE BURNING

The afternoon was drawing to a close when Alyen and her companions reached the fork where Brother Hugh would turn off toward Castle Dúr, and Alyen and Nah'dar would continue on to Brann Dala.

Alyen's spirits were low as she dismounted to say farewell to the former monk who'd been a constant companion on both her previous journeys. "Are you sure you won't come?" she asked, trying to keep the plea out of her voice.

Brother Hugh's smile was tinged with regret. "I'm afraid not, my dear. The pull of domestic bliss is too great to overcome this time, and I've promised Nellie I'll leave the adventuring to others. Though just between you and me ..." he leaned in conspiratorially, "I also think I shall miss the fun."

Alyen nodded and embraced her eccentric friend. "Be well, Brother Hugh. It really won't be the same without you."

Brother Hugh patted Alyen's cheek fondly. "Never fear, my dear. I have full faith that you shall emerge victorious as ever."

Nah'dar and Brother Hugh clasped arms, and the three remounted. Alyen and Nah'dar watched from the fork as Brother Hugh disappeared down the road in the slanting afternoon light, his loud singing slowly fading until he was gone from sight.

Once Brother Hugh had gone, the journey was largely a silent one as Nah'dar had never been much inclined to conversation. But it was a companionable silence, and after months alone in the forest, Alyen found she didn't mind the quiet. In fact, as the days passed with the Mountains of Geal sliding by on her left, she welcomed the space to think about the meeting with Aaron ahead and what, exactly, she wanted—or needed—to say.

She had spent the majority of her time in the Keeper's cottage trying to avoid thoughts of the Slayer, focusing instead on regaining her sense of peace. But the truth was, it had been nearly impossible to stop her mind from turning endlessly over the events of the past few months. In reality, she now realized she'd done practically nothing *but* dwell on memories of Aaron since leaving Illya, but as she'd been trying to concentrate on other things, she hadn't allowed herself to delve too deeply beneath the surface or to formulate any kind of plan as to what she would say to him when they inevitably met. Now she had a week to process what she'd so painstakingly avoided, and as the sun grew hotter with each day they moved farther south, she found that there was, in fact, quite a lot she wanted to say to Aaron. And that whatever peace she'd thought she'd found in the forest had merely been covering up the simmering anger that was all too ready to reignite as her thoughts prodded at it.

On a day approaching late summer, under a sun hot

enough to make everyone slick with sweat and grime, the mountainous sandstone canyons of Brann Dala came into view. As the shadows lengthened, heralding the approach of sunset, they reached the base of the mountains and saw Aaron's stallion, Soran, tethered in the shade of a grove of trees. They reined in their horses, and Nah'dar turned his gaze to Alyen.

"Leave Lusa's care to me, sanahara. Contact Aaron. You may have a long night ahead of you."

Alyen smiled wryly at the frankness of her companion and slid off Lusa's back. "You needn't trouble yourself, Nah'dar. I'll let Aaron know we're here, and I can tend to Lusa while we wait."

"Alyen. Nah'dar."

The voice Alyen hadn't heard in months sent a stab into her chest that was some mixture of excitement and anger and pain. She whirled around to see Aaron walking toward them, his skin tanned from the summer sun, his eyes flashing hazel in the slanting light.

"I saw you coming from the cliffs," he said by way of explanation. "The phoenix burning is tonight, or I would have arranged an inn for us."

"Greetings, Slayer," Nah'dar said, clasping Aaron's offered arm. "An inn will not be necessary. I will be content here with the horses if you and Alyen would care to discuss Trianid matters privately."

Aaron turned his gaze to Alyen and their eyes met. His expression was unreadable, and Alyen felt her limbs tingle with apprehension. When he spoke, his voice seemed formal. "Alyen. Would you care to watch the phoenix burning from the cliffs with me? It's a sight not many see in their lifetimes."

Alyen cleared her throat and nodded. "Of course. Lead the way."

Without further discussion, Aaron turned and began making his way back up the canyon, Alyen following behind. Neither of them spoke as they climbed, and Alyen was glad for the extra time to collect herself before the discussion she knew was coming began. Aaron followed a narrow path that wove between boulders and skirted around cliff ledges that Alyen tried hard not to look down as she passed. The ground beneath them rose steadily upward, and with the mountains blocking most of the remaining sunlight, it wasn't always easy to make out the path in the deepening dusk.

At last, the rocky path opened up onto a wide sandstone cliff that seemed to overlook all of Brann Dala. The rays of the setting sun threw fire across the ruddy sandstone canyons, making Alyen's breath catch at its beauty. Aaron sat down, clasping his arms around his knees, and Alyen followed suit, leaving a bit of distance between them.

They sat in silence for a while, then Aaron spoke, keeping his eyes trained on the canyons. "The sun will set soon. Once it's dark, we'll be able to see the fires of the phoenixes as they ignite and burn. They're already nested in the cliffs."

Alyen was quiet for a moment. "Does it hurt them? The burning?"

"I don't know." Aaron paused, then added, "Maybe. But I think mostly it comes as a relief. Their lives are finished. It's time to let the old fall away so they can start anew."

The last crescent of the sun dipped beneath the mountains, sending blazes of red and orange through the sky. As the colors slowly dimmed and the light faded, Alyen saw glowing salamandars—first only a few, then in ever greater numbers.

The fire spirits danced past them into the canyons, presumably to aid the phoenixes in their rite of death and rebirth.

All at once, a sound began to rise, echoing through the canyons before reaching their perch above. It was eerie and beautiful, a song full of memories—of joy and grief and hope.

"What is that?" Alyen asked. "Is it the phoenixes?"

Aaron nodded. "They always sing a final song before burning."

They listened in silence as the phoenix song grew, swelling as more and more of the immortal birds joined in, then slowly diminishing as one by one they ended. Alyen was glad for the gathering darkness that hid the wetness on her eyelashes from view—not that Aaron was looking at her, anyway. When the last solitary strain of song ended, fading once more to silence, nighttime had fallen, only a thin line of pale light still visible on the distant horizon.

Suddenly there was a flash of light from one of the distant cliffs, and an orange fire sprang into existence. Another flash from another direction, and a second fire ignited. One by one, fires flashed into being throughout the dark and silent canyons until all of Brann Dala seemed ablaze with light and flame.

"It's beautiful," Alyen whispered. "And the salamandars are helping, did you know?"

Aaron nodded, thoughtful. "Makes sense. I always wondered how the fires started to begin with."

"It's a good reminder, I suppose. Nothing in nature really functions well alone."

Something in the air between them shifted, and Alyen suddenly knew that she'd inadvertently brought their impending conversation to the fore.

"How's Faer Dinnán?" Aaron asked. Alyen could hear the chill in his voice already.

"I assume he's fine," she replied, matching his tone. "I haven't seen him since Illya."

"You haven't?" Alyen heard his surprise with a grim satisfaction she tried to ignore.

"No. I haven't."

Aaron paused a moment, then took a breath. "Look, Alyen, I can't get back together with you. Not yet, at least."

"What?" Alyen asked, genuinely taken aback.

"I just can't … I can't get over what you did to me. I know you had your reasons—we've been over all that already. But I can't find a way to feel all right being with someone I can't trust, who doesn't trust me, and someone who will always choose me last. I'm sorry, but I can't."

Alyen nodded slowly, anger stirring in her chest. "I see," she said. "Well, the thing is, Aaron, I didn't come here to ask you to get together again."

"You didn't?"

"No. I came here on the orders of my parents to fix things enough to prevent the Trianid from complete collapse."

"Of course, it'll always be about the Trianid for you, won't it?" Aaron said bitterly.

Alyen refused to take the bait and continued as if he hadn't spoken. "In fact, to be honest, I don't know if I ever want to get back together with you at all."

She could sense Aaron's shock in the silence that followed her words. "You … you don't?"

"No," Alyen said. She took a breath, feeling the dam that had held her anger at bay all summer threatening to give way. "Aaron, being with you was wonderful. Perfect, in fact—as long as everything was going well. You were fantastic when it came to kisses and firelight and picnics in the glen. But things can't always be easy. Sometimes things get really, really hard. And when things got hard for us, you *left*. You wouldn't consider my opinions or listen to my ideas—"

"I didn't *agree* with them, Alyen. There's a difference."

"Fine. But the main point is that instead of working through things with me, you ran away. Twice."

"*Twice?*"

"Yes, twice. You stormed out when I tried to tell you about Faer Dinnán's proposal at the cottage—"

"I needed to calm down! You still had no right—"

"*And* you left me on the beach at Illya! Saints, Aaron, do you have any idea what it took for me to do everything I did that day? I had barely regained consciousness, and you *left me* alone and vulnerable on a deserted beach with barely any food ..." She shook her head. "No, Aaron, you were good at playing the faerie tale, but when it comes to real life, I need to be with someone who will be there with me through the good *and* the bad."

Silence followed her words, and Alyen didn't know whether she was glad or regretful that she couldn't clearly see Aaron's face. The phoenix fires had dimmed and were slowly winking out, deepening the surrounding darkness. The sight was still beautiful, and under any other circumstances, Alyen knew that she would be eager to witness the next part of the ritual—the hope and promise of rebirth. But all she felt now was bitterness.

"Alyen, I—"

But Alyen never knew what Aaron was about to say next. At that moment, heat flared against her skin, and she started, reaching for the hearing stone that rested against her chest. By the fumbling coming from Aaron's direction, she assumed that he'd felt the same from his own stone. They each clasped their stones in their hands and the words they heard had them suddenly scrambling to their feet, Alyen calling hastily for salamandars to light their way down from the cliffs as quickly as they could manage.

The phoenix rising—and their discussion—would have to wait.

Alyen and Aaron emerged from the canyons at a run, Alyen's boots skidding on pebbles and dirt as she finally reached level ground. Their haste was enough to make Nah'dar spring to his feet, his scimitar ringing as he unsheathed it in one fluid movement, his eyes scanning their surroundings, searching for danger.

"What has happened?" he asked, his voice sharp.

"It's Lirianna," Alyen said, her breath coming in gasps. "She's been abducted by pirates in Tiragel."

Nah'dar's brow drew into a scowl. "Tiragel does not rest on the shore," he observed.

"She was drugged and taken down the river," Aaron explained. "It happened last night, just after the Gathering."

"Does she know why they have taken her?" Nah'dar asked.

Alyen shook her head. "Not yet, but she thinks she'll find out soon."

"And she is on their ship now?"

"Yes."

Nah'dar slowly replaced his scimitar in its sheath. "This is troubling news."

"We have to go after her," Aaron said. "How far away is the closest port?"

Alyen frowned. "We? Shouldn't one of the kingdom's ships go? With a contingent of warriors?"

"And do what?" Aaron said, an edge in his voice. "Destroy the ship Lirianna's on? We're closer, we already have the Captain of the Guard with us, and we have magic. It should be us to go, and we should go now."

Alyen hesitated. Part of her hated to agree without a fight —particularly as she had just made a point of complaining about him not listening to her ideas. On the other hand … this time, she didn't have any better ideas.

"The Slayer makes good points," Nah'dar said, his voice uncharacteristically gentle. "Dunmaer and Tírann are the two closest ports in that direction. Dunmaer is a shorter ride, but our ship would need time to maneuver out of the bay before heading out to sea. Or we could take an extra few hours of riding to reach Tírann, but it's a straight voyage to the Eastern Sea once on a ship from there."

"Then let's head for Tírann," Alyen said quickly, wanting to voice an opinion before Aaron. "Hopefully a few hours won't make that much of a difference, and the quicker we can get to the Eastern Sea, the better."

Aaron hesitated a moment, as if he felt just as reluctant to appear agreeable as Alyen, but he nodded. "Fine. We'll leave at dawn."

"Dawn?" Alyen said. "Shouldn't we leave now?"

Aaron shifted his weight, folding his arms across his chest. It was a gesture Alyen knew meant he was getting ready for an argument. "We won't be any help to Lirianna if we run ourselves into the ground and show up useless. And the horses can't run all night either. We need to take the night to rest and hopefully get more information from Lirianna once she has a better idea of what's going on."

Alyen huffed, unable to deny the logic of Aaron's words. "All right. I just … it feels wrong sitting here when she's in trouble."

Aaron eyed Alyen for a moment, then lowered his arms. "I know. But she's a long way away. We have to pace ourselves. For all our sakes."

Alyen nodded but said nothing more, and Aaron turned away to tend the fire.

Nah'dar studied Alyen's face, his expression impassive. "Best to sleep while you can, sanahara. We seem to find ourselves on a quest once again."

7

CAPTAIN VOROS

It had grown dark on the *Belladonna*. Lirianna's stomach had finally settled, and she sat cross-legged on her cot, back resting against the hull of the ship that continued to rock and creak in the waves. One of the other sailors had descended the stairs to leave a mug of water and a candle, but that had been at least an hour ago, judging by how far the candle had burned down since he'd left it. Lirianna hadn't touched the water.

She was terribly weak from her ordeal, but she knew that the prickles and shivers running through her body had just as much to do with nerves as exhaustion, poison, or lack of food. If what Tom said was true, the pirate captain of this vessel would be summoning her soon, and despite the bravado she'd shown in front of her former friend, in truth, the idea terrified her. She'd never met a pirate—not until Tom, that is—but she'd heard stories. None of them were good.

What could he possibly want her for? It was that question

that scared her most of all. Tom had said that he hadn't known she was the one he'd be taking. Did that mean the pirate captain didn't know she was the Seer of Strands? If that was the case, why had he sent Tom to the Gathering? As she turned over the events of the past two days in her mind, Lirianna was convinced that Tom hadn't been looking for her specifically. But if it wasn't her weaving the captain wanted, why had she been taken at all?

Lirianna almost didn't notice when the music started. As the night grew darker, a sound broke through her string of anxious thoughts, making her lean forward on her cot, ear turned toward the stairs. Someone was playing a tune—a simple melody she recognized as a lullaby from the southern coast, haunting and beautiful. It had started with a lute, but others were joining in now. There were pipes—that was Tom, she'd recognize his playing anywhere—and she heard a concertina, a few viols, and percussion as well.

They were good. They were all good. Good enough to be bard-trained.

The *Belladonna* was crewed by musicians.

Lirianna listened in stunned silence until the lullaby ended. Then, before she could make any meaning of this latest revelation, she heard boots on the stairs and Tom appeared, his face tense. Lirianna scrambled off her cot and stood at the door to her cell, gripping the iron bars.

"Tom, why is the crew made of bard-trained musicians?" she hissed.

Tom ignored her question. He thrust an iron key into the lock on her cell door, rattling it until the bar slid open. He glanced at her, his voice urgent. "Remember: don't speak unless it's needed and don't give any information that's not strictly necessary. Above all, don't let the captain know that you're the Seer of Strands, or that we have a history."

A part of Lirianna wanted to contest the use of that phrase, but she sensed time was limited. "But he'll know we're both from Tiragel, won't he? Obviously, we'd know each other."

"We'd be acquainted, of course," Tom acquiesced. "But nothing more than that. We weren't friends, we meant nothing to each other, we barely knew each other at all. Understand?"

The fear she saw flickering in Tom's gray eyes frightened Lirianna more than anything. "Why?" she breathed.

Tom's fingers grazed hers as he took hold of the door and he leaned close to whisper, his breath warm on her ear. "Because he'll use it. Anything you give him he will use against you, against me—against both of us. Information is his greatest weapon. So, don't give him anything he can use."

With that, Tom stepped back, pulling the cell door open. Lirianna dropped her hands from the bars as they swung away from her and she stepped out, fingers trembling.

She followed Tom up the stairs and emerged on the deck, eyes sweeping her surroundings as she took in her first look at the *Belladonna*. It wasn't a terribly large ship, but sizable enough. Lirianna didn't know much about ships, but she thought it might be built to an eastern design. Sure enough, the flag resting idle at the bottom of the mainmast showed the colors of one of the Eastern Kingdoms—she couldn't remember which. Her eyes trailed up to the top of the mainmast, where she saw another flag flapping above the sails. It was too dark for her to make out its pattern, but she had no doubt that it bore the colors and symbols of the pirate lord who'd captured her. *So,* she thought to herself grimly. *They fly a pirate flag when they want to be feared at sea, and a flag from the Eastern Kingdoms when they don't want anyone to know they're a pirate ship. That's why no one raised an alarm when they docked for the Gathering.* She wasn't sure whether to think it clever or cowardly.

The crew was gathered around a single lamp on deck. They sat or stood silently, men of all ages, each holding an instrument, their faces trained toward Tom and Lirianna as they made their way to the captain's cabin. Lirianna chanced a few glances at their expressions as she passed by. Many of them were blank or cautiously curious, but others looked at her with expressions of suspicion or something that looked like pity. It made her still-delicate stomach turn. *But they all look Dúramairian,* she realized. *Why is an eastern-built ship flying the colors of the Eastern Kingdoms crewed solely by Dúramairian musicians?* Curiosity nudged at her despite the fear that continued to crawl through her veins.

Tom stopped before a door leading to what must be the captain's cabin. He knocked on it sharply, and a voice from within called out in summons. Lirianna turned wide eyes to Tom, who gave her one last brief glance filled with warning. Then he pushed open the door, and they stepped inside.

The door closed behind Lirianna with a finality that sent shivers down her spine. She made no further movement forward, but surveyed the room as rapidly as she could. It was spacious for a ship and showed its owner's fine taste. The furniture was made of dark polished wood; the bed and chairs were covered with pillows and cushions of fine silk in vibrant colors. A case of shelves with glass doors held a larger number of books than she would have expected, and on its top stood numerous navigational tools, all made of pristine brass that shone in the lamplight.

Whatever fear Tom had shown to her below deck seemed to have vanished the moment he stepped inside. He strode to the desk that faced the door, his gait confident. "Captain, sir," he said, stopping smartly. "I've brought the harper, Lirianna of Tiragel."

The harper? Lirianna thought, utterly bewildered, then forced herself to focus on the man who came into view as Tom stepped aside.

He wasn't at all what she'd expected from a pirate captain. He was younger, for one—surely not more than thirty. And he was entirely too ... clean. In all the songs and stories she'd heard, pirates were always dirty and rough with missing body parts or blackened teeth. But this man could have passed for a wealthy merchant or an ambassador from the Eastern Kingdoms. Like the upholstery, his clothing was expensive: a rich brocade vest over a garment of finely woven linen. A jeweled signet ring rested on one finger, and his face, though somewhat angular and showing a shadow of stubble, could have been considered handsome. Only the gold rings in his ears—rings bearing the same markings as Tom's single earring—marked him as anything other than the proprietor of a prosperous trading enterprise. But his eyes, cold with an emptiness deeper than the fathomless waters below, struck a terror in her stomach greater than any number of scars or gold teeth could have produced.

The captain's gaze rested on Lirianna, his eyes trailing over her figure from head to foot and back again. He paused, expressionless, before asking. "Are you certain of your choice, Tom? She doesn't strike me as one who could be exceptionally ... experienced."

"I'm sure, sir," Tom replied, his tone confident as ever.

"She gave the finest performance of the night; I heard several of the elder bards say as much myself. Hobart and Renneth heard her as well. I'm sure they'd agree if you care to ask them."

The captain waved a hand. "No need. If she's as good as you say, it won't matter." He rose and came around to stand in front of his desk, eyes never straying from Lirianna's form. He paused a moment, then gave a small bow. "You honor us with your presence, harper. Welcome to the *Belladonna*."

Lirianna hardly knew what to respond, so she opted for silence and merely nodded.

The captain considered her again, then gestured to a table that Lirianna now noticed was set for three with platters of roasted chicken, root vegetables, fresh bread, and crystal dishes of olives and preserves. "Please, join me for dinner. It's late, I realize, but I understand you've not eaten in quite some time. Tom, you may join us if you like."

It was clearly an order, rather than an invitation. Lirianna stole a glance at Tom, who moved immediately to the table and stood behind one of the chairs. The captain pulled out the chair nearest Lirianna and gave her a smile that did not reach his eyes. Behind his back, out of the corner of her eye, she saw Tom give the smallest nod of his head. Suspecting she had little choice in the matter, Lirianna walked slowly to the table and sat as the captain adjusted her chair beneath her.

The captain took his own seat at the head of the table and began dishing food onto his plate. Tom sat last and followed suit, but Lirianna, still uncertain of her stomach's stability and unable to banish the lingering fear that she may be poisoned again, made no move toward the food. The captain noticed and paused, his lips stretching in an amused expression.

"You needn't fear the food, harper. In fact, I must insist you eat. It will stabilize your stomach much better than the fare served to the rest of the crew, and a fainting harper will do me no good. Now, please …"

The captain gestured to a platter of chicken, and Lirianna chewed her lip, hesitating.

Then she noticed Tom's hand.

It rested, seemingly casually, on his wine glass, but his fingers moved, positioning themselves in a manner only Lirianna would understand.

He was using their secret language. The one they'd made up to communicate silently during lessons at the barding school. It was a series of hand gestures, and they'd only ever come up with a dozen or so. But it had been enough then to keep them entertained when they found the instruction boring, and it was enough now to relay Tom's message: *Yes.*

Keeping her eyes carefully directed away from Tom, Lirianna reached for a platter of chicken. She may have lost a good deal of trust in Tom, but deep down, she didn't believe he'd ever want to see her truly harmed, and he was certainly more trustworthy than the captain. She found herself irritatingly grateful for his guidance.

They ate in silence for a time, Lirianna chewing slowly so as not to upset her stomach once more. Eventually, the captain sat back in his chair, twirling his wine glass between his fingers as he watched Lirianna finish her meal. His constant gaze made her want to squirm or shrink, so she put down her utensils, hoping that if she stopped eating, he would stop staring.

The captain studied her a minute longer, then took a draught from his glass and set it down. "I imagine you must have many questions, harper, and I'll do my best to answer them, but first, I'm afraid, I have a few questions of my own. Tom was good enough to arrange your passage on the *Belladonna* for me. Tell me, did you know each other well in Tiragel?"

Lirianna didn't have to look for Tom's hand signal to know what he wouldn't want her to say, and she forced herself not to look in his direction. "No, sir," she said, hoping her voice wouldn't betray her by wavering. "We were acquaintances only, both students at the barding school." She sensed Tom shift in his chair and wondered if he already felt she'd said too much.

"I see. And as a student of Dúramair's barding traditions, did you ever study the music of the rather well-known harper, Andair the Bard?"

The shock of hearing the name of her disgraced ancestor rattled Lirianna more than anything thus far. She attempted to hide her surprise by frowning and turning her head as if in confusion, just enough to make out Tom's hand on his glass out of the corner of her eye.

No.

"Not really, sir," Lirianna said, though Andair the Bard was famed enough that she felt it was a risky lie to tell. "I learned of him, of course, but studied only a few of his most notable ballads."

"I see. A pity."

But he didn't sound like he thought it was a pity. If anything, he sounded pleased. The captain paused, and Lirianna felt her nerves rise once more in the silence.

Abruptly, the captain rose from his seat and strode to his desk. He opened one of the drawers and pulled from within a folded piece of parchment, which he brought back to his seat at the table. He made no move to open the parchment, but traced its edges with his fingers as he studied Lirianna once more. Suddenly he smiled—a smile which, again, did not warm the chill in his eyes.

"I don't believe I've introduced myself properly," he began. "My name is Captain Jácomo Voros. I'm sure you've deduced by now that the *Belladonna* is a pirate vessel. When I find it more convenient, others know it as the *Red Falcon*, a trading ship from the Eastern Kingdom of Lyndros."

The captain paused, and Lirianna said nothing as she saw Tom's hand move.

Wait.

The captain seemed to be considering something as he fingered the parchment in his hands. "I have a business proposition for you, harper, one I think you'll find rather attractive. But first, if I may ask you to indulge me, I'd like to share a little story with you."

Yes.

Lirianna nodded, and Captain Voros began.

"The story concerns the same Andair the Bard. I imagine that you've heard tales of Dúramair's most legendary bard in his youth. In fact, you probably know more about his early life than I. Would you care to tell me what you know already?"

Be careful.

Lirianna swallowed. Of course she knew the stories of Andair the Bard. She probably knew them better than most Dúramairians—even better than most of the bards. But Captain Voros didn't need to know that. "You said it yourself, sir. Andair was Dúramair's greatest bard. It's said his music could tame the winds and calm the seas, that even the mountains would weep with his harp. He was revered throughout the kingdom, destined to be the greatest of barding legends, until he abandoned his post and took to piracy." Her voice dropped almost to a whisper as she ended this recitation, and Captain Voros's mouth curled in a smile.

"Precisely. I imagine his change of career is not viewed favorably by the barding guild."

Generations of inherited shame clawed at Lirianna's stomach as the word *traitor* bloomed in her mind, but she said nothing. After a moment, Captain Voros continued. "Do they speak in Dúramair of why such an illustrious artist would have made so drastic a choice?"

No.

Lirianna shook her head, relieved that this time Tom's guidance wasn't a lie.

"I thought not." Captain Voros poured himself more wine and lifted the bottle in offering to Lirianna. She shook her head in refusal, and Captain Voros set the bottle down with a shrug. He didn't offer any to Tom. "Allow me to fill in the gaps for you. You see, prior to Andair the Bard's abrupt departure from barding, he visited Lyndros as part of the Dúramairian ambassador's retinue, no doubt to impress the king with his considerable talents. And impress he did."

Captain Voros took another swig of his wine. "The king and his court were enchanted by Andair's music, but none so much as the king's youngest daughter, Princess Nerina. Happily for her, she was not the only one entranced—Andair was completely taken with her as well, and soon, by all accounts, they were deeply in love."

A small frown appeared on Lirianna's face. She'd never heard anything about a foreign romance in any of the stories she'd heard, but the captain's next words explained why.

"Of course, their love was kept completely secret from the Dúramairians. We, in the east, do not have quite so many rules around how and with whom we share our … affections. However, the Dúramairians would have seen such conduct as an embarrassment to the ambassador and his profession, so their affair was hidden. Apparently quite well. When it came time for the ambassador and his retinue to depart, Andair returned to Dúramair with them, but found he could no longer live happily without the woman he'd come to cherish even more than the music he loved. So, without leave or explanation, he fled Dúramair and returned to Lyndros, intending to spend his life with Nerina. And so you see, Andair the Bard did not originally abandon Dúramair for a life of piracy, but for a life of love."

Lirianna felt herself growing curious despite herself. "So, what happened?"

Captain Voros flashed a satisfied smile that reminded Lirianna of a cat who'd just caught a mouse. "What happened, harper, is that life is cruel and favors neither the suffering nor the blessed. Shortly after Andair's arrival in Lyndros, his princess fell ill. All the best doctors were called, but it seemed there was no cure. As desperation in the palace grew, Andair and the king began to entertain 'healers' of increasingly questionable credibility, until they met one who swore he could cure the princess, but only for an astonishing amount of gold that even the king had no hope of paying. And so, as all desperate men do, Andair the Bard did what was once unthinkable: he took to the seas and became a pirate lord. A rather successful one at that."

"He needed the gold. For the princess," Lirianna said

almost to herself as stories she thought she'd known reshaped themselves in her mind.

"Yes, well … sadly for him, it did not work."

Lirianna looked up, hating the indifference written across the captain's face. He shrugged.

"It's true. Andair and his ship became a new kind of legend: the terror of the Eastern Sea. Even the Dúramairians learned of his new occupation and his crimes. He amassed a staggering amount of gold and treasure from the ships and ports he raided. But in the end it was for nought. No amount of gold can stop death, and by the time he'd gathered the healer's requested sum, the princess had already journeyed into the next world."

Lirianna said nothing as the captain set down his wine glass once more and tapped the parchment on his fingers. "So, harper, what do you think a broken man with a broken life does with an unfathomable amount of treasure?"

Tom's hand remained still, so Lirianna judged it safe to answer. "I don't know. I suppose he could have left it to the king in memory of his daughter."

The captain's eyes crinkled, and he laughed in a way that made the color rise to Lirianna's cheeks, though she didn't know why she felt ashamed. "My word, you are an innocent, aren't you?" he said. "How delightful. No, I'm afraid that tidy, sentimental endings exist only in stories. Andair knew that he'd become the most wanted pirate on land or sea, and it was only a matter of time until his enemies united against him. Not even the king could protect him from his own crimes, and accepting the blood money would only invite disaster to the throne and the kingdom. Andair was left with one option—the pirate's option: hide the treasure and disappear, leaving the name Andair the Bard behind forever. And that's exactly what he did.

"As the story goes, Andiar the Bard split his treasure into seven chests, each buried in a different place. He left a letter containing the clues to their locations for the king, then disappeared into the night and was never heard from again. The king, however, consumed by grief over the loss of his daughter, never retrieved the treasure and hid the clues so he would never be reminded of his tragedy. Thus was the treasure lost to time, and there the story ends."

At this point, the captain leaned forward, his eyes growing suddenly intent. "As the years passed, the story of the bard and the princess faded into legend, told only as a bedtime tale to children like any other faerie story that no one truly believes. Until one boy heard it—a boy who thought that perhaps there was truth in legends and tales. A boy who would scour the archives for hours looking for stories and maps from times forgotten until one day he stumbled upon the clues left to his great-grandfather so long ago. A boy who was, himself, desperate and willing to do the unthinkable."

Understanding lit in Lirianna's mind. "You found the clues. You're a prince of Lyndros?"

The captain's mouth curled in an ugly smile. "I was the *youngest* prince of Lyndros. Too far down the line of succession to ever dream of possessing power, with too many siblings to inherit much wealth. Had I left Destiny to her own devices, I would have been doomed to an insignificant life and a marriage of convenience, a royal face to fill the royal hall on feasting days, and nothing more. So, I took my fate into my own hands. I found the clues, abandoned my family and my royal life, and begged employment with a Sandamarian trader.

I learned the workings of a ship and the ways of the seas, taking every opportunity to advance myself until I came into possession of the *Belladonna* and was free at last to roam the waters, seeking out and claiming the treasure that would make me the greatest pirate lord this world has seen. For not only did I find the seven chests, untouched and filled with riches you cannot, in your wildest fantasies, envision, I found an eighth clue."

With this, Captain Voros set the parchment lightly on the table before Lirianna, whose eyes widened. She looked back up at the captain. "There's an eighth chest?"

"Oh, much more than a chest, I think," Captain Voros whispered. "Read it and tell me what you think."

Lirianna hesitated only a moment to register Tom's hand movement. *Yes.* She reached out, noticing the quiver in her fingers and the way the captain's mouth curled in satisfaction as he noticed it as well. Irritated, she grasped the parchment as firmly as she could and opened it, scanning the single page in surprise.

It was music. A song actually, written in the common language, but with distinctly Dúramairian notation. She looked up, confused. "It's a ballad?"

The captain leaned close. "It's a map."

Lirianna looked back down, unsure of what to say.

"Read it," Captain Voros commanded, then sat back in his chair to wait.

The lyrics were scrawled and faded, and Lirianna had to lean closer to the lamp on the table to make them out.

If you would find my greatest treasure,
Heed my words in equal measure.

I'll lead you to an island fair:
That which I lost is resting there.

Follow true the eastern mark
That rises only after dark,
And when you reach the Dragon's Mouth,
Choose your passage, north or south.

Beware the maelstrom and the snake,
But let them not your courage shake,
For one of these you must survive
If you're to reach the isle alive.

And when the shore is in your sight,
Wait for evening's gentle light.
There rests a cove 'neath seagulls' cries.
'Tis there my greatest treasure lies.

To you who seek, remember this:
Be grateful for the raindrop's kiss,
The sighing wind and warming sun,
But most the arms of your loved one.

For tomorrow is guaranteed to none.

Lirianna read over the words several times, sure she must be missing something. When she could find nothing more, she looked up.

"And …?" the captain asked.

Tom's hand was still in its *yes* position, which she took to mean it was safe to be honest. "It seems straightforward to me.

There are directions to an island, and the treasure should be buried in the cove."

"Precisely as I thought." Captain Voros inclined his head in agreement. "However, I followed the instructions exactly, found the island, and dug throughout the entire cove. I found nothing."

"Perhaps ... perhaps it was already found?" Lirianna suggested.

"I doubt it," Captain Voros replied, eyeing her keenly. "None of the other chests had been disturbed, and this one was to be the least known of all. No, there must be something I am missing; some part of the clue so well hidden that only a select few would be able to notice it. Something only a fellow Dúramairian bard would see."

Lirianna's stomach sank as realization dawned. "Your crew," she said. "That's why everyone on your crew is a musician."

"Right, again," Captain Voros said, raising his glass toward Lirianna. "And yet, no matter how many bards and musicians I have collected, none seem able to decode the message left by one of your own in the language you all claim to share."

Lirianna shook her head, not noticing that Tom's hand shifted to *be careful*. "Dúramairian bards don't write like this," she explained. "Sure, music is written down by the guild scribe, but only to ensure nothing ever gets truly lost. Most bards don't even know the notation—everything is taught and learned by ear."

"Yes, I've gathered as much," the captain said, a dangerous edge to his voice. "Which is why I knew that if I am to claim the last remaining treasure of Andair the Bard, I would need Dúramair's very best bard to guide me."

There was a silence as Lirianna gaped a moment. *"Me?"*

"I have it on Tom's authority that yours was the finest performance at the Gathering. Surely, the bard whose playing stirred the souls of the entire guild in an event that won't repeat for another ten years would have a depth of skill and knowledge equal to the task I require?"

"But—but I'm not a bard," Lirianna blurted, realizing too late that Tom's knuckles had turned white as they clenched his glass. *No!*

"I mean—" she faltered, trying to backtrack and collect her thoughts. "I mean to say, I trained as a bard, but never finished." The statement sounded weak even to her own ears.

Captain Voros studied her for a moment. "I see," he said. He shifted in his chair, setting his wineglass on the table, then leaned toward Lirianna, placing his elbows on his knees, his expression cold. "Let me be clear, harper. I don't care about you or your past or the technicalities of the Dúramairian barding traditions. I have a task I need a bard to complete, and you're the one Tom brought. I would certainly hate to think what your fate would be if you prove ... unhelpful."

Lirianna's heart was pounding. She couldn't see Tom's hand anymore, not with the captain leaning so close. "I thought you said this was a business proposition," she breathed.

There was a moment of silence during which Lirianna thought she might faint. Then suddenly, Captain Voros burst out laughing, a mirthless sound, his breath sour as it hit Lirianna's face. He leaned back in his chair, an amused expression on his features.

"So I did. Here, then, are the terms, harper. You decipher this clue and lead me to the treasure, and I'll give you one tenth of it along with your freedom."

"And if I fail?" Lirianna asked, wishing her voice didn't sound so meek.

The captain's eyes were hard as stone. "Then I have no further use for you. Understand?"

Lirianna nodded mutely, not trusting herself to speak.

The captain's eyes never left Lirianna as he addressed Tom. "Tom, take our guest back to her quarters. See that she gets an instrument."

"Aye, sir." Tom rose immediately, and Lirianna stood to follow him, the parchment clutched in her fingers.

"And Tom." The captain's voice stopped them at the door. "I'd hate to think what *your* fate would be should your harper prove useless."

Lirianna saw Tom's face pale, but when he spoke his voice was steady. "Understood, sir."

With that, Tom opened the door and escorted Lirianna back into the bowels of the *Belladonna*.

8

THE HARP

Despite her exhaustion, Lirianna slept poorly. Throughout the remainder of the night, she tossed and turned on her uncomfortable cot, trapped in a restless doze filled with swirling thoughts of treasure, music, legend, and generations of family shame. Finally, she gave up the struggle for sleep as dawn gave what feeble light it could to the dim hold of the *Belladonna*. She sat up, her unsettled night leaving her certain of three things.

One, if this whole misadventure was about her disgraced ancestor, Andair the Bard, then Tom's betrayal ran much deeper than she had known.

Two, she had no interest in claiming even a single gold coin of the supposed treasure.

And three, she would never, ever, help the likes of Captain Voros with anything, least of all something that would bring shame to the barding guild.

What that meant for her, exactly, she didn't know.

Her thoughts were interrupted by footsteps on the stairs. Tom appeared, carrying a tray of food in one hand and a harp in the other.

Lirianna's eyes tracked him as he crossed the hold and leaned the harp against the bars of her cell. She studied the instrument as Tom rattled the key in the lock. It was small— just a lap harp, suited for a bard traveling on foot—but it seemed in decent repair.

Tom swung open the door and set the tray on a small stool. Lirianna noted that the food it bore was similar in quality to the dinner she'd received in the captain's cabin— presumably far better than what the rest of the crew was served, if Captain Voros's words were to be believed. Lirianna wondered how long she would get to enjoy such a privilege once it became apparent that her intentions were less than cooperative.

Tom retrieved the harp and brought it inside the cell. He held it in front of him, almost uncertainly.

"I know it's not what you're used to," he said, sounding apologetic. "But it's the best we have."

Lirianna said nothing. After a pause, Tom tried again.

"It's not bad for a lap harp. Just a bit limiting, I guess. What do you think?"

Lirianna glared up at him, making no move to take the offered harp. Tom's lips thinned with concern, and he set the harp down against the hull of the ship.

"You're angry."

"Well spotted," Lirianna snipped.

Tom took a breath and sat on the cot. "All right, then. Let me have it."

"I don't want to speak to you."

"I'm quite sure you do," Tom said with half a chuckle that only served to make Lirianna angrier.

"Is this funny to you?" she asked, her voice rising. She turned her burning gaze on Tom and was gratified to see the humor slide off his face.

Tom was silent for a moment. "No," he said softly. "No, this isn't funny at all."

Lirianna stared furiously in front of her for a moment. Part of her didn't want to give Tom the satisfaction of confronting him the way she knew he expected. But she also knew that she wouldn't be able to hold it back for long. Not when she was this angry. Best to get it out and over with. Besides, Tom deserved it.

"You knew the story, the ballad—all of it—before you took me, didn't you?"

Tom nodded slowly. "I had the same night you did—the dinner, the story, the deal—when Captain Voros took me. But I couldn't figure it out. Neither could anyone else on the crew. That's why he sent me to the Gathering. To get someone better."

Lirianna chose to ignore this last statement. "So, you knew that this whole thing centered around Andair the Bard, and still you took me? Knowing everything you know about my family? Knowing what it took for me to even be allowed into the school at all?"

Tom nodded again. "Yes."

Lirianna finally looked at him again, fire in her eyes. "Ten generations, Tom. Ten generations of my family were supposed to be banned from the school, from the guild, from playing music at all—all in punishment for the betrayal of my great, great uncle, Andair the Bard. And then I came along, wanting music so bad it hurt …" Lirianna dashed angry tears out of her eyes with the back of her hand. "Do you know how hard it was for my parents to go to the school to beg for my entrance? After the shame my family had been carrying for generations? The only reason I was ever allowed to touch a harp is because Master Oram is kind. And even so, I had to endure slights and judgements for years before I'd proved myself enough to be respected by the guild. Even the other students …"

Tom was nodding again, his face serious. "I remember."

"And *you*," Lirianna said, her voice breaking. "You and Tris were my only friends. The only ones in the beginning who saw me for who I was instead of the lineage I came from. You were *important* to me. And now …"

This time, Tom said nothing.

Lirianna took a moment to catch her breath and calm her voice. "So, knowing all that … how could you do this to me? How could you put me in a position that forces me to shame my family again? To betray the guild again? You could have taken anyone from the Gathering. How could you do this to *me?*"

Tom looked at her, his expression unreadable. "Do you really believe that?" he finally asked. "You really think I could have chosen to take someone else?"

"Of course! Every bard in the kingdom was there. You could have taken anyone—even an apprentice."

Tom shook his head in a disbelieving manner. "You really don't know how good you are, do you?" he asked, then continued quickly when Lirianna started to glare again. "Lirianna, I was told to bring back the *best*, and I wasn't sent alone. Both men who came with me heard you, too. If I'd taken anyone else, it would have been obvious that I'd disobeyed orders and if I ruined the captain's chance of getting who he needed from the Gathering—the Gathering that wouldn't happen again for another ten years ... Well, I wouldn't be sitting here breathing today, that's for sure."

Lirianna tossed her head, unwilling to be softened. "And I'm to believe that your fellow musicians would have turned you in?"

Tom's face was serious. "Yes, if it would have saved their own skins. Everyone on this ship looks out for themselves first."

Lirianna snorted bitterly. "Well, not everyone," she said. "You can just take that harp back, because I'm not doing a single thing that insane captain wants me to do."

Fear flickered in Tom's eyes. "Lirianna, you have to. You don't know what you're saying ... what he'll do."

"So, what *will* he do? Throw me overboard?"

"Maybe," Tom said, steel entering his voice. "But only if he was feeling kind."

The words sent a shiver down Lirianna's spine, and for a moment, she wasn't sure how to respond.

"Look," Tom said, raking his fingers through his hair, flustered now. "You heard the captain last night. He won't hesitate to punish you if you don't cooperate, and it won't be just you. It'll be me, too. And I know I'm not your favorite person right now, but *please*. Just do this thing, and I'll protect you the best I can. I promise. Just ... please."

The desperation in Tom's eyes took Lirianna aback, cooling her anger just enough to let some thoughts trickle through. Perhaps it would be better if she went along—just long enough to give Alyen and Aaron time to reach her. If she could stall the captain and avoid punishment, aided by Tom's protection, perhaps she could play the part just long enough to be rescued from this mess before anything terrible happened.

"Fine," she said quietly, noting the relief that rose in Tom's eyes. "You can leave the harp."

Tom let out a breath. "Thank you." He nodded, apparently at a loss for anything more to say. When Lirianna remained silent, he rose from the cot and stepped out of the cell, keys jangling reluctantly in his hand. He paused. "I'd leave it unlocked," he said, his tone apologetic again. "But the captain might send someone else down, and if they find it open ..." He shrugged helplessly, his eyes asking for understanding.

"Yes, I'm sure that would be dreadful for you," Lirianna said, her gaze cold.

Tom lowered his eyes, his shoulders slumped as he worked the lock. It slid in place with a clang, and Tom pocketed the keys with a defeated shrug. "I'll see you later, then," he said, and turned to go.

"I'll be right here," Lirianna called to his retreating back, unable to hold back one last jab.

Tom's steps faltered for a moment, but he ignored the comment and made his way back above deck.

Lirianna sat on her cot, staring angrily at the bars of her cage. She eyed the food tray, but she was too riled to eat. She stood, walked the two paces to the door, and tried the handle. She'd heard it lock, but thought perhaps Tom had had a change of heart at the last moment. But there was no such luck. The door held fast.

There were only two other things in her cell: the bucket which, now that she'd stopped vomiting, had been left under her cot for other purposes. She was trying very hard to ignore it—and the smell. And secondly, the harp. She walked over to it, her fingers running lightly over the curves of the neck.

"Well, this certainly is a fascinating turn of events."

The voice startled Lirianna, and she whirled around to find Faer Dinnán standing not far from her cell, surveying his surroundings with an air of astonished curiosity.

"*Fascinating?*" Lirianna said, incredulous. "I've been taken by *pirates!*"

"Yes, it's not at all the solution I would have thought of. But the ways of Destiny have always been mysterious. Even to me."

Lirianna felt as if her mind were suddenly on fire, making connections she had never considered. "Wait. You mean to tell me that all this happened because of my weaving at Monstar? The one *you* convinced me to make?"

The faerie king turned to Lirianna and met her fierce gaze. "I believe so. The sensation of fate is strong."

Lirianna felt herself begin to seethe. "When you asked me to weave," she said through clenched teeth, "you didn't make it clear that I could be endangering myself by doing so."

Faer Dinnán managed to look mildly surprised. "Of course not. I had no possible way of knowing what would happen when you wove. I knew only that something had to be done to avoid a future that I believe you agreed was most unappealing."

"Well, next time, you can do it yourself," Lirianna snapped. She turned away and sat back upon her cot, rather harder than she had intended.

The hold was silent for a moment, Lirianna too upset at

this most recent revelation to care whether she had offended the faerie king. After a while, Faer Dinnán spoke again.

"I'm not sure there has ever been a Trianid with whom I have been less popular," he said. His musing tone made Lirianna wonder if he'd actually meant to direct the statement to her, or if he was simply thinking out loud. She decided to respond anyway.

"Has there ever been a Trianid you meddled with more?"

"Meddled?" Faer Dinnán sounded genuinely taken aback.

Lirianna swiveled around to face him again. "Yes, meddled," she confirmed. "And don't act so surprised—you said it yourself. You meddled with Alyen and Aaron's relationship, insinuated you wanted Alyen to be your queen, tampered with Aaron's memory, convinced *me* to tamper with Destiny, breaking my vows as Seer … The very messy state of things right now has really quite a lot to do with you, so don't stand there acting shocked if we're a bit upset."

Faer Dinnán listened to Lirianna's tirade, his face showing lines of concern by the end of it. There was a silence when she finished, and for a moment, Lirianna wondered if, in her anger, she'd truly overstepped her bounds.

"What you say is all true," Faer Dinnán said, finally, his voice soft. "Though, in my defense, I might remind you that I did many of those things while under the influence of the darklings."

Lirianna studied the faerie king's face. "Unfortunately, that doesn't make them any less impactful," she said.

"It is strange to me …" Faer Dinnán began, confusion lining his features. He hesitated, then tried again. "Nature moves instinctively toward balance. If something goes amiss, it knows how to heal itself. I find it hard to understand how such conflict can arise from merely doing my best to remedy a terrible situation and restore balance."

In the silence that followed, Lirianna smiled grimly. "Well. You sound almost human." She stared at him.

Faer Dinnán returned her stare, his expression making it impossible to tell what he was thinking. Finally, he spoke. "What very uncomfortable lives you must lead. Tell me, Seer. What is it that keeps you humans steady amidst such chaos?"

It was a question she wasn't ready for. Lirianna was tempted to give a flippant answer, but something in Faer Dinnán's expression—something open and almost vulnerable—gave her pause.

"We steady each other," she said at last, opting for the most honest answer she could find. "Family, friends, loved ones … we all hold each other up." For some reason, her words brought Tom to mind, and her heart gave a painful twinge.

"You speak of love. Human love," Faer Dinnán said, and for a moment, his eyes took on a faraway look. "As Alyen explained—the thing that makes living worthwhile."

Something in the faerie king's voice as he spoke of her friend caught Lirianna's attention. Her eyes narrowed a fraction as she studied Faer Dinnán's face.

"Alyen said it was all a ruse—you wanting her to be your queen. But was it? Did you really want her to choose you?"

Faer Dinnán went still as he regarded her, his eyes as fathomless as the ocean's depths. "Alyen chose wisely when she took up the Keeper's mantle," he said. "She walks her path with competence and grace."

"Yes," Lirianna agreed, silently noting that the faerie king had not answered her question. "But she won't be happy upon it without Aaron, and you've practically forced them onto different paths."

Faer Dinnán inclined his head. "Then I find myself in your debt once again, Seer. For it would seem that Destiny has chosen you as the instrument of their reunion."

"Yes, well, if I ever meet Destiny, I'll have some words to say about that."

"A conversation I sincerely hope I am present to witness," Faer Dinnán said, the shadow of a smile flickering over his face.

Lirianna snorted and looked away, noting that her ire had, at least for now, simmered down to irritation. At least Faer Dinnán admitted his fault, and twice had proclaimed his indebtedness to her. Surely, some good must come of that— though she had no idea how one went about collecting on favors owed by a faerie.

Wondering if it would be wise to ask about it, Lirianna looked back to the faerie king, but found that he had gone. She sighed and surveyed the now-empty hold and her tiny cell. The harp still stood silently against the hull of the *Belladonna*. If Lirianna felt any tug toward the waiting strings, she pushed it away, refusing to be tempted into gratifying Captain Voros's desires. Instead, her eyes settled on her breakfast tray. She'd formulate a plan on how to delay Captain Voros as she ate, but first she had a message to relay. She paused to listen for footsteps, then drew her hearing stone out from inside of her dress.

9

THE BALLAD

Alyen slept fitfully and woke before dawn, the sky showing only a faint line of light where the sun would soon break above the horizon. She rose quickly, relieved to see that her companions were stirring as well. By the time Aaron and Nah'dar had risen and stowed their bedrolls, Alyen was waiting with bread and cheese and a cold tea brewed from some fortifying herbs she'd brought in her saddlebags.

"How long will it take us to get to Tírann?" she asked, already itching to be on the road.

"The journey would usually take two days," replied Nah'-dar. "If we push the horses, we may be able to make it in slightly less."

Aaron glanced up briefly from his tea before averting his eyes again. "If we don't stop for the inns and just go as far as we can today, I think we could make it by late tomorrow afternoon. If we find a ship quickly, we'd be at sea by nightfall."

Alyen nodded, though she cringed inwardly. The pirates were so far ahead of them already, and two days seemed an eternity. "Then let's go," she said, tossing the remains of the tea and hastening toward Lusa without further comment.

She worked quickly and silently, adjusting and buckling the straps of Lusa's tack, avoiding the eyes of her companions. She hoped her tense manner would be interpreted by the others as worry, and in part, that was true. But she knew it wasn't the whole story. Her conversation with Aaron had been cut off at a distinctly unresolved moment, and now she felt the weight of words both said and unsaid straining the air between them in a way that made her edgy and short-tempered. She glanced quickly in Aaron's direction, noting how terse his movements seemed as he adjusted Soran's bridle. If she wasn't mistaken, it seemed that he was feeling the same way—a fact which served only to irritate Alyen further.

It was a long, hard ride. Once the sun had risen, the temperature rose swiftly until the road became one long stretch of insufferable, shadeless heat. Had the situation been any less dire, Alyen would have determined the conditions unfit for travel and taken shelter at the nearest inn. Instead, she plowed on alongside the others, trying to ignore her discomfort, and soaking her sleeves and hair whenever they paused to water and rest the horses.

Thankfully, there was one distraction which came later that morning. They had stopped at a stream and were just about to remount and continue on when Alyen and Aaron both felt their hearing stones flare at the same time. Knowing it would be Lirianna, they passed their reins to Nah'dar and stepped into the shade of a thorny tree, eager to hear what had transpired while they were sleeping.

The story Lirianna told was bizarre enough to make them momentarily forget to ignore each other, and they exchanged expressions of disbelief as they clutched their stones and followed the words of their abducted friend.

"*So, that's why they took me,*" Lirianna concluded. "*Captain Voros thinks I'm some sort of genius bard who can lead him to a treasure trove of riches, and all I have to go on is this ballad, which seems completely straightforward.*"

"*Are you sure it's as straightforward as you think?*" Aaron asked, his brows constricting. "*There was a lot I didn't understand … things about dragon heads and snakes and such?*"

"*Apparently it makes sense if you're a sailor,*" Lirianna said. "*Captain Voros said he followed the clues and made it to the island once before. He just couldn't find the treasure.*"

"*Can you read it out to us again?*" Alyen asked. "*We're going to have to follow the same clues if we're going to find you, so we better be sure we have it right.*"

They spent the next quarter of an hour memorizing Andair the Bard's ballad until they could recite it without error, at which point Lirianna heard footsteps approaching and had to hide her hearing stone away quickly. Alyen and Aaron both dropped their hearing stones back beneath their clothing.

"Well, that's interesting," Aaron said. "We're going to have to give the verse some thought before we set sail if we want to know where to go."

It was an obvious statement, which, for some reason, made Alyen irrationally angry all over again. She narrowed her eyes at the sky, unwilling to risk making things worse than they already were by sounding waspish. "Let's talk about it tonight," she said, avoiding Aaron's gaze. "We've already stopped for too long. We should get back on the road."

Without waiting for a response, she made for Nah'dar and Lusa, ignoring the fact that Aaron looked as if he had been about to say something just as she stalked off.

They made good time, riding until darkness had almost completely fallen. When, at last, they stopped to make camp, Nah'dar and Aaron concluded that, indeed, they would be able to reach Tírann by mid-afternoon of the following day, provided that they left at first light and ate in their saddles.

"What will we do with the horses in Tírann?" Alyen asked, then whispered to the salamandars, coaxing the flames of their small fire a bit higher.

"We can board them," Aaron said, sounding hesitant. "I hate to do it, and it'll be expensive, but I don't know of any other option. I can't imagine taking Soran on a ship."

"There is one alternative," said Nah'dar. "I can take the horses to Tírann's military outpost and ensure that they will be cared for there. Perhaps I can even arrange for their safe return to Castle Dúr in case our own return is ... delayed."

Alyen caught the true meaning of Nah'dar's subtle words, and for the first time, a stir of alarm snaked through her. "Do you really think that's likely?" she asked. "It's only pirates, after all. Surely between you and Aaron and a bit of magic as backup ..."

Nah'dar looked up, his black eyes frank. "That is certainly my hope, sanahara. But a wise warrior knows to expect victory, yet prepare for defeat. And I do not believe it is 'only pirates' we shall face. The verse that the Seer relayed to you— did it not specifically reference serpents and maelstroms and dragons?"

Alyen chewed her lip. Nah'dar was right. She'd been so intent on getting to Tírann quickly that she hadn't given much thought to the ballad's insinuations of what awaited them. But they'd shared the verse with Nah'dar that morning, and he'd clearly paid more attention.

Aaron set his food to the side and fixed his gaze on Alyen. "As it's nighttime, perhaps now would be a good time to review the ballad and make plans for our next steps?"

She didn't miss his pointed tone repaying her for her shortness that morning. She decided to ignore it. "Of course," she said coolly. "Would you like to recite, or shall I?"

Nah'dar's eyes were flicking between the two of them, yet his face remained stoic as ever.

Aaron gestured at Alyen as he retrieved his bowl, and Alyen cleared her throat.

"There's nothing much in the first verse other than establishing that we're looking for an island where the treasure is hidden. The real clues start in the second verse:

> *Follow true the eastern mark*
> *That rises only after dark,*
> *And when you reach the Dragon's Mouth,*
> *Choose your passage, north or south.*

So, does anyone know what the eastern mark is?"

"It's obviously an instruction to sail east," said Aaron. "The question is, is it *exactly* east or not?"

Alyen felt her irritation rising again. "Obviously not. Otherwise, it would have just said 'sail east' without referencing a specific landmark."

"It could just be poetic, though, couldn't it?" Aaron retorted. Alyen noted that his jaw was tensing. "It's a ballad, not a recipe."

Nah'dar cleared his throat, heading off further argument. "I believe the bard is referring to what is known in Sandamar as the Cradle of the Sun. Have either of you made a study of astronomy?"

Alyen and Aaron both shook their heads, and Nah'dar continued. "The Cradle of the Sun is a constellation of stars that rises in the east each evening after sunset. It is shaped like a crescent moon turned on its side, so that when the sun rises in the morning, it 'fills' the hollow of the crescent—hence its name. And no, it is not *exactly* east; it lies slightly to the south of true east."

Alyen felt a tiny surge of triumph at these last words and looked at Aaron, brows raised. "That sounds likely to me. The island probably lies under the crescent—which we would miss if we went directly east."

Aaron scowled. "I never said we *should* go directly east. I was just thinking through the possibilities."

"Well, we don't have a lot of time to waste thinking through hypothetical possibilities that likely aren't relevant."

Aaron stood suddenly, surprising Alyen. "You know, if this is how the discussion is going to go, I'd rather not have it. Let's just get to Tírann, figure out a ship, and head toward the crescent. We'll figure out the rest as we go."

With that, he stalked off to retrieve his bedroll.

Alyen was silent. Guilt was trying to creep into her

stomach—a sensation not at all helped by Nah'dar's eyes resting on her from across the fire. She ate a few more bites slowly, and when it became apparent that the captain was not going to move on, she looked up to meet his gaze.

The former assassin stood and moved closer to her, crouching down to stoke the fire. "You know, sanahara," he said quietly as he sent sparks swirling into the darkness, "you will not succeed in hurting him more than he already hurts. You will only succeed in making yourself more miserable."

Alyen's expression turned sour at the criticism. "Well, he's not the only one who's hurt," she said. "Besides, I'm your sanahara. Aren't you supposed to be on my side?"

"I am always on your side," Nah'dar said evenly. "Even when I must oppose you to accomplish it."

He sent one final shower of sparks into the air, then rose and left Alyen to her bitter thoughts, and a heart that felt like weeping.

IO

TEMPTATION

Relaying the ballad to Alyen and Aaron had been a far greater relief than Lirianna had anticipated. Now that her friends knew her plight, and she knew that rescue was on the way, Lirianna felt that a weight had been lifted. It had been good to talk, the three of them again, and it brought to mind happier times from Monstar Abbey and Castle Dúr when they had basked in the joy of each other's company, the bonds of the Trianid weaving them together in ways both profound and inexplicable. As bad as her current situation was—and it was, indeed, terrible—if it led to a world in which they could return to that harmony and camaraderie … well, no one would be happier than she.

Lirianna had extracted the parchment containing the inscribed ballad from her pocket in order to recite the lines to Alyen and Aaron, and now it rested next to her on the cot. She glanced down at it, an unwelcome curiosity niggling at her mind. These were the words of her own ancestor. Not only her ancestor, but the legendary Andair the Bard—a ballad unknown to the guild that might shed light on the curse her family had endured for generations. She was still determined not to aid Captain Voros in any way—there would be no negotiation on that point. But another part of her—a part that was growing by the minute—wanted desperately to delve into the music and uncover its mysteries.

For many hours, Lirianna resisted temptation. She ate her breakfast in silence, refusing to be lured into studying the parchment as she chewed. When one of the other pirates descended to her cell to remove the tray and, thankfully, the chamber pot bucket, she refused to look at him, hoping he didn't notice how her face burned, and thanking each and every saint that it wasn't Tom who'd been sent to do it. When he returned with the now-empty bucket, Lirianna was sitting on her cot with the harp in her lap as if intent on her task. It gave her a reason to avoid making eye contact until the bucket was once more well out of sight, and perhaps he would mention above deck that the harper was taking her duty seriously, buying her some time.

For the rest of the morning, Lirianna lounged on her cot with the harp, her fingers idly drifting over the strings, getting the feel of the instrument without seriously playing anything. She was surprised to find that it worked to distract her from her ancestor's riddle far better than she'd thought it would. Once her mind was trained on her fingers traversing the harp strings, she sensed the musical stirrings of something else growing inside her. A new song, perhaps? Or a ballad of her own? She wasn't sure, but whatever the music was, it pushed at her with an insistence she'd never felt before. Enticing as the sensation was, something told her she didn't want to give into it. Not here, not now. It would have to wait, but now that it was occupying so much of her mind, she knew she'd have to force her thoughts to something else entirely or she would eventually give in. With no other source of distraction, her attention gradually drifted back to the parchment and the riddle it contained.

For the first time, she let her mind turn toward the uncomfortable questions that would make delaying her captor difficult. How much of the ballad did Captain Voros—or the rest of the crew, for that matter—know? Had the others at least learned the melody? If she played something she'd made up herself, something only she would know, would anyone on the ship know that it wasn't the ballad she was working on? She supposed she could just learn the ballad even if she never meant to give any useful information about it … But how long could that last? As the morning slipped away, Lirianna's list of questions grew, with few answers to accompany them.

Her thoughts were interrupted when Tom returned around midday with a new tray of food. It looked like she was still being served from the preferred menu, which Lirianna took as a good sign. Tom left the door open and set down the tray, his eyes taking in the sight of Lirianna with the harp on her lap. His eyes strayed to the parchment resting beside her, and his face lightened with relief.

"You're working on it, then?" he asked.

Lirianna debated how much of her scheming to let on. "You were always better with notation than me," she hedged. "Did you ever learn it?"

Tom shrugged and picked up the parchment, sitting beside Lirianna as he looked at it. "I learned the melody," he admitted. "But that's all I could really do, just with pipes. I studied the words for hours, but I couldn't find any hidden pattern or anything. Maybe there's some clue with the harmony … a harper might have an easier time spotting that than me."

Lirianna nodded. If Tom had learned the melody, it was safest to assume that everyone on the ship also knew at least that much. "What about the others? Did any of them find anything?"

"I don't really know," Tom said, his face losing some of its levity. "We don't talk much. Especially not about the ballad."

Lirianna frowned. "Why not? Don't you have friends among the crew?"

Tom paused a moment. "Not friends, no. The captain makes sure no one gets too close to each other. I think he's paranoid that, as we're all musicians, we could band together and stage a mutiny if we get overly familiar."

"But couldn't you?" Lirianna asked, excitement rising. "Mutiny, I mean. There's so many more of you—shouldn't it be easy to overpower him?"

Tom's voice went flat. "Remember when I told you that information is Captain Voros's weapon of choice?"

"Yes."

"Well, he has information on all of us. On our families and on our homes. And he's made it clear that he has agents on the mainland who've been instructed to exact revenge on everyone we most love should news ever reach them of a mutiny at sea."

"Tom, that's … that's *evil.*" Lirianna was horrified. She sat for a moment, her mind reforming her understanding of Tom's true situation as her heart pulled toward him almost painfully. "So, what, none of you talk to each other? You're all together, but you're completely … alone?"

Tom gave a light shrug to his shoulders, his face still blank. "For the most part. But there's one way we can communicate without the captain realizing what's happening."

"How?"

"Music," Tom said, and Lirianna heard how he said the word. How it sounded like a prayer or the name of a loved one on his lips.

"What do you mean?"

"Well, the captain wants us to keep in shape on our instruments in case competent musicians are needed by whomever is tasked with solving the riddle of the ballad. So every few nights, we're allotted a couple of hours to play together. We don't dare talk much, but we each take turns leading the sessions, and each sailor picks tunes from his home region when it's his turn to lead. The leader gets one evening being reminded of home, and the rest of us sort of … support him. Hold him up with the music. I don't really know how to explain it better than that."

Tom sounded awkward and unsure, but Lirianna understood. She understood perfectly, and in that moment, she thought it was the most beautiful thing she'd ever heard anyone say about music in her life. She gulped at the lump that rose suddenly in her throat. "And what do you pick when it's your turn to lead?" she asked.

Tom was silent for a moment, then listed the songs quietly. "'Ballad of the Bards.' 'The Shepherdess' Lament.' 'Two Coppers for the Ribbons Blue.' And 'The Road to Tiragel.'"

For a moment, Lirianna couldn't speak. They were the perfect choices. If she'd wanted to remember Tiragel with the best of its music—and to weep from homesickness at the same time—they were the perfect songs to do it. "Tom," she said, and reached out to lay a hand on his arm. "I'm sorry. I didn't realize."

Tom said nothing. He was so much quieter now than he used to be. His eyes held hers for a moment, then trailed over her face, lingering a moment on her mouth. Lirianna held her breath, suddenly remembering the one stolen moment they'd shared behind the Hall of Bards ... but Tom suddenly dropped his gaze and shrugged, avoiding Lirianna's eyes. "Doesn't matter. Maybe you'll have better luck than the rest of us." He glanced back at her, as if gauging whether she would listen to him without anger this time. "You should give it your best, you know. The rest of us were all forced to stay when we couldn't solve the ballad, but ... I honestly don't know what he'd do with you."

His words sent ice trickling down her spine. She hadn't thought that far ahead, and the unanswered question filled her with dread. Now, more than ever, she needed to find a way to stall the captain until her rescue arrived.

Tom rose from the cot, and suddenly Lirianna didn't want him to leave. "Tom," she said, a sudden idea striking her. He turned, his eyes questioning. "You said the crew has sessions every few nights?"

Tom nodded. "Next one's the day after tomorrow."

"Do you think ... do you think the captain would let me join? If I need them to play the ballad?"

Tom's eyes searched hers, and she couldn't tell if they held hope or wariness. He nodded. "He might. If he thought it would help. Shall I ask him?"

"Please," Lirianna said. With any luck, it would buy her a couple of days. And if she could stall the captain long enough, perhaps she wasn't the only one who could be rescued.

Tom nodded again, the faint lines of relief returning to his face. "I'll let you know what he says."

He retreated above deck, and Lirianna turned to her tray of food. She ate quickly, glancing over the parchment as she did so, her mind working over the notation that she'd never truly mastered. Then, wiping her fingers on her dress, she turned back to the harp. She had a new piece to learn.

II

THE SEA SPARROW

The *Sea Sparrow* was a small ship, sturdily built and easily sailed by two. It had seemed extravagant at first to buy a boat rather than booking passage on a larger ship, but as Aaron pointed out, a ship with a docking schedule would only slow them down. If they wanted a vessel that answered only to them, then a small boat they could crew themselves was the more affordable and time efficient way to go rather than hiring a large crew. It would be lighter and faster in the water as well.

"But do either of you know how to sail?" Alyen asked, still unconvinced. "Because I don't."

Aaron and Nah'dar looked at each other.

"I know some things. I did grow up on the docks, after all," Aaron said, sounding faintly petulant.

"Yes, but only until you were eight," Alyen pointed out. "Have you ever actually been on a ship?"

"Well ... no." Alyen could tell Aaron's frustration was

growing. "But it can't be that hard, can it?" He looked again at Nah'dar.

The warrior hesitated a moment before speaking. "I have been on a ship once before, and I learned a few basic sailing skills. I do not claim to be a knowledgeable seaman, but I believe I can be of some assistance."

Aaron looked back at Alyen as if he thought that settled the matter. "And we do need the speed of a small boat," he said.

"What we need is to make it to Lirianna alive," Alyen retorted, unwilling to give in. "We should at least hire one or two seasoned sailors—ones who know how to navigate. We'll still have the advantage of a small ship running on our sched-ule, and it will be faster and safer if it's crewed by people who know what they're doing."

Irritation lined Aaron's face, but he relented. "Fine. We'll get things settled on board first, and then we'll go hire two experienced sailors. Will that satisfy you?"

"Perfectly," Alyen quipped, then made for the wooden gangplank that led up to the deck of the *Sea Sparrow*.

Once aboard their small vessel, Alyen turned to look back at the port city of Tírann. Dwellings, shops, and inns sprawled over the hills and cliffs that lined the narrow inlet of water that led to the sea beyond. She sighed as her eyes sought out the Dúramairian flag, just visible above the military outpost with its adjoining stables. It felt odd continuing their venture without Lusa. Alyen's horse had been a constant throughout her life; even more so in the years since she'd left Castle Dúr. It didn't seem right continuing on without her, and Alyen hadn't liked leaving her behind.

As if reading her thoughts, Nah'dar joined her at the rail

of the deck. "I have arranged for the horses to be taken back to Castle Dúr. They will be well cared for."

Alyen squinted up at the captain's face. "Thank you. I suppose they wouldn't have liked being at sea in any case."

"Indeed not," Nah'dar agreed. "Nor do I, to be honest."

"Why not? Do you get seasick?"

"No. But Sandamarians are superstitious about water that cannot be drunk. The sea is avoided by most."

"Ah. Is that why there aren't many Sandamarian merchant vessels?"

Nah'dar nodded. "Only those born with very little magic and therefore little other prospects venture to create a life for themselves at sea. It is not a respected profession."

It wasn't the first time Nah'dar had mentioned his people's tradition of determining the amount of magic a child was born with—a determination that would dictate most of the child's life and opportunities. Alyen was about to inquire about it, but just then Aaron, who had been studying the ropes and sails, joined them at the rail.

"Everything looks like it's in shape. The tide's going out and the wind is strong, so we should be able to leave as soon as we hire our crew and clear things with the dockmaster."

As if on cue, a neatly dressed man with an air of importance marched down the dock at that moment, his steps clipped and business-like. He stopped in front of the *Sea Sparrow* and squinted up at them. "Permission to board?"

"Please." Alyen gestured, and the man made his way up to the deck. The dockmaster opened a large leather-bound ledger and settled a pair of spectacles firmly on his nose. Quill poised over the page, he scanned his entries, then looked up at the trio over the tops of the spectacles. "I see your fees are paid, and everything seems to be in order. When do you plan to set sail?"

"As soon as we hire two crew members," Alyen replied.

The dockmaster frowned. "You mean today? This evening?"

"Yes ...?" Alyen said, looking to her companions for confirmation. "We're in a bit of a rush."

"Yes, but the tide is already half out. With a small boat like this, you *might* make it past the shallows without scraping the bottom if you left immediately, but you're cutting it very close. And you certainly won't make it if you still need to hire a crew. Better to wait for high tide. The next high tide after the storm, that is."

Aaron turned in a full circle, scanning the cloudless blue sky. "Storm?"

The dockmaster gave them a severe look and shut his ledger with a snap. He removed his spectacles and faced them squarely. "Do you mean to tell me that none of you knows a thing about sailing? Or the sea?"

The three companions were silent for a moment, then Nah'dar said. "It is true that we are rather ... inexperienced."

"Why do you think there's a storm?" Aaron asked, still unable to erase the skepticism from his face.

The dockmaster eyed Aaron in a manner that reminded Alyen forcibly of her former tutor, Professor Glibb, when she had managed to make him particularly irritated. He held up his fist and began ticking items off with his fingers.

"One: the gulls have been flying inshore from the sea all day, taking to their nests. This means that there is a storm brewing, from which they feel the need to take cover. Two: the wind is not blowing steadily. It's coming in spurts and strong gusts. This means that there is a storm brewing, and we're already feeling the effects of the changing wind. Three: have you noticed how heavy and wet the air is today, despite the wind? It's not usually like that, and it means that—"

"There's a storm brewing," Aaron concluded, interrupting the man's lecture.

The dockmaster sniffed and hoisted his ledger under his arm. "I could go on," he said. "But I will be unable to provide you with a lifetime's worth of maritime knowledge in the next few minutes. Suffice it to say, that I strongly advise against your departure until such time as the conditions are more favorable. Any experienced seafarer will say the same, and you will be hard-pressed to find anyone willing to venture into the open sea until the storm has passed. However, if you do insist on departing immediately, I am unable to stop you, and you will not need to wait for a scheduled time as no other sailor in their right mind will be leaving the harbor simultaneously."

Alyen shifted uneasily. "And how long would it take for the conditions to be favorable?"

"It's hard to say," the dockmaster said, not unkindly. "If it was only the tide, then the next window would be just before dawn. But with a squall on the way ..." He shrugged. "Some blow themselves out in a couple of hours, others last for days at a time. If I were a betting man, I'd say we're in for a big one."

"May we have a moment?" Alyen asked.

The dockmaster gestured his consent, and the three companions turned to each other.

"I don't think we should go," Alyen began. "None of us really knows what we're doing, and if we can't hire anyone, it's too risky."

Aaron scowled. "We can't wait, Alyen. It's already been two days since Lirianna was taken, and you heard what he said. If we get caught here in the storm, it could be days more before we can even leave port. We'll have to risk it on our own."

"I can count days as well as you, Aaron, but we won't be any good to Lirianna or anyone else if we're dead at the bottom of the sea!"

Frustration emanated from Aaron in a nearly palpable wave. "But we have *you*, Alyen! We have elemental magic on our side. Surely you could—I don't know—calm things down a bit if things start to look dicey?"

"*Calm things down?* Exactly how do you expect me to *calm down* an entire storm?"

"You did it once before."

"That wasn't a natural storm, and I was lucky to survive!"

Their voices were rising, and Alyen saw the dockmaster's eyebrows raise as he turned away, awkwardly pretending to examine the deck rail.

Aaron drew a deep breath through his nose, then spoke in a deliberately measured tone. "Alyen, we're running out of time. For once, could you just agree with one of my plans and trust that it will work out?"

Alyen's eyes narrowed, as she realized with a new stab of anger that he was referring not to their present circumstance, but to the morning in the Keeper's cottage when Faer Dinnán had enchanted him. "Not until your plan consists of something better than acting against all reason and advice to the contrary while 'hoping things work out' and relying on me to fix everything magically when they don't."

Aaron's eyes flashed, but he was stopped from speaking by

Nah'dar clearing his throat. "It seems to me that a decision must be made quickly. If you are unable to come to an agreement, may I suggest drawing straws?"

Alyen couldn't miss the dry note in the captain's voice and her lips pursed. She looked once more to Aaron, but he merely raised his own eyebrows, half in question, half in challenge. She clenched her jaw, despising what she knew she was about to say. Much as she hated to admit it, being stuck for days at the dock when there was the possibility that she *could* aid their safe passage was unappealing. And they did have to catch up with the pirates.

"Dockmaster," Alyen called, her eyes never leaving Aaron's. "We sail immediately."

The dockmaster didn't even bother to hide his disapproval. "In that case, be on your way. And may the Saints protect you—though I think this one may be out of even their reach." With that, he retreated back down the gangplank, his boots clopping away down the dock.

"Thank you, Alyen," Aaron said pointedly, sounding anything but grateful.

"You can thank me later once I've saved all our lives from your *trustworthy plan*," Alyen snapped, then turned away, wishing she knew how to sail so she could make a point of busying herself with the ropes rather than staring angrily at the sea.

Nah'dar turned away silently and began loosening the knots that held their new purchase to the dock. Aaron stood where he was, neither speaking nor moving. Alyen knew he was watching her, but she refused to look his way. She was sure he wanted to say something, and for an aching moment she wished desperately that he would, because even fighting felt better than the silences that formed the walls of the gulf between them. But Aaron said nothing, and after a while, he turned away and joined Nah'dar at the rail.

With the sun lowering behind them, the *Sea Sparrow* drifted away from Tírann into the shallows. Alyen watched the land slip by from the prow, pretending that the salty wetness on her face was from the spray of the sea, rather than her own stinging eyes.

12

THE STORM

Navigating the shallows was slow and nerve-wracking. The dockmaster had been correct—with the tide quickly ebbing, the jagged rocks beneath the surface could be seen more and more clearly, some even jutting out of the water like dark, angry claws. Nah'dar and Aaron tried to curb their speed as best they could, unfurling only a fraction of the sail, but the gusting wind kept catching what little they gave anyhow, sending the *Sea Sparrow* lurching forward in barely controlled bursts that left Alyen sucking in her breath, bracing for impact and the crunch of rock ripping through wood.

It seemed a miracle when, at last, they reached the end of the shallows where the land opened up and gave way to the sea. Aside from a few heart-stopping bumps against the rocks, they seemed to have made it out in one piece. Alyen let out her breath, Aaron gave a triumphant whoop, and even Nah'dar looked relieved. But their jubilation was short-lived.

Now that they could see beyond the land, it was clear that the dockmaster had been correct on his second count as well: straight ahead of them, the eastern sky was blotted out by a towering mass of black clouds. The surface of the water was already growing choppy; frothy white foam capping the peaks of the restless waves.

"What should we do?" Alyen called over the rush of the wind. "How can we follow the Cradle of the Sun if we can't even see it?"

"We wouldn't be able to see it even without the storm if it doesn't rise until nightfall," Aaron answered. "But if the storm is coming from the east, we'll just aim for that."

"You want us to sail directly into the storm?" Alyen yelled.

Aaron gestured at the wide bank of clouds, lightning now flashing from within. "It's a pretty big storm, Alyen. We're going to get hit by it either way. Might as well aim in the right direction." He ignored Alyen's incredulous expression and looked to Nah'dar, who was manning the wheel. "Are you ready, Nah'dar?"

The captain nodded tersely, eyes trained on the ominous clouds.

Aaron looked back at Alyen. "Are you ready?"

Do I have a choice? she thought, but settled for a sour expression and a nod.

"Then, here we go," Aaron declared, and pulled the rope that would unfurl the sail.

The rush of the *Sea Sparrow* lunging forward took Alyen's breath away again. For a short time, the small ship moved steadily enough, cutting through the agitated waters with only a bit more turbulence than Alyen would prefer. But as they neared the edge of the towering cloud bank, Alyen's heart started to pound. The wind was roaring in her ears, and raindrops were stinging her arms and face as they lashed against her skin. Yet it was the waves she saw ahead that caused her knees to turn weak.

The ocean ahead of them looked like a dark landscape of undulating hills. The waves towered above their small ship, and Alyen knew beyond a doubt that it would be impossible for them to survive the crossing—not without elemental assistance, and even with it, she had her doubts. Panicked, she looked to Aaron and finally saw a similar unease written across his face. The waters beneath them were becoming more turbulent by the second, and already the *Sea Sparrow* was bucking up and down over the smallest of the waves edging the storm.

Aaron's mouth thinned to a line, and he hurried to close the sails, rain and saltwater plastering his shirt to his chest. "Nah'dar!" he shouted. "Keep us aimed straight at the waves so we meet them head-on. If they catch us on the side, we'll capsize."

Nah'dar nodded grimly, but Alyen could see that his knuckles were turning white where they gripped the wheel.

"Alyen!" Aaron's shout drew her attention back to his face. Her eyes widened in horror as she saw a wave about to crash into the ship's prow just behind him. Reading her expression, he grasped onto the rail just in time, Alyen following suit and clenching her eyes shut as water crashed over the deck, sweeping their feet out from under them and leaving them coughing and soaked to the bone.

"Alyen, we need you now!" Aaron shouted, and there was no way over the howl of the storm for Alyen to detect whether his voice carried fear or regret or apology beneath the order.

Fear throbbed in her veins, but the past spring with the darkling storms had trained her well. Giving her fear a nod of acknowledgement, she steeled herself with its ice and fire. Then, gripping the rail with all her might, she closed her eyes, and sent her singing speech out into the storm.

"Undines of the salty seas, sylphs who ride the wind and breeze, to all who rule this mighty squall, hear my voice and heed my call!"

Magic slammed into her with a shock that almost swept her from the ship. Never would she have guessed that so large an elemental force was involved in the creation of a single storm. She'd thought it would be similar to entering the darkling storm on Illya, but that had been an unnatural tempest born of elementals in need of healing. This was altogether different. This was elemental magic at its strongest and most potent. This was a force of nature—vast and far more powerful than anything one human could hope to harness.

Gasping, she clutched at the rail, willing her mind to stabilize, to corral the magic that threatened to overwhelm her. Before she'd had a chance to orient herself, another wave hit the ship, and she gagged on a mouthful of seawater. By the time she'd regained her footing and her breath, she knew one thing with certain clarity: she could not calm this storm. Not without risking a catastrophe similar to the one she'd created at Norhelm. And she'd sworn never to do that again.

But what was the alternative?

Panic battled the elemental magic, each determined to be the first to overwhelm her. Despair rose within her, but just as she felt that she was unable to hold the warring forces at bay, suddenly Alyen was no longer alone. All at once, her magic surged in a way it hadn't in months, not since Illya, not since Aaron had last connected his magic to her own.

"I'm here," his voice sounded in her mind, and he was next to her, one hand gripping the rail, his other arm wrapping tightly around her, anchoring her body to his as his magic anchored her mind, defying both storm and fear.

Then, as it always had, memories slid across the thread of their connection, Alyen's to Aaron and Aaron's to her, and the images bloomed before her mind's eye.

They were in the Keeper's cottage, standing near the bed, and Aaron watched, enthralled, as firelight flickered across her skin in patterns of orange and gold. It was beautiful enough to make his chest ache.

He was sitting by the campfire, trying not to watch the green glow from the moor where he knew she was with the faerie king. Trying not to imagine what they were doing together each night, because blocking out the thought was the only way to keep the rage at bay.

He was standing on the beach near Illya, staring at her wet, pale face, her eyes angry yet beseeching as the bitterness of betrayal seeped through his veins. Knowing that no matter how keenly it would shatter his heart, they could never return to the way things had been. Finality hung around his heart like an anvil.

The memories flashed before Alyen, each one clawing and rending her own heart until she almost wailed aloud. And she knew that next to her, Aaron was experiencing the same thing, the montage of her own memories of their journey to Illya and their ensuing separation causing his arm around her to clench as if in pain.

Another wave, the largest yet, suddenly slammed them

back into the present. Aaron was forced to grasp onto the rail with both hands, Alyen clutching onto his soaked shirt as he pressed against her, pinning her to the rail. Dashing the salt-water from her eyes, Alyen saw the unmanned wheel spinning freely, the *Sea Sparrow* listing dangerously parallel with the waves. Fear for Nah'dar rose, sharp in her throat, and she craned her neck, searching wildly. She spotted him, thankfully still on board, but struggling to regain his footing where the wave had slammed him against the railing at the stern.

"Aaron, I can't calm the storm," she said, hopelessness edging the thought.

Aaron's voice was steadier in her mind. *"Maybe you don't need to. Can you find land?"*

Hope sparked in Alyen's chest as a new plan crystalized around Aaron's words. She sent her mind out again, this time seeking not the magic of the watery undines nor the airborne sylphs, but the earthy solidity of the gnomes.

At first Alyen could sense only water, wind, and storm, the raging magics of undines and sylphs swirling together in a pattern that was at once chaotic and ordered, fierce and beau-tiful. She strained, stretching her thoughts and her magic outward as far as she could, and finally she found it, merely a whisper, but unmistakable: a hint of sand, of wet earth, of rock and solid ground.

"I have it," she said. *"And I think I can get us there."*

"What do you want me to do?" Aaron asked.

"Nothing," Alyen said, trying to ignore the way her heart was still aching from their shared memories. *"Just keep the connection steady. I might need to rely on your magic as well."*

"Be careful," was Aaron's only reply.

Alyen quickly took stock of their situation. Nah'dar was

still struggling to regain the wheel, but with the *Sea Sparrow* essentially unmanned and bucking aimlessly on the waves, he was forced to maintain his grip on the railing simply to avoid being thrown overboard. They'd been lucky thus far, she realized, and for a moment she wondered if Faer Dinnán could be shielding them from the worst of the storm as he had once before. But it didn't matter if he was. She'd learned the hard way not to rely on the faerie king, so she'd get them to shore herself one way or another. She could use the singing speech —she felt the undine and sylph magic still pressing upon her —but melding would be easier and more powerful.

Thunder suddenly rent the sky. In the accompanying flash of lightning, Alyen saw a towering wave, black against the darkened clouds and heading straight for the *Sea Sparrow*. It didn't take a sailor to know that it would certainly capsize their ship.

She needed to hurry.

Alyen closed her eyes and sent her mind out once more to the waiting undines and sylphs. *"Water, wind, air, and sea, lend your magic; meld with me!"*

It was brief and perhaps inelegant, but it did the trick. Alyen felt the familiar void, praying that the *Sea Sparrow* would remain afloat while the melding took hold. She felt her body shift, taking on the characteristics of the elements around her —scales glittering on her limbs while her body suddenly rose an inch off the deck, weightless as the wind. Then, once the elemental magic thrummed in her veins, mixing with Aaron's magic and her own, she gathered it all up and sent it out around the *Sea Sparrow*, encasing the ship in a shield of blue, green, and golden light.

The shield finished forming not a moment too soon, then

the massive wave crashed over them, the sound deafening. Alyen braced herself for the end, but it didn't come. Instead, the water cascaded over her shield, the *Sea Sparrow* bobbing back up above the waves like a cork in a vat of wine.

Alyen breathed a sigh of relief, but her task was only halfway done. Knowing the *Sea Sparrow* was protected—for now—she turned her mind back to the place she'd sensed the gnomes' earthy magic. She found it once more, steady and beckoning, and, not quite sure how she was doing it or if it would work, she concentrated her melded magic and pulled the ship toward the place she knew land awaited.

The *Sea Sparrow* rushed forward, their speed far greater than any ship could manage, even in the calmest of seas with the most favorable wind. Skimming over the water, the ship mounted and descended the rolling waves, their passage seemingly smooth and effortless, as if detached from the storm that howled around them. Even the sounds of the storm and the flashes of lightning seemed muted, as if the shield were made of solid glass and they watched through a window pane rather than the thin shimmer of magic.

But it was not as effortless as it seemed. After only a few minutes, Alyen felt her body begin to strain as the magic took its toll.

"Are we getting close?" Aaron asked, sensing that Alyen was weakening.

"We're getting there," she replied, gritting her teeth.

Aaron said nothing more, but Alyen felt his arms tighten around her, and his magic flared again as he redoubled his efforts to bolster her. It took the edge off the strain, but Alyen knew it wouldn't last for long.

Another few minutes passed, then Alyen noticed with a

twinge of triumph that the sea began to calm and the clouds parted, revealing the gleam of stars hanging in the now night-time sky. Judging that they no longer needed protection from the waves, she let the shield fall, and her body sagged with relief. The *Sea Sparrow* glided silently into still waters, and just ahead, land beckoned them to shore.

But perhaps they needn't land just yet.

With the weight of the shield removed, it wasn't nearly as taxing simply to propel the *Sea Sparrow* forward. It would be a shame to dock now, when they could take advantage of their speed under the cover of night. Perhaps they could continue east for a time and reduce the substantial lead the pirates had on them? Lirianna might not be safe on that ship for long—it was certainly worth a try.

"What are you doing?" Aaron asked as the *Sea Sparrow* angled east with a fresh burst of speed.

"I'm saving us time," Alyen said, ignoring the sweat forming on her brow.

"Don't overdo it," Aaron said, concern sharp in his tone. *"You can always meld again later, after you've rested."*

"Just a little farther," Alyen insisted, and she gave the *Sea Sparrow* another push forward.

But it was too much. Alyen suddenly swayed, vertigo hitting her as her body rebelled against the drain of too much magic held for too long. Dimly, she felt Aaron's arms clasp her against his body. The heat from his torso melted into her shaky limbs, momentarily steadying her.

"Alyen, you need to unmeld. Now!" Aaron's voice was firm in her mind.

"Let me just get us to land," Alyen replied, noting how her own voice sounded distant to her.

"There's no need. We can sail there ourselves ..."

But Alyen had stopped listening, concentrating all her attention on the welcoming magic of earth and sand she sensed ahead of them. Using her last bit of strength, she turned the *Sea Sparrow* toward the waiting shore. Sinking into the relief of knowing they were safe, Alyen felt her mind begin to slip into unconsciousness.

"Alyen!" Aaron's voice was sharp, almost angry, jolting her back to the present. *"We're coming in too fast! You need to unmeld or slow down!"*

Blearily, Alyen looked up and saw what had Aaron so worried. Straight ahead, the dark outline of the shore was fast approaching, and the *Sea Sparrow*, propelled by magic, was going to crash into the rocks that guarded its coast.

"I need to unmeld," she thought, her mind sluggish.

"Now, Alyen!"

Alyen nodded in bemused agreement. Her mind a haze, she sent her thoughts back to the sylphs and undines, whispering thanks and a farewell she barely registered. She felt the magic leave her, and her body slumped in exhaustion.

Aaron shouted to Nah'dar—something about dropping an anchor and angling away from the shore—but it was too late to change course. By the time Nah'dar had lowered the anchor, the *Sea Sparrow* was already in shallow water, hurtling for the inevitable crash into the shore. The anchor did little to arrest their forward momentum as it bounced and skidded along the ocean floor, serving only to wrench the ship into violent jolts. Alyen was hurled from Aaron's grasp. There was a resounding crash of splintered wood as the ship smashed into the rocks, then something collided with her head. For a second she saw the flash of stars and felt the warm, sticky sensation of blood trickling down her face. Her body was flung into the air, helpless as a child's doll, then she slammed onto something solid that smelled of sea and stone. She had time to register only the sensation of coarse wet sand pressing into her cheek and palms before the world went dark and she knew no more.

13

SANDAMAR

Alyen woke to darkness. At first, she wasn't sure whether she had actually opened her eyes or not, as everything seemed to be black either way. Perhaps she wasn't even conscious, but merely dreaming. She blinked slowly a few times, her mind slowly registering her senses: damp sand, coarse on her palms; the crash of waves on rocks; the taste of salt on her lips. Gradually, as her eyes adjusted to the darkness, she began to make out certain shapes: the splintered ruins of the *Sea Sparrow* run aground on the shore, and Nah'dar pacing in the sand, his movements more agitated than she'd ever seen.

Her fingers curled against the sand. It was unpleasant, this grainy wetness, but at least it was only on her hands. She frowned. Why was it only on her hands? Shouldn't she feel it on her face, too? Hadn't she felt her cheek hit the ground before she lost consciousness? Memories fell sluggishly into place, and she remembered hitting her head on something as they crashed. She raised a hand to her head and tried to sit, but pain seared through her skull and spine, and she cried out, falling back onto whatever it was she'd been lying on.

"Nah'dar, she's awake!"

It was Aaron's voice, shouting—far too loudly—from just above her. Alyen realized that the thing she was lying on was, in fact, Aaron's leg. Furthermore, his hand was on her arm, his fingers moving in gentle circles. Vaguely, she thought she should probably feel certain things about that, but she was in far too much pain to give it any attention. The only feeling she had room for was relief—relief that they were alive, and that Aaron was with her.

The shadow that was Nah'dar suddenly appeared in her vision. She couldn't make out his features clearly, but the way his silhouette moved made her suspect he was considerably unnerved.

"Sanahara." His tone was soft, but his voice held concern and something else. Fear? "Are you well?"

"I—I'm not sure," Alyen said. "My head … I hit it, and it hurts."

"We need a light," Aaron said, and something warm lit in Alyen's chest as she heard a note of desperation in his voice.

"Salamandars, burn bright, bring us light," Alyen whispered, unable to manage anything more than the bare minimum in the singing speech.

Aaron immediately hushed her. "Don't do that. Save your strength."

But it was enough, and a few dancing salamandars sprang to light before them, casting their golden-orange glow over their haggard forms.

Alyen looked up into Aaron's face, the sight of him

instantly causing her body to ache anew. The salamandars' light swirling over his features as he looked at her took her straight back to the Keeper's cottage, the way she'd seen it in Aaron's memories she'd just shared—and the way it lived in her own mind as well. For a second, she longed to reach out to him, to feel his arms around her, his skin against her own, knowing that she was safe and home and adored.

But the waves crashing against the rocks, the sand, and the shore reminded her instead of Illya and all that had transpired there, and the bitter taste of abandonment rose suddenly in her mouth.

One glance at Aaron and Alyen knew his thoughts were traveling the same road as her own. How could they not, given the memories they'd just witnessed? The way their connection had communicated their joint heartbreak better than if they'd sat and talked the entire night at Brann Dala? For a frozen moment in the glow of salamandar light, Aaron's face registered that same war of emotions, and once more, Alyen sensed that there was something he wanted—needed—to say. But his eyes caught and rested on a spot on the side of her head. He frowned, and the moment was gone.

"Your head is bleeding," he said. "There's a cut—I can't tell how bad it is."

Alyen raised her hand once again. "Where is it?" she asked, and Aaron guided her fingers to the wound. Gingerly, she probed around the injury. She'd been lucky, all things considered. A couple of inches lower and the blow would have hit her temple. That would have been a stupid way to die, considering everything they'd been through. As it was, a mighty lump had formed, but the cut didn't feel too deep, and there were no obvious breaks to her skull.

Reassured that the head wound was nothing terribly serious, she turned her attention to her back. She didn't like the way pain had shot like fire through her spine when she'd tried to sit, but perhaps it was just muscles battered by their shipwreck.

"Can you help me up?" she asked.

Nah'dar grasped her hands, Aaron supported her back, and slowly they pulled her to a sitting position. Her muscles still protested, but without the burning sensation of her previous attempt. Alyen flexed her limbs and gave a few cautious twists to either side. She breathed another sigh of relief—it didn't seem that anything was broken. Nothing a hot bath and some healing balm wouldn't cure.

"My healing bag," she said suddenly, her hands springing automatically to her side and shoulder where it usually hung. "I was wearing it …"

"It is here," Nah'dar said, handing her the soaked leather bag. "It must have been thrown from you in the wreck, but I found it on the shore."

"Thank you," Alyen breathed. The bag was drenched, and likely everything in it was ruined, but at least it wasn't at the bottom of the sea. Perhaps it was silly to feel so relieved that she hadn't lost it—nothing it contained was irreplaceable, after all. But her healing bag was an extension of herself now. She would feel like she was missing an arm without it.

"I think I can stand up," she said, reaching awkwardly to sling the strap of her bag over her head.

"Here, let me carry that," said Aaron. "Are you sure you can stand? We can wait for you to recover more."

Something shifted in Nah'dar's face as if he desperately wanted to disagree, but he said nothing.

"It's all right," Alyen insisted, trying to decipher Nah'dar's behavior. "It's probably best if I don't let my back get too stiff."

With Aaron's help, she stood, grateful that she felt no sense of vertigo or sickness upon rising. She looked around, trying to guess their whereabouts, but could still make out little else but darkness. "Do either of you know where we are?" she asked.

Nah'dar's jaw tightened and the same fearful glint flashed once again in his eyes. He gestured to the sand below their feet. "We are in Sandamar," he said.

Alyen looked down at the sand and realized that it was not only the darkness of night that made everything seem black. The sand *was* black. The famed black sands of the Sandamarian desert.

Alyen looked up, scanning their surroundings with new awareness. It was still too dark to see properly, but in every direction she could detect only the black sands stretching the length of the shore and rising in obsidian dunes behind them.

"Sandamar," she whispered, then looked to Nah'dar. "But that means …"

Nah'dar nodded. "We must find shelter before dawn. We have little time."

Aaron frowned. "Why do we need shelter? Can't we just follow the coast to a port?"

Nah'dar looked back at the sand, his expression making it seem like he was about to spit on it. "When the sun rises, the black sands of the Sandamarian desert will absorb its light, heating to such a degree that any who touch it will be burned as though by the sun itself. To be caught during the day in the desert is certain death."

"I've heard as much, but surely, here by the sea—"

"No." Nah'dar shook his head. "Even the sands of the shore will scald. We would have to stay in the water until sunset, and even then, we would suffer severe burns from the sun and risk dehydration."

"Where do we go, then?" Alyen asked.

Nah'dar nodded toward the dunes. Every muscle in his body was rigid, and Alyen didn't think it was only concern about the impending dawn. "We must head inland. With any luck, the road will not be far into the desert. We must hope we landed near an oasis."

They took a few minutes to scour the wreckage of the *Sea Sparrow* for their belongings, the sight of the ruined ship sending waves of guilt coursing through Alyen's trembling limbs. This was her fault. She'd pushed her magic too far and lost control—again. Given her past, she should have learned by now never to test the limits she knew were unnegotiable and unforgiving. She felt she should make some sort of apology to the others, but Nah'dar seemed far too unnerved to approach, and Aaron ... Aaron was complicated. So, she gulped down the lump of guilt in her throat, and concentrated instead on picking through the wreckage for anything salvageable.

In the end, there was little to be found. Everything of value—coin and weaponry—had been on their persons and had thankfully arrived on shore still attached. As Nah'dar had already retrieved Alyen's healing bag, they saw little point in wasting time searching for a few items of clothing or food that was certainly ruined, so they turned their backs on the splintered ship and headed up the dunes into the desert sands of Sandamar.

Traversing the dunes without a road was difficult, even more so exhausted and battered as Alyen was. She struggled to gain footing in the shifting sands, wincing as her back wrenched with each step. Aaron hovered close, patient with her slow progress, though he said little. Often Alyen would stumble, and Aaron's hand would be there on her back or arm, gentle but strong. She remembered when being touched by him like that would have sent thrills through her entire body. Now, they just made her heart hurt.

As they made their slow progress, Nah'dar strode before them, his impatience impossible to mask. Agitation marked his every movement, and he was constantly turning to wait for them as his pace outstripped theirs time and again. His behavior perplexed Alyen. She'd become accustomed to his keen attention to her comfort since she'd asked Faer Dinnán to save his life after the Battle of the Second Slayer, and now she found his disregard of her struggle brazenly out of character. Part of her wanted to stop and insist he tell her what was bothering him so deeply, but she knew better than to ask in front of Aaron. Nah'dar had told her things in private, things about his past and about his homeland, things he'd made her promise not to share with anyone, and Alyen was certain that the former assassin's discomfort sprang from an ocean of pain of which she'd only glimpsed the surface. Besides, they needed to find an oasis quickly. There was no time for words.

Thankfully, Nah'dar had been correct, and it wasn't long before their path intersected with a road. They followed it to a high spot in the dunes and Alyen was heartened to see lights in the distance: the glow of a port city not more than an hour's walk away. With relief written across her face, she looked to Nah'dar and was taken aback. Rather than mirroring her relief, the captain's face showed something more akin to terror or rage as he stared at the distant glow with burning eyes.

"Nah'dar, what's wrong?" Alyen asked, unable to keep silent any longer.

Ignoring her question, Nah'dar turned in place, his eyes holding desperation as they raked over the desert sands in every direction. But there were no other cities, nothing to be seen save for the black sand stretching to a horizon that was showing the first hints of dawn. He turned back to the glow of the oasis, shaking his head, and Alyen couldn't decipher whether it was denial or disbelief or dread she saw written on his face.

"I need—I need to know which oasis we are approaching," he said. Without further explanation, he strode forward down the road, leaving Alyen and Aaron to exchange a glance, completely nonplused, and hurry after him.

The line of light on the horizon before them had turned to orange and pink by the time they reached a square stone pillar standing erect in the sand at the side of the road. Writing was etched across its surface, but despite the imminent dawn, it was still too dark to make it out.

"A light!" Nah'dar cried as he rushed to the pillar, his fingers tracing the engraved words. "Alyen, I need a light!"

Shocked more by Nah'dar's request for magical assistance than by anything else that had transpired thus far, Alyen hastily moved next to him, whispering a request to the salamandars to hover closer to the pillar, their warm glow cascading over the windswept stone.

Nah'dar's eyes scanned the writing, and even in the half-light, Alyen could see his face drain of color. Then suddenly,

Nah'dar shoved away from the rock, cursing violently in the most uncontrolled display of rage Alyen had ever witnessed from her stoic warrior companion. Alyen and Aaron stared, aghast, as Nah'dar shouted at the sand, finally ending with his hands gripping the top of his head, his breathing labored as he stared out into the desert.

There was a moment of silence, then Alyen stepped toward him, one tentative hand reaching for his arm. "Nah'-dar? What's wrong?"

Nah'dar lowered his arms and turned to meet Alyen's alarmed gaze. The turmoil in his eyes made her heart constrict. After a moment, he spoke, his voice tight and barely controlled. "The oasis in which we must take refuge is the port city of Lunalor."

Aaron stepped forward to join them. "And why is that bad?"

Nah'dar looked to the oasis as the sun broke over the horizon, bathing the city's white walls in a fire that reflected the burning in the former assassin's eyes. "Because the kalsheera who rules Lunalor Oasis is my mother."

14

THE SESSION

Captain Voros gave his permission for Lirianna to join the bards' session just hours before it was to begin.

"I've been assuring him that you're working diligently on the ballad," Tom said when he came to tell her the news and leave her dinner tray. "You have been, haven't you?" Concern etched his features, pinching it in a way Lirianna didn't like.

"Of course," she said, trying to convince herself that it wasn't really a lie. She *had* learned it—she'd spent the better part of the last two days studying it until she thought she might crawl up the walls of the hold from boredom. She just hadn't given much thought to what the ballad could mean. Still, her efforts seemed to have delayed any further action from her captor, and with any luck, the session tonight might make her look invested enough to buy her a few more days. She'd figure out her next steps then.

Lirianna finished her dinner alone as usual, then sat,

absently picking through melodies on her harp as she waited to be summoned above deck. Her stomach felt jittery, and she couldn't quite discern if it was nerves or excitement—or some strange effect of the music that still hovered at the edge of her mind, begging to be played, which she was still firmly ignoring for reasons she couldn't quite define. Finally, when the light in the hold had faded until Lirianna sat in almost complete darkness, a wavering orange glow appeared from the top of the stairs, heralding Tom's arrival with a lamp. Lirianna rose to meet him, hoisting the harp into her arms and waiting near the door as Tom rattled the lock.

"So, how does this work, exactly?" she asked. "I don't want to get anyone in trouble if you're not allowed to speak to one another."

Tom swung open the door and Lirianna stepped out. Tom faced her, the light from the lamp casting odd shadows across his face. "You'll be fine," he assured her. "You're to lead the session tonight, so you can speak more freely than the rest of us." He hesitated. "I'm assuming it's not just the ballad you want to play with everyone?"

Lirianna looked away, sheepish. "Is it all right if we play other things as well?"

Tom chewed on his lip. "It should be. But be smart about it. It has to look like the main purpose of the session is for you to make progress on the ballad, all right?"

Lirianna nodded, suddenly uneasy. It didn't sound like she'd been able to convince Tom of her dedication, not if he was warning her like this. True, he knew her better than most, so he'd known she'd be itching to play anything and everything with a group of bard-trained musicians. But even if she hadn't convinced him, she'd have to make sure that no one else suspected her motives. "We'll spend most of the time on the ballad," she assured him. "I promise."

Tom nodded, unable to erase the traces of uncertainty from his features, and led the way above deck.

The crew was waiting for her, instruments in hand. They stood or sat on crates and barrels in a semi-circle around an empty chair she assumed had been reserved for her. Lamps hanging from the mast and sitting on deck gave the only light, save for the silver moonlight that glinted off the water around the gently rocking ship. Captain Voros was nowhere to be seen—a fact that afforded Lirianna a small sigh of relief.

Tom gestured her to the chair, then turned to his fellow pirates. "To lead tonight's session, may I introduce Lirianna of Tiragel," he said simply, then took a spot leaning against the mast, pulling a small pipe from his pocket.

A dozen pairs of eyes fixed on her. A few sailors nodded in greeting. Some looked on her with curiosity, some with skepticism, others with blank expressions. No one smiled. In Lirianna's experience, this was strange behavior from a group of musicians about to play together. She cleared her throat, hoping she didn't sound nervous.

"Good evening," she ventured. There was no reply, so she continued. "If there are no objections, I'd like to start with 'The Road to Tiragel.'" Briefly, she caught Tom's eye, gauging his reaction at her choice of one of his favorite songs from their home. His expression remained closed, but he gave the tiniest of nods and raised his pipe to his lips.

Lirianna drew a breath and began playing the traditional introduction. One by one, the other instruments joined in, their music quickly swelling in the still nighttime air. By the time the song truly began, Lirianna had to catch her breath, biting down on her lip to keep her eyes from tearing.

How long had it been since she'd played with a group of bards? She hadn't realized how much she'd missed it, not even when she'd played at the Gathering, intent as she'd been on her own performance. She'd forgotten how it felt, the things it did to her soul, how it both lifted her up and laid her gently down. How music knew her inner state better even than she did, how it stretched her heart until it lay open and bare, broken and yet never more complete. Lirianna felt the music swell around her, an ocean of harmony and sound, her harp a floating ship at sea, gliding above it all.

Once through, then twice. Traditionally, the song was played three times in all, and Lirianna closed her eyes for the last round, her fingers moving over the strings in a pattern she knew better than her own name. Without her vision to distract her, she could sense each instrument, each thread of the music —and the musicians behind them. She felt the pain of their fate, their longing for home, their love of the sea that had grown in spite of it all. She felt the unique tingle of each instrument in its owner's hands, as if music-making was its own kind of magic, and she felt it all directed her way, flowing through the space that separated them in patterns that were honest, raw, and beautiful. And she felt her own magic, flowing from her heart through her hands and into her strings, where it joined the dance of light and sound that was 'The Road to Tiragel'.

Lirianna barely noticed when, halfway through their last round, the tapestry of the music began to thin. One by one, instruments fell silent until only a few remained, then even they fell away and Lirianna was left playing alone. As her senses began to return to her, she realized that she was no longer one voice of many. Confusion prickled in her mind, an unwelcome distraction, and as the last notes sounded from her instrument, she opened her eyes.

Her heart nearly stopped.

Magic was pouring from her fingers, her hands glowing like beacons in the darkness, plainly visible for all to see.

Panicked, she looked up, scanning the faces of her fellow musicians. They were all staring her way—how could they not? But they were also … weeping.

Lirianna was speechless, her mind racing. What had she done? Her magic had never shone so brightly, and certainly not while playing. Should she say something? Ask the sailors to keep it a secret? Certainly, she should hide it from the captain. She clenched her fingers into fists, her eyes seeking Tom's. He met her gaze, and though his lashes and cheeks were wet with tears, his eyes held a terror she'd not yet seen.

"Lirianna," he breathed. "What are you doing?"

"I …" But she didn't know what to say. She didn't know what she *could* say. She didn't even know what the answer to his question was.

Suddenly, the door to the captain's cabin slammed open. Captain Voros strode out, quiet fury etched on his face. His eyes burned into Lirianna's, but when he caught sight of her glowing hands, he stopped in his tracks, eyes narrowing. "Witchcraft," he hissed, and made a sign with his fingers that Lirianna could only assume was meant to ward off dark magic.

Hastily, her hands fumbling, Lirianna set the harp down and stood. The captain's eyes were scanning the tear-streaked faces of his crew. Eager to escape his scrutinous gaze, the bards all hurried to stow their instruments away and return to their posts—all save for Tom, who stood stock still, his face blank, but his eyes still fearful.

"What have you done to my crew?" the captain demanded of Lirianna.

"I'm sorry, sir," Lirianna said, breathless. "I didn't mean … it was unintentional."

"I asked *what*, not why!" he snapped.

"I don't know," Lirianna replied quickly, panic rising. "It's … I don't really know how it works."

The captain's face darkened. "I have no use for a witch on my ship, bard or not." His hand strayed to the dagger hanging at his waist.

"Tom!" Lirianna cried, and without thinking, she stepped toward him, her hands reaching for his arm as if he could somehow shield her from the captain's wrath.

Captain Voros froze, his hand on the hilt of his dagger. Tom's head bowed in defeat, and at once Lirianna realized her mistake. The captain's eyes flicked between Lirianna and Tom, realization igniting in their depths. His lip curled, and Lirianna felt herself go cold.

"Does this boy mean something to you?" Captain Voros gestured toward Tom, who swallowed, his eyes never leaving the deck. Dreading the truth, yet fearful that a lie would be even worse, Lirianna nodded.

Captain Voros advanced toward Lirianna, his slow footsteps echoing on the ship's wooden planks. He stopped before her, and it was all Lirianna could do to hold his gaze.

"That was not the ballad you were playing," Captain Voros said, his voice calm and dangerous. "Have you even learned it?"

Lirianna forced herself to speak. "I learned it, sir. We were only playing something to warm up. The ballad was going to be next."

"I see. You were going to play the ballad with my crew reduced to weeping? Was that a necessary component to solving its riddle?"

"As I said, sir. I don't know how that happened. I'm sorry."

The captain paused, his eyes boring into her, and Lirianna said nothing, barely daring to breathe. Suddenly, his eyes narrowed almost imperceptibly. "Brutin!" he snapped, his gaze never leaving Lirianna's face. "Five lashes for Tom."

"No!" The word escaped Lirianna's lips, but no one paid any heed. A swarthy pirate Lirianna hadn't seen before emerged from the throng of sailors, seized Tom and dragged him across the deck. Tom's shirt was ripped off, and he was bound tightly to the mast, his face pressed against the wood. He did not meet Lirianna's gaze.

Brutin approached with a black coiling rope, and before Lirianna could protest again, the whip cracked through the air, Tom grunted, his face flinching in pain, and a line of blood blossomed on his back.

"Stop!" Lirianna cried, but the whip cracked again, and then again, Tom's groans becoming less controlled with each strike until all five lashes had been dealt.

When it was over, Brutin retreated with the whip, and there was silence broken only by the sounds of the sea, the creaking of the ship, and Tom's panting breath.

Captain Voros circled around Lirianna until he stood behind her. He bent forward until his mouth was close to her ear, and when he spoke, his voice was soft enough to be heard only by her. "So, you see how it is, harper. Today it was five lashes. Tomorrow it will be ten. The next day twenty-five, then fifty. Should you fail me again on the fifth day, the punishment for poor Tom will be one hundred lashes. I very much doubt he'd survive that, and it would be a long, painful, messy death. I am not a cruel man, so I would offer the kinder alternative of simply throwing him to the sea. I'll let you pick. But I'm sure it won't come to that, will it? Because now that I've certainly left no more room for misunderstandings, you'll be working very hard on the riddle I've given you. Not for me, but for Tom. And whatever witchery you thought to use against me will never happen again. Am I correct?"

Lirianna's breath was coming in shallow pants and she didn't trust herself to speak. She simply nodded quickly, trying to blink away the tears that threatened to spill out of her eyes, tears that burned with salt and wind and fear.

"Good," the captain purred in her ear. Then he straightened and strode for his cabin. "Take her below," he growled to Tom's assailant as he passed.

Lirianna tried to catch Tom's gaze, but his eyes were closed as he slumped against the mast, his back dripping blood onto the planks beneath him. Before she could say anything, her arm was grabbed roughly, and she was half-dragged back down to her cell, the harp left lying on the deck above.

To Lirianna's surprise, it was Tom who descended the stairs to her cell not long after his lashing above deck.

"Tom," Lirianna breathed, rising quickly and striding to the edge of her cage, hands grasping the cold iron of the bars.

"What are you doing down here? Won't the captain punish you again?"

Tom unlocked and opened the cell door, his movements slow and pained. He shrugged to indicate the items he was carrying—a steaming teakettle, a bowl, and a bundle of linen—then winced at the movement. He shook his head. "Captain's orders, actually. You're supposed to fix me up. I'm sure it's his way of making sure the guilt rubs in and sticks."

"I'm so sorry, Tom," Lirianna said, near tears. "You warned me, and I didn't listen. This is all my fault."

Tom uttered a groan as he bent to set his things down, then straightened and settled on the edge of the cot, tilting his head back, his eyes closed. "It's not your fault," he said. "It's never been your fault. I'm sorry I got you into this mess …"

He sounded so dejected Lirianna felt her insides melt. She walked over and joined Tom on the cot. "It's all right. It's not your fault either."

Tom opened one skeptical eye and swiveled it toward Lirianna. She rolled her own eyes. "All right, so it's a little bit your fault, but … I forgive you. And nothing you've done justifies this. Here, let me help you with your shirt."

"You don't need to …"

"Lift up your arms," Lirianna said in a tone that allowed for no further objections.

Tom said nothing, but Lirianna thought she saw the corner of his mouth quirk upward. He raised his arms halfway in compliance, and Lirianna went about carefully removing the garment that was already sticking to the wounds beneath. She worked slowly, trying not to hurt her friend, but nevertheless, Tom jerked or inhaled sharply on several occasions. When finally she was able to lift the shirt up and over his head, she saw why.

Tom's back was crisscrossed by five angry gashes, each swollen and red. Blood had smeared over his skin between the wounds, but though the open cuts continued to glisten wetly, it seemed that the bleeding had mostly stopped. Lirianna could see that at least a few places should be stitched—Tom would scar terribly without it—but that was Alyen's specialty. The best Lirianna could do was to clean up the blood.

"Oh, Tom," she said, hating the tremor in her voice.

"That bad, huh?" Tom said, with a gallant attempt at humor.

Lirianna cleared her throat to banish the impulse to cry. "Why don't you lie down? This will take a while."

Tom lay face-down on the cot, and Lirianna was glad he couldn't see her expression. For a moment, gazing at his ruined back, Lirianna's face crumpled. Then she drew in a steadying breath. *I can cry, or I can be angry,* she thought.

She chose angry.

Lirianna poured hot water from the kettle into the bowl and soaked the cloths. She wrung one out, then, as gently as she could manage, she dabbed at the dried blood crusting Tom's back. Tom flinched, and Lirianna jerked her hand away, then carefully tried once more. Slowly, Tom became accustomed to the sensation, and Lirianna was able gradually to clear away the blood and grime.

For a time she worked silently, but the anger she'd chosen grew with each dab of the cloth until she felt her eyes stinging again, this time with tears of helpless fury. "I can't believe a fellow musician would do this to you," she said, her voice shaking. "It makes me sick."

Tom made a movement that would have been a head shake if he'd been sitting upright. "Brutin isn't a musician. Only one who's not. He's a thug, through and through, and Captain Voros just keeps him around to do his dirty work."

"If you ask me, it should have been Captain Voros," Lirianna seethed. "If you're going to do something like this to a person, you should do it yourself. He's a coward."

"He's not," said Tom, then he snorted. "But there's a reason he keeps Brutin around so he can avoid being violent himself."

Lirianna frowned. "Is he squeamish?"

"Not at all. He'll kill a man—or woman—without blinking. I've seen him do it. But remember, he was raised to be a prince, not a soldier."

"What, can't he fight?"

"He can," Tom said. "Enough to be dangerous, at least. He knows the basics of swordplay and combat, but he's just not very good at it. His balance is off."

"How do you know?" Lirianna dabbed at a particularly angry slash and Tom flinched.

"I've watched him," he grunted. "The crew sometimes plays at knife throwing when we've been at sea a while. Sometimes Captain Voros joins in. His aim is decent, but every time he throws, his left leg shoots back and to the side. I wouldn't have thought much of it, but I've caught a few of the crew smirking about it behind his back. Even a bunch of musicians can tell he looks ridiculous."

Somehow this mockery of the captain took the edge off Lirianna's rage, and she managed a half-smile. "Well, speaking of musicians, you sounded good tonight. I always did love the way you play."

Tom was still for a long moment, and in the silence Lirianna could feel the weight of lost dreams heavy in the air.

"Thank you," he said at last. "And … you were right. I should never have left the school. I miss it … so much."

Lirianna wiped away a tear, then dabbed the last of the blood from his skin and said softly, "You would have made a great bard, Tom."

Her hand was resting gently on Tom's bare back, and, though her ministrations were done, she didn't lift it away. For a moment the air seemed to shift between them, and time froze, Lirianna's heart in her throat.

But then Tom drew a deep breath and rose, and the moment was broken, Lirianna's hand returning to her side. Gingerly, his movements hesitant and jerky, Tom shrugged his shirt back on over his wounds.

Suddenly, Lirianna couldn't let Tom leave. Not without trying to erase the hopelessness from his face. "You still could be, you know," she said, abruptly.

"What?" Tom sounded confused.

"A great bard," Lirianna said, earnest. "Once this whole business is done, we could leave. We could find a way together. Go back to Tiragel, and …" she trailed off as Tom slowly turned toward her and she saw his expression.

"We?" he said quietly, a burning in his eyes. "Together?"

Lirianna swallowed. "At least until we get back safely."

Tom shook his head slowly, the fire in his expression fading back to numbness. "It's too late for that, Lirianna."

"Don't say that. You, of all people, should know there's always hope for a good ending. Think of all the ballads we know."

"The ballads," Tom scoffed, his expression suddenly lined

with bitterness. "The ballads aren't real, Lirianna. We were fools to think they were."

"What do you mean?" Lirianna asked, shock at his words hitting her in the stomach.

The look Tom gave her was pitying. "Think about it. How do the ballads always end? Either in a blaze of glorious victory and an idealized happily ever after, or in such terrible tragedy that even the most stoic of warriors is weeping in his cup by the time the song ends. That's not real life. Real life rarely falls to either extreme. Real life usually lands somewhere in the middle: imperfect, complicated, and messy. And never interesting enough to sing about."

"Tom …" Lirianna said, wanting to object, but finding herself at a loss for words.

"Thank you for your care," Tom said, cutting her off, his face returning to the expression Lirianna now thought of as his pirate face—miserable gray eyes in an emotionless face.

He turned toward the stairs, but Lirianna's voice halted his steps. "Maybe you're right, Tom. Maybe the ballads aren't always true. But happy endings do exist. In real life. Love, joy, redemption—those are all real things and some stories do end well."

Tom remained motionless for a moment, Lirianna unable to gauge his expression with only the back of his bloodied shirt facing her. Then his head turned a fraction, just enough for her to be able to make out his half-whispered words.

"Pirates don't get happy endings."

Without further comment, he trudged back above deck, leaving Lirianna to wonder in the dark if she still truly believed her own words.

15

LUNALOR OASIS

It had been several minutes, and Nah'dar still stood glowering in silence at the oasis before them. Alyen would have been inclined to leave him to his thoughts as long as needed, but the golden disk peeking over the horizon was making her nervous. It would still take some time to reach the city, and daylight had come.

Alyen looked at Aaron, a silent question on her features. Aaron shrugged uncertainly, but she could tell by the way he glanced toward the sunrise that he shared her concern. She looked back to Nah'dar and sighed. There was nothing for it: she'd have to talk with him.

With tentative steps, Alyen joined the captain on the black sand next to the pillar that, in the growing light, now clearly showed the words "Lunalor Oasis" in several languages. She stood a minute, half-hoping the former assassin would say something first, but she was met only with more silence. "Nah'dar?" she ventured. "The sun is up."

"Yes," Nah'dar replied, his voice flat. "We should leave. We have only an hour or so before the gates will close, and we must take shelter for the day."

"We can always ... avoid your mother, can't we?"

Nah'dar shook his head, his expression dark. "I don't know. All visitors to the oasis must present themselves for registration and approval at the palace. *I* may be able to blend in for a day, but you and Aaron will be too noticeable. Trying to evade procedure would likely result in more trouble than it is worth."

Alyen swallowed, his words making guilt twist her stomach. "I'm sorry. Is there no other way?"

"There is not."

Alyen was silent for a moment, raking her mind for something to say. She was saved by Nah'dar abruptly turning away from his scowling to address them both.

"Come. Dawn has broken, and we have little time. We will register at the palace, find lodging in which to take refuge during the day, and find our way back to sea come nightfall. While we are in Lunalor ..." He paused, and Alyen saw a war of emotions cross his features. "While we are there, you must leave the talking and arrangements to me. I have a plan that I have no time to explain, so I will need your trust. Follow my lead and do not perform magic of any kind while we are there. Above all, mention nothing of my previous occupation as the First Assassin of the Bahari. It is ... a matter of life and death."

These words sent a shiver of both surprise and dread down Alyen's spine, but it was Aaron who spoke first. "What do you mean? Will we be in danger there?"

"Not so much the two of you," Nah'dar said. "But if it is

discovered that the First Assassin who abandoned his country, his tribe, and his brethren has returned, the price will be my life."

"But … Nah'dar," Alyen protested, her mind still trying to process the news that Nah'dar had apparently abandoned his previous life illegally. "What if we see your mother? Won't she recognize you?"

Nah'dar met Alyen's eyes, and in them Alyen saw a coldness she hadn't seen in months. "I have not seen my mother since my childhood, and she is unaware that I ever belonged to the Order of Assassins. It must remain that way. With any luck, she will think nothing of three partners in trade passing through to establish their business."

"She doesn't know … But surely your own mother wouldn't turn on you."

Nah'dar held Alyen's gaze for a long moment before he spoke. "You do not know my mother." Then, "Come. We must walk quickly if we are to make it to the city gates in time." Without further ado, Nah'dar turned and strode toward the oasis, Alyen and Aaron hurrying after him.

Nah'dar's pace was brisk, and while Alyen knew it was necessary, she found it difficult to match, taxed as she was from her melding at sea. The sun had only just risen, but already she could feel the heat beginning to radiate from the black dunes surrounding them, making her almost glad that her clothing was still damp. Urgency propelled her on, yet despite her best efforts, she soon lagged behind the former assassin, her breathing labored.

Aaron stayed by her side, glancing at her frequently, concern etched on his face. "Are you all right?" he asked finally. They'd covered perhaps half the ground to the oasis, and Alyen felt sweat start to trickle down her back.

"I'm all right." She gave Aaron a tight smile, then returned her focus back to the approaching city. "I'm just tired. And hot."

Aaron took in her sagging form. "You need to sleep. That's always helped before."

Alyen shrugged. "Well, we'll have to see how this goes. Something tells me it might not be the most restful stop on our journey."

"What do you think happened to him here?" Aaron asked, his voice low as his eyes trained on Nah'dar's retreating back. "Do you think we should be worried?"

Alyen didn't reply right away. It occurred to her that she'd never told Aaron about Nah'dar's confession to her concerning his answer to the sphinx's riddle in Norhelm: the fact that his mother had never loved him. Nor had she conveyed the few details the new Captain of the Guard had shared with her about his past on the way to Illya that spring. "I think," she said slowly, "that we need to trust Nah'dar. But we probably shouldn't expect to be welcome guests."

To Alyen's relief, Aaron let the conversation drop. Likely, he wanted to allow her to save her strength in the rapidly growing heat, a necessary consideration that she appreciated. But it was more than that. They had connected magically again on the *Sea Sparrow*. The parts of each other that they'd seen now rested silently between them, demanding resolution. It would need to be discussed at some point, but Alyen didn't think she could do it properly now, not with her exhaustion, their haste, and the unknown trials that may await them in the city. Perhaps Aaron felt the same, for he remained silent for the remainder of the hour until they reached the entrance to Lunalor Oasis.

The gates of the city were manned by two guards, both wearing expressions of impatience as the trio crossed into the shade under the alabaster archway. The elder guard fixed his eyes on Nah'dar, as if sizing him up, and Alyen thought she could detect a faint trace of disdain in his eyes. "You are cutting it close," he said in the common tongue, which Alyen could only assume he used for her and Aaron's benefit. "We saw you coming and held the gates. You should not be so careless—the desert does not show mercy."

Nah'dar inclined his head. "Then we must thank you for yours."

The guard's gaze swept over the three of them, his sharp eyes taking in their bedraggled appearance and lack of baggage. He nodded down the street leading into the city, paved in the same pale alabaster stone as the gates. "The road leads straight to the palace. You must hurry, though. They will close soon for the day, and it will be difficult to find lodging without the proper documents."

Nah'dar nodded his thanks, and the three hurried past the gates into the city.

Brisk though their pace remained, Alyen tried to take in as much as she could as they passed by shops, inns, and dwellings, moving ever closer to the palace at the center of the oasis. The entire city, from the buildings to the roads, seemed to be constructed of the same pale stone, and Alyen could understand why. Despite the fact that the sunlight glinting off the streets and buildings made everything uncomfortably bright, it was significantly cooler within the gates than it was in the black desert sands. To counter the glare and the temperature, tall desert trees lined the roads, their long, waving fronds casting welcome shade over their path. Alyen could imagine that during the night, the streets would be bustling with the citizenry, traders, the smell of exotic food, and Sandamar's famed moon markets. But now the streets were nearly deserted, windows shuttered, and shops closed, with only a few stragglers hurrying to make their way indoors before the worst of the heat hit.

They made it to the palace in good time, and Alyen was relieved to find that the doors were still open. They quickly climbed the long flight of stairs leading to the palace entrance, eager to be indoors despite the relative comfort of the shady streets. For a moment at the top, Alyen chanced to pause and glance around at the sudden view of the oasis from their higher vantage point. The city lay before them, a circle of alabaster dotted with greenery set in the vast black sands that stretched to the southern horizon. On the north side, however, she could still make out the glimmer of the sea, as well as the masts of the ships docked at the port, banners fluttering in the ocean breeze.

Alyen looked away and caught Nah'dar staring intently in the same direction, his eyes scanning the emblems on the ships' standards. His eyes froze, and for a moment, Alyen saw something like hope spark in their depths. Then he turned away and led them through the palace doors.

The interior of the palace was cool, pristine, and oddly quiet, Alyen thought, until she remembered that most people in Sandamar were readying themselves for bed at this hour. They were standing in a round foyer with high, vaulted ceilings and decorative gaps in the walls, which let a cooling breeze drift in from the sea. The gentle sounds of trickling water could be heard—perhaps from a fountain nearby, though Alyen couldn't see one. Directly in front of them stood a desk, occupied by a clerk who wore a near-identical expression of weary impatience as the guards they'd encountered at the gate. The clerk's eyes flickered over them as they approached, the same hint of derision lining his features. Alyen forced herself not to frown, but made a mental note to ask Nah'dar about it later.

"Were you the last through the gate?" asked the clerk without preamble.

"We were," Nah'dar confirmed, and the clerk made a satisfied sound as he refilled his quill and held it poised over a new line in the large ledger book before him.

"Your name?" he asked without looking up, his voice bored.

"Shal'han," Nah'dar answered.

"Tribe?"

"Bahari."

"Home oasis?"

"Norsari."

"And the names of your companions?"

"Elynn of Dunmaer and Ewan of Tírann. My partners in trade."

"And your purpose in Lunalor?"

"We are here to establish our trade route and to negotiate with suppliers."

The man scribbled on some papers before handing them over to Nah'dar. "Are you in need of lodging?"

Nah'dar nodded. "If you could direct us to the nearest—"

"Nah'dar?"

The new voice startled Alyen, and she quickly looked

around, hoping her face hadn't given them away. Next to her, she could sense Aaron's muscles stiffen, and she could see Nah'dar's jaw clench, though his expression remained otherwise unchanged. Nah'dar looked up, taking in the man who'd spoken. He was rather short in stature, skin a shade darker than Nah'dar's, and he was peering at the former assassin as though uncertain of what he was seeing.

The clerk looked up, his face showing interest for the first time, his brow constricting. He turned to the stranger. "Nah'-dar? That is not the name he registered under. Do you know this man?"

The newcomer stepped forward, his eyes scrutinizing Nah'dar's face. "I am not sure. If he is who I think he is, I have not seen him since childhood. But if I am right, he should have a scar on his left forearm in the shape of a crescent moon."

The clerk looked to Nah'dar, curiosity rather than suspicion in his eyes. "Well?"

Slowly, Nah'dar extended his left arm and pushed back his sleeve.

"It is on the underside," his accuser said, and Alyen felt Nah'dar tense.

The clerk's gaze sharpened. "Well?" he repeated.

With only a hint of reluctance, Nah'dar turned his arm to expose the underside. Alyen couldn't see it from her position, but she saw recognition light on the clerk's features, and triumph flared in the other man's eyes.

"I knew it!" he said. "Even after all these years, I knew it was him. Do you know who this is, Nim'seer? This is Nah'dar, son of Shan'dar and Neri'dara."

There were daggers in the clerk's eyes as they turned back

on Nah'dar. "Is that so?" he said softly. "The son of Shan'dar and Neri'dara? How is that possible?"

The other man shrugged. "Who can say? But it is him, and if he has given you a different name, then …"

"Then he must have some reason to lie," the clerk concluded, now studying Nah'dar with calculated interest. "What are you hiding, Nah'dar, son of Shan'dar and Neri'dara?"

Nah'dar's answer was calm, and Alyen wondered if the others would be able to detect the faint hint of tension that ran through his voice. "I hide nothing. As my old friend here, Tam'bir, has so accurately pointed out, our childhood was a long time ago, and I have since taken a different name."

"What?" Tam'bir nearly scoffed. "Why would anyone take on a different name?"

Nah'dar's eyes were cold as they fixed on his acquaintance. "Perhaps if one considers my childhood, the reasons would not seem so mysterious."

At this, the man's gaze faltered, and he seemed to shrink under Nah'dar's stare.

"Be that as it may," the clerk said, his tone businesslike, "this is no longer a matter of simple registration. You will have to present your case to Kalsheera Neri'dara."

Alyen thought she detected a spark of anxiety flash across Nah'dar's features.

"I would not want to disturb the kalsheera at such an hour," he said quickly. "Perhaps if we can find lodging for the day, I can return to complete our registration this evening?"

"I am afraid not," the clerk said, rising with the clear intent to lead them farther into the palace. "Kalsheera Neri'-

dara enjoys taking in the waters of the oasis and does not retire until late in the morning. If you will follow me?"

It was an order, not a request. Nah'dar's mouth thinned, but he said nothing and made to follow the clerk, sparing no further attention for Tam'bir, who watched him pass with an almost wary expression. Alyen and Aaron exchanged a glance, then followed Nah'dar into the heart of the palace.

They passed through corridors and passageways, nerves clawing at Alyen's stomach despite her tranquil surroundings. The palace interior was pleasantly cool; shades had been pulled down over all the windows, casting the halls in a muted light, and the sound of trickling water grew louder the deeper into the palace they moved. Eventually, they reached a set of tall, ornately decorated doors guarded by two Sandamarian warriors, both of whom looked considerably more formidable than the guards at the city gate.

"Wait here," the clerk ordered. "See that they do not leave," he added to the guards, then passed through the doors, which swung shut behind him.

It was a tense few minutes, standing awkwardly in the quiet palace. Obviously, Nah'dar couldn't say anything in front of the guards, and Alyen didn't want to invite suspicion by appearing worried. She tried to school her features into a mask of unconcern, breathing slowly to settle the churning of her stomach. She was keenly aware that their situation was further taxing her already frayed nerves, and that exhaustion was threatening to overwhelm her once again. She could think of no worse time for that to happen, so she tamped down on the feeling, trying to concentrate instead on the calming sounds of water and wondering where they were coming from.

At last the doors opened again, and the clerk stood aside to wave them through. Nah'dar strode forward, and Alyen and Aaron followed him into one of the most beautiful rooms Alyen had ever seen.

The hall was spacious and airy, with beautiful carvings of flowers and the boughs of orange trees decorating the walls and the arches of the vaulted ceilings. There were no shades, and sunlight spilled through the high windows, dappling the fronds of the palms and other exotic foliage that grew in large alabaster vessels lining the room. In the center of the floor, a pool of crystalline water glittered, scattered with lotus flowers and bubbling softly where the water seemed to rise up. Realizing it must be the mother spring of the oasis, Alyen suddenly understood that the trickling she'd heard throughout the palace was likely water from the spring being pumped through the walls and out into the city. An unexpected stab of envy and stubborn loyalty to her own kingdom twisted in Alyen's belly, but she quickly doused it. Dúramair had plenty of beautiful places, and such sentiments were surely below her.

At the far end of the pool sat a dais on which rested a graceful chair that looked rather like a throne. Sitting on the chair was a woman, her striking appearance only enhanced by the white streaks in her hair and the fine lines around her eyes. She sat regally, almost haughtily, and for a moment Alyen could see how she must have looked in her youth: dark, lustrous hair against an alabaster complexion, her features beautiful and proud. Suddenly, Alyen was reminded forcefully of Ylvain, and she quickly pushed that thought away, too. This was not the time for unwelcome distractions from the past.

Neri'dara eyed Nah'dar with a sharpened gaze that spared

barely a glance for Alyen and Aaron as they skirted the pool and approached the dais. Her face showed no trace of emotion, yet somehow Alyen still felt a cold sweat bead on her palms as they came to a stop before her.

"Nah'dar," Neri'dara said, her voice rich but without warmth. "I had thought not to see you again in this lifetime."

"Mother," Nah'dar replied with an incline of his head, his voice stiff. "The assumption was mutual."

Neri'dara's mouth twisted, an expression that exuded distaste and coolly controlled anger. "My clerk tells me you have attempted to gain entry to my oasis under a false name. Is this so?"

"I used a name different from the one I was given at birth. If this makes it false in your mind, so be it."

Neri'dara's eyes narrowed, and Alyen couldn't help feeling that perhaps angering the kalsheera so early in the conversation wasn't the wisest choice given all that was at stake.

"Do not attempt to toy with me, Nah'dar. I have far more important things to attend to than entertaining the word games of a grown child. I should not have to tell you that evading registration is a crime."

Nah'dar's lip curled. "And if my answer is not satisfactory, what then? Will you throw your own son in prison, Mother?"

"Yes," Neri'dara said without hesitation. "I am the kalsheera of this oasis, and my obligations as such far outweigh whatever maternal sentiments you may be counting on." Neri'dara's eyes flickered over Alyen and Aaron, disapproval and suspicion written on her face. "Who are your companions? And do not give me the lies you told my clerk."

Nah'dar turned to Alyen and Aaron, and Alyen saw the warning in his gaze as their eyes briefly met. She tried to step forward, anticipating an introduction, but suddenly her exhaustion got the best of her, and she stumbled, her head spinning. Aaron's arm was around her instantly, catching her before she could fall, and Nah'dar was supporting her on the other side, alarm flashing in his eyes.

"I'm all right," Alyen mumbled, cursing inwardly at her weakness.

The kalsheera raised one eyebrow as she studied the three of them, her eyes calculating. "Is she ill?" she asked without sympathy.

"No," Nah'dar replied, his voice terse. "But she is exhausted from travel and needs rest."

"Your concern is surely greater than that of a trading partner." Neri'dara's features resembled that of a cat who has caught a mouse. "Is she your lover?"

Oh, Saints, Alyen thought, struggling to clear her head. At her side, she felt Nah'dar bristle, and Aaron's hand tightened a fraction on her arm.

Nah'dar looked back at his mother, his eyes burning. "Crassness does not become you, Mother. I am alive today because of her, and so, as is her right, I fulfill the sacred obligation of sanhar."

The room went still, and Alyen could tell that Nah'dar's pronouncement had not been received well. The kalsheera's face was rigid, all traces of amusement gone. When she spoke, her voice was quiet.

"Are you telling me that you play at sanhar to this girl? To an *outsider?*"

"I play at nothing," Nah'dar snapped.

"The rites of sanhar are sacred and pertain only to

Sandamarians," Neri'dara said, her voice cold. "You dishonor our family with this mockery."

"In that case, I see that nothing has changed in my absence," Nah'dar said, a quiver in his voice betraying his rage. "For I cannot remember a time in which I was not an embarrassment to you in one way or another."

Neri'dara's eyes flashed. "And what did you expect, Nah'-dar? What would you have done in my place, bound to a son who had little hope of ever leading an honorable life, let alone of being counted among the great Sons of the Desert? Sending you to the masters was the best thing I ever did for you, and more than you deserved."

"The best thing you ever did for me," Nah'dar snarled, "was to send me away from *you*."

The kalsheera stared at Nah'dar, a quiet triumph settling over her. "Guards," she called. She barely raised her voice, yet immediately two warriors were standing at her side. It rattled Alyen more than anything thus far. She hadn't seen them waiting at all, and it made her wonder if the palace was filled with hidden places with watchful eyes. "Show my son and his companions to a room and ensure it remains guarded. They shall remain our guests until I receive the respect that is due a kalsheera of the Bahari."

Alyen's stomach dropped, and she nearly fainted again, saved only by the strong arms of her companions propping her up. Unless she was very much mistaken, it sounded like "guests" was just another word for "prisoners."

Without further confrontation or words of farewell, they were ushered out of the beautiful hall with the peacefully trickling water, and though she could not see it, Alyen was quite sure that the eyes of the kalsheera followed them like knives in their backs.

16

THE DESERT AND THE MOON

Alyen's fears were soon confirmed. The guards led them through the corridors until they reached a room with high wooden doors intricately carved like so much of the palace. Inside, the room was spacious and richly furnished, with a large bed and several lounge chairs, all made from polished wood and cool silks. Alyen's first reaction upon seeing the room was a flutter of hope, for surely prisoners would not be treated to such lavish accommodations. But the click of a key in the lock as the guards closed the doors behind them left no room for uncertainty as to what their situation truly was.

Aaron and Nah'dar helped Alyen settle onto the bed, Aaron glancing up at their Sandamarian companion with consternation as he eased Alyen back onto the pillows.

"Nah'dar, was that really wise—"

But Nah'dar cut him off with a sharp motion of his hand. He pointed silently to the doors and walls, then to his ears. *So there* could *be eavesdroppers,* Alyen thought grimly. Then Nah'dar drew out his hearing stone from beneath his clothing, motioning for the others to do the same. Once they all had their stones in hand, the former assassin's voice sounded in their minds.

"Yes, Aaron, it was wise, though I am sure it did not seem so. I had to anger my mother enough to ensure that she would place us in one of these rooms. There was no way to explain it to you ahead of time."

Alyen very much doubted that Nah'dar's show of temper had been merely an act to rile his mother, but she said nothing. In any case, Aaron was already questioning again. *"Why these rooms? What are they used for?"*

"These are the rooms reserved for visiting dignitaries, either from other tribes and oases, or from foreign nations. Sandamarians are a suspicious people at best and combative at worst. Competition for control of the oases is fierce, and though much is made of the warriors who battle for their tribes and their kalsheeri, in truth, the opportunities for open combat are few and brief, given the climate. Often it is easier to dispense with an enemy in ways that are less public—hence the existence of the Order of Assassins."

"And how does that relate to this room, exactly?" Alyen asked, fearing she would not like the answer.

Nah'dar's eyes scanned the room darkly, as though remembering things that had once happened there. *"These rooms were designed for assassinations. Each has hidden entry points known only to those ranking highest in the Order. Not even the kalsheeri know how their commands to the Order are fulfilled, and the builders and architects were executed upon the palace's completion to preserve the secret. To most people, these rooms are a prison. But to a royal assassin, they are the rooms with the safest and most secret exits."*

Alyen and Aaron stared blankly at Nah'dar for a moment,

shock at his words temporarily rendering them speechless. Then Aaron frowned, casting about the room as if searching for the hidden entry points. *"But Nah'dar, you said that if your identity was discovered, the Order would come to assassinate you. Doesn't that mean that we're in danger?"*

Nah'dar strode to the windows and began pulling down the shades, casting the room in shadow as he spoke. Alyen wished he wouldn't—the light had been comforting. *"Not yet. Sandamarians are also a superstitious people, and they will not move against me without observing procedure. First, it will take time for news of my arrival to reach the Order. Then, they will consult the oracle to seek guidance from the spirits—who will say that I must be killed. They will then confirm this interpretation with the Order's priest and high master. Only then will an assassin be assigned to my death, and they will go through the ritual preparations. As such, we have several hours before we must flee. We would be wise to use the time to rest."*

Nah'dar turned back to his companions and was met with two incredulous stares. *"Rest?"* Alyen said. *"How can we possibly rest knowing assassins are on the way? And even if we make it out of the palace, where do we go then?"*

"We will go to the docks. My sister's ship is anchored in the port."

Alyen's head jerked backward. *"Sister? I didn't know you had a sister."*

Nah'dar nodded. *"Jah'dara. My twin."*

"You have a twin?"

Nah'dar's face was impassive, and in the darkened room Alyen couldn't tell if he was perplexed by her surprise or simply ignoring it.

"So your twin sister, Jah'dara, owns a ship?" Aaron asked. *"And we're going to ask her for safe passage out of Lunalor?"*

"That is my plan, yes," Nah'dar confirmed.

Aaron chewed his lip for a moment, seeming to consider his next words. *"Nah'dar, how certain are you of her loyalty to you? I wouldn't ask, but … your mother seemed less than …"* he trailed off, unable to find words that would be both accurate and sensitive.

Nah'dar's answering voice in their head was soft, but edged in steel. *"Jah'dara and I are loyal to each other until death. I trust her more than any other soul in this world or the next."*

There was a silence, and Alyen felt a small kernel of jealousy twinge in her stomach. Somehow she'd come to think of Nah'dar as a lone warrior, and she—his sanahara—as his most trusted companion. He'd confided in her, after all, about his past and more. Now it seemed there was someone higher in his esteem, and it hurt. Another loss in a year of losses.

But this wasn't the time or the place to sort through those feelings. She hid them away with the rest, wondering briefly if there would ever come a time when life was settled and slow enough to feel things as they came, rather than stashing them away in the hidden places of her heart for later.

The moment stretched almost uncomfortably, then Aaron nodded in deferment. *"All right. We make for the docks. When do we leave? Why don't we just go now?"*

"We cannot go now," Nah'dar said firmly. *"For one, no one will be out at this time, and we would attract too much attention by wandering the empty streets. Secondly, Jah'dara and her crew will also likely be resting through the heat of the day. If we go too early, we will be forced to rouse them—which could draw unwanted eyes—or else to wait in the open as easy targets. Thirdly, we do all need rest after the ordeal of last night—Alyen in particular. So we will stay here for a few hours, then leave through the tunnels in the late afternoon. I will lead you to a safe place where you can wait while I find Jah'dara alone.*

Once I have arranged for our passage, I will return to take you to the ship."

"*We couldn't wait in the tunnels now?*" Alyen asked, still unenthusiastic at the thought of waiting in the palace where assassins would be imminently arriving.

"*Until someone is sent for me, we are far safer in this room than we would be in the Order's labyrinth. Trust me, Alyen. I would not endanger my sanahara.*"

There was something vulnerable in Nah'dar's eyes as he held Alyen's, and she suddenly regretted her jealous thoughts. "*Of course,*" she said, emphasizing her words with a nod. "*I trust you.*"

Nah'dar nodded back as if satisfied that things were in order. "*Rest, then. I shall keep watch and wake you when the time comes.*"

"*Don't you need to rest, too?*" Alyen asked.

"*Yes, we can take turns with the watch——*" Aaron agreed.

But Nah'dar cut them off, a sharpness entering his tone. "*This watch is mine to take. Rest, and prepare for what is to come.*" He released his hearing stone, turned away, and sat—peculiarly, Alyen thought—against one of the walls near the far corner of the room, his face inscrutable in the shadows.

Alyen and Aaron looked at each other, neither knowing what to say. Alyen shrugged, and Aaron nodded in reply.

"*Will you be all right?*" Aaron asked. His voice sounded like it used to, gentle and protective. It sent a stab through Alyen's gut, agitating the growing storm of things left unresolved between them.

Alyen swallowed and nodded. "*I'll be fine,*" she assured him. As if to prove her point—and to avoid anything that might further rile what she needed to stay dormant inside her

—she dropped her hearing stone back beneath her dress and lay down as if to sleep.

Aaron stood for a moment, indecision lining his face. Alyen held her breath, fearing what he might say, yet desperate for the words. She closed her eyes to block out his form, unable to bear the sight of him standing so close to the bed with arms that she knew still ached when they remembered holding her and eyes that darkened when she was near. For a few heartbeats he hovered, then seemed to sigh, and Alyen heard his footsteps retreat from the bed to claim a spot on one of the lounge chairs.

Alyen let out her breath, and she didn't know whether it was exhaustion, relief, or tears unshed that made it shake as it left her lips.

Exhausted as she was, Alyen found that she could not sleep. The room was too strange, their circumstances too fraught to relax. For what seems like hours, Alyen alternated between staring at the walls, and lying with her eyes closed, ears straining for any sound that might herald the arrival of Nah'-dar's would-be assassins. She hoped that if she at least rested her body, she would avoid a complete collapse long enough to make it to the supposed safety of Jah'dara's ship. But eventually she gave up, unable to tolerate the interminable tense stillness of the room any longer.

She sat up on her bed, cringing with distaste at the way her dress seemed to crackle, stiff and caked with salt from the sea. Her eyes trailed over to Nah'dar. He had not moved since taking up his post, arms clasped around his bent knee in a posture that seemed relaxed, but from which, Alyen guessed, he could be on his feet in an instant, scimitar in hand. How he could sit there, knowing that at this very moment his former Order was planning his own assassination was beyond the limits of Alyen's reasoning. Not for the first time, she wondered how much turbulence her sanhar carried beneath his stoic demeanor.

Alyen rose and crossed the room, careful not to wake Aaron, whose breaths were coming slow and deep from where he lay curled up on his lounge chair. She settled herself next to Nah'dar, raising her eyebrows and drawing out her hearing stone when the former assassin's eyes flicked up to hers. He reached for his own stone and clasped it in his palm.

"You cannot sleep?"

Alyen shook her head. *"I don't know how Aaron does it, honestly."*

"He sleeps too deeply for a warrior," Nah'dar observed. Then, sounding somewhat abashed, added, *"It is my only critique."*

Alyen grinned. *"I won't tell him."*

Silence stretched between them. Alyen took in the unhappy lines of Nah'dar's face, wondering how much she could ask without upsetting him further. Or perhaps he would welcome the chance to talk about the past that he carried like a knife in his heart?

In the end, it was curiosity and her need for distraction that won out.

"The man at registration—the one who recognized you," Alyen said. *"Who was he?"*

Nah'dar's mouth turned downward. *"He was … a friend. When we were very young. Another born with little magic, though a bit more than me. He betrayed me in order to further himself in the eyes of those who could offer him a better position than what he would otherwise enjoy."*

"I'm sorry."

"Do not be. I likely would have done the same. Anyone born with little magic would if they thought it would secure them a better future."

Alyen frowned. "What is the reason for the way Sandamarians view magic? Forgive me, but … it seems cruel."

Nah'dar glanced sideways at her. *"You have never heard the legend?"*

"No."

Nah'dar drew in a deep breath, and let it out—a sound that seemed heavy and resigned. Instead of the anger Alyen expected, sadness deepened the lines of his face. A pause, then his words came, quiet and flowing.

"In the time before time began, Desert stretched, black and rich with magic, over Sandamar. By day, Desert's magic unleashed in a blaze of heat and power so strong that only the sun could bear to look upon him. But at night, while Desert slept and his magic cooled, Moon, drifting pale and beautiful from high above, could look down and admire Desert for his strength and the magic that was so different from her own.

"Moon fell in love with Desert and longed to join their magics together. But Desert could not leave the earth, nor could Moon leave the sky, and so it seemed their union could never be.

"Heartbroken, Moon wept, and her tears fell upon Desert's black sands. Thus could the magic of Desert and Moon at last entwine, for wherever Moon's tears fell, a pool of cool water formed, cradled in Desert's dark embrace. And around each oasis, life sprang into being: first plants, then beasts, and finally the Children of Sandamar. These were the Sons of the Desert and the Daughters of the Moon, called thus for the magic of their parents flowing beneath their skin. Men carried the black

magic of Desert's blazing sands, while the women carried Moon's pale and beautiful power."

Nah'dar paused in his recitation, and when he continued, his voice held a bitter note. *"It is this legend that led Sandamarians to the belief that for men, darker skin indicates a greater gift of magic from our father, the Desert. And a woman's power is reflected by the Moon's alabaster glow in her complexion. For those of us who do not fit the mold ..."* Nah'dar's voice trailed off and his hand made a flippant gesture. *"We are cursed to a magic-less existence. Unworthy. Unwanted. Despised."*

Alyen was silent for a long moment, logic and an urge to console warring with her desire not to offend. *"But why couldn't there be a Daughter of the Desert? Or a Son of the Moon?"*

Nah'dar's eyes glinted, a deeper black in the already shadowy darkness. *"Because that is not how the story goes. And a person will cling more fiercely to the stories they believe than almost anything else in the world."*

Alyen shook her head. *"Nah'dar, you are the greatest warrior I've ever seen—probably one of the greatest warriors the world has ever known. Surely you can't believe—"*

"What I believe will not make sense to you." Nah'dar's tone was dismissive.

"Try me," Alyen pressed.

Nah'dar was silent for a time, his gaze resting in the gloom on things Alyen couldn't see. When he spoke, his voice was a near-whisper in her mind. *"I know the stories are not true. But I believe them still."* He turned his face to Alyen, and in the shadows that were his eyes, she watched the heart of a small boy break anew.

Alyen swallowed back the lump that rose in her throat.

"But you changed your story," she said. *"How did you come to be the First Assassin of the Bahari if you were supposed to live a rejected life?"*

Nah'dar's mouth thinned. *"I did something ... irreversible. At the time, I thought it proved to someone important that magic is not the only thing that determines a person's potential. But I am not sure that is true. He had much to gain from me, and if letting me believe that I was leading a noble life gave it to him ..."* He shrugged, letting the words trail off.

Alyen frowned, not liking the defeated sag to her sanhar's shoulders. *"But then you changed your life again. Twice you rebuilt yourself in ways that most people never do, even once. That must mean that somewhere deep down, you believe you deserve better."*

"And what if I do?" Nah'dar asked, looking frankly into Alyen's face. *"It makes no difference to my people. Most of them cannot ever know the things I became or the life I have led. And even if they did ... I do not think it would change their minds. It is why I hoped never to see my mother again. I have spent far too much of my time seeking things from her that she will never give."*

Alyen paused, wondering if the question on her tongue would be crossing a line. *"Does it bother you? That your mother will never know what you've accomplished?"*

Nah'dar was still for a moment, his face impassive as he studied his hands. *"As I said. It would not matter. To her I will always be the son who shamed her by being born magic-less."*

"How is that possible? After everything you've done?"

Nah'dar's eyes rose to meet Alyen's, his mouth a bitter line. *"Because it is the story she believes."*

17

LIGHTSTONE

Despite everything, Alyen must have fallen asleep, because she suddenly found herself nudged awake, her head jerking groggily off of its resting place on Nah'dar's shoulder.

"Come, sanahara," Nah'dar's voice spoke, still inside her head. *"We must leave."*

Alyen hastily rose, attempting to clear her head as she stuffed her hearing stone back into her dress. Aaron was already moving about the room, checking that they'd forgotten nothing, and he brought Alyen her healing bag. His eyes held hers for a moment as he helped her sling the strap over her head. *How are you?* he mouthed, his hand lingering on her shoulder.

The storm in her chest awakened at his touch, and emotions coursed through her, chaotic and conflicted. Anger at what he'd done to her. Yearning that bordered on anguish. Grief at what they'd lost. Guilt over her part in it. Fear that it

175

could never be fixed, and resentment that it was her task to do so. Part of her wanted to push him away, another part wanted to cling to him, losing herself in his arms forever. She looked into his eyes—eyes that were opening again, searching and hesitant—and knew that she hadn't a clue how to even begin sorting through everything that was roiling inside her, let alone how to mend things. And she knew that, once again, she had no choice but to push it all aside, to let the storm simmer for another day.

Alyen gave him a wry expression and a shrug, a reassuring gesture that belied nothing of her inner turmoil, then turned to Nah'dar, willing herself to focus only on their escape.

Nah'dar was crouched by the corner of the room, his fingers moving over the seams between the alabaster stones of the palace wall. His hands paused on the largest slab on the bottom, then he struck the stone sharply with the heel of his hand in three different places. The stone shifted, and Nah'dar lifted it away to reveal that it was not, in fact, a solid stone in the wall as it appeared, but rather a thin slab acting as a facade that hid a dark hole in the bottom of the wall.

He stuck his head into the hole and froze as if listening, then withdrew it and moved aside, gesturing for Alyen to enter first. Skeptical, Alyen approached the opening, and, peering inside, saw a series of rungs attached to the inner wall leading from the mouth of the hole down into the darkness below the palace.

Alyen looked at Nah'dar doubtfully, and her sanhar nodded in confirmation. Cringing inwardly at the thought of squeezing herself into the tight, dark space, Alyen set her mouth in a determined line, and lowered herself backward into the hole. Her feet found their footing, and she began to climb downward, slowly feeling for each step, and wondering how far down the shaft went and what they would find at the bottom.

As it happened, it wasn't a very far climb downward. Alyen was soon surprised by her foot hitting solid ground as it reached for another rung, and she stumbled from the ladder, her hands groping around her in the dark. Her palms connected with a rock wall, and she froze, huddled against it as she waited for the others to descend.

It was pitch black in the tunnel, and Alyen was tempted to ask the salamandars for some light, but thought better of it. If there were assassins moving through these passageways, she certainly didn't want to attract them. Above her she could hear feet descending the rungs once again, and soon the scrape of boots against rock announced that one of her companions had reached the bottom.

"Alyen?" Aaron's whisper sounded in the dark.

"Here," Alyen whispered back, reaching out in the direction of Aaron's voice. A few shuffling steps, then Aaron's hand connected with hers, and she pulled him over to join her against the wall. She relaxed her hand, expecting him to let go, but he didn't. Instead, he stood close by her in the dark, hands still clasped, and Alyen was reminded forcefully of the day they had found the tunnel in the back of the tool-shed at Monstar Abbey. Her heart wrenched. How simple things had been back then, how minor her worries, how inno-cent the thoughts that had preoccupied her mind. She closed her eyes against the swirl of the storm within, focusing her attention instead on the feel of Aaron's hand in hers, the way it was hardened from swordplay, yet gentle as it encircled her palm. Almost involuntarily, her fingers tightened around

Aaron's—just a fraction—and she felt Aaron's soft squeeze in return.

From above came the scrape of the slab being replaced in the wall, then Nah'dar's boots on the rungs as he descended. Alyen heard his feet meet with the floor and take a few steps away from them before stopping all together. Silence filled the darkness, and Alyen was just about to ask Nah'dar what was happening when a faint light bloomed and spread throughout the space, casting a greenish glow through what appeared to be a long stone tunnel. As the light hit them, Alyen and Aaron instinctively released each other's hands.

Nah'dar was standing opposite them, and the light, they saw, was being emitted from a sphere of glowing rock embedded in the stone wall. "Sandamarian lightstone," he explained softly. "It glows when rubbed, but only for a minute or two. There are spheres embedded at intervals throughout these tunnels. Follow behind me and I will lead the way to the port."

They set off through the tunnel, Alyen following close behind her sanhar, with Aaron following her. As they walked, the green glow steadily dimmed, but always before it extinguished completely, Nah'dar would reach another sphere, pause to rub it, then lead them down the next stretch of tunnel in the eerie half-light. As they progressed, Alyen became aware that it was not simply one tunnel, but a warren of interconnected passageways running beneath the city, with tunnels frequently branching off in all directions. Several times, Nah'dar turned to lead them down a different passage, always confident in his direction, and Alyen wondered how long it had taken him to memorize the twisting labyrinth.

They made good time, and soon came to a passage that

angled upward, presumably back toward ground level. Nah'dar stopped and turned to face them.

"I must go on alone from here," he said, his voice still low and soft. "Wait here for me. Do not ignite the lightstone, and try to remain quiet. When I have settled things with Jah'dara, I will come for you."

"But why can't we come with you?" Alyen asked.

Nah'dar hesitated, and Alyen was unsure how to interpret his expression. "It has been a long time since I saw my twin," he said. "It will be better if I approach her alone. Besides, one person will attract less attention than three."

"I thought you said you trusted Jah'dara," Aaron said, frowning.

"I do," Nah'dar confirmed. "But I know my sister, and she will feel better if I warm her to our cause before bringing strangers to her ship. As we are in need of her assistance, it is prudent to make her as comfortable as possible."

"All right. Be careful," Alyen said. "And … are you sure we'll be safe here?"

The lightstone was dimming, throwing everyone's faces into shadows of green and black. Nah'dar nodded, the odd lighting making his face look mask-like. "We should still have some time, and I will try to be quick. And even if trouble were to find you, sanahara, you have a warrior at your side. One of the best."

With these words, he turned and disappeared into the shadows of the ascending passage.

Alyen looked at Aaron, but the Slayer seemed to be avoiding her gaze. Perhaps Nah'dar's words had made him feel awkward? He'd never been one to preen under praise, but it wasn't like him to be shy either. The lightstone was barely glowing now, and Aaron took the moment to settle himself on the floor of the passage, his back leaning against the rock wall. Alyen followed suit, resting against the wall opposite. No sooner had she done so, than the lightstone extinguished, and they were plunged once again into darkness.

They waited in silence. Half of Alyen listened intently for any sound of an approaching assassin. The other half skirted the edges of the storm inside her. Memories of their connection at sea flooded her mind, her heart a turmoil in her chest. She wondered if Aaron was thinking similar thoughts, if he, too, was feeling the strain as his own desire and pain warred with each other. She supposed she should have expected it, yet still she jumped when Aaron's voice sounded, soft yet sudden in the dark.

"I'm sorry. About asking you to calm the storm. It wasn't fair, and … it wasn't a good plan."

Alyen swallowed, unsure if she was relieved or disappointed he hadn't brought up the deeper void between them. Regardless, she was somewhat gratified that he'd offered an apology. She knew it was time to offer one of her own as well. "I'm sorry I shipwrecked us. I should have listened when you told me to unmeld instead of pushing us farther. I suppose I should know better by now."

Silence stretched between them again. Alyen found herself hoping he would say more, that somehow he would make her feel seen and cherished the way he once had. But things were different now. They couldn't return to that time or how they once were, could never erase what had transpired, and Alyen had to stop wishing they could. It only led to more pain and an inner storm she could barely contain.

"I came back."

Alyen started, jarred from her thoughts by Aaron's sudden words. She frowned. "What?"

"To the beach," Aaron said, sounding defeated. "I … when I left you there after Illya. I came back, but you had already gone."

Alyen was silent for a moment, his words echoing against her in the dark. Her breath was suddenly coming quicker, the storm swirling. Of all the things he could have said—of all the things she'd imagined or hoped he would say—this was one she'd never anticipated. Finally, she said, "You knew where I'd gone. You could have followed."

"I know," Aaron replied, his voice barely above a whisper. "I—I'm not sure why I didn't. It was the biggest mistake I've ever made and … I'm sorry."

The brokenness in his voice made Alyen's heart shatter. The storm sensed the crack in her armor and fought for release. She wiped away the tears on her cheeks, grateful for the darkness. The silence hung between them, heavy with hurt and regret, until Alyen added her own whisper to its depths, the words rising unplanned and unsought, but heavy with truth.

"I made the wrong choice. I never should have let Faer Dinnán alter your memory. I was afraid, and … I should have had more faith in you. I should have had more faith in us."

Aaron said nothing. She heard a sniff from his side of the passage and wondered if he, too, was silently weeping.

This was not how she'd ever envisioned this conversation to go. There was no triumph, no vindication, no reconciliation, nor really any relief on either side. Whenever Alyen had fantasized about this exchange, there had always been a sense of resolution at the end. A return of equilibrium, and perhaps even of love.

But this was no happy ending. True, they had seen and felt each other's pain, and they had both atoned for their misdeeds. But rather than joy or renewal, sorrow now surrounded them, and they could only sit in its embrace, grieving together, yet still apart.

Suddenly, the lightstone ignited once more, and Nah'dar's form could be seen returning down the passage. Alyen glanced at Aaron, and for a moment, their eyes met. He looked as she felt—raw, broken, and sad, with cheeks that shone wetly in the green half-light. Alyen lowered her eyes and wiped a sleeve against her face as she stood to meet their third companion.

If Nah'dar noticed their shattered state, he made no comment. "Come," he said. "All has been arranged, but we must make haste. The ship is ready to depart on the tide, and our absence will soon be noticed in the palace."

Without further instruction, he turned and led the way up the passage.

Alyen's limbs trembled as she walked, unable to withstand the exhaustion of the past two days much longer. She concentrated on her steps, placing one foot after another, taking note of how the tunnel changed as they ascended. Already the lightstone was dimming, but she found it did not matter as much. A different kind of light—daylight—was filtering into the passage from ahead, and she felt herself drawn to it as a moth to a flame.

At last, they came to a wall of stone where the passage ended. Once more, Nah'dar ran his fingers over the stones, searching for something Alyen could only assume was some small indication of which slab marked the hidden doorway. As before, his hands suddenly paused on one block of stone, then he rapped sharply on its corners, and lifted the slab away to reveal an opening just large enough for a grown man to slip through.

Alyen crawled through the makeshift door and staggered to her feet to find herself at the back of what appeared to be a shop that had long since gone out of business. A dilapidated structure of empty shelves stood behind a dusty counter, and old, weathered signs hung haphazardly from the walls, their writing faded and peeling. With her rudimentary skills in Sandamarian, Alyen gathered that the small store had once sold fishing supplies and bait. A breeze carrying the sharp tang of the sea blew in through the door that hung half off its hinges, and she realized that they must be close to the docks.

Aaron emerged from the passage just behind her, followed by Nah'dar, who swiftly replaced the slab over the entrance to the tunnels. It immediately camouflaged with the rest of the wall, leaving no trace of the doorway it concealed. Nah'dar straightened and strode swiftly to the door of the shop, peering out through its cracks, his face tense. Apparently satisfied that their way was clear, he motioned Alyen and Aaron to follow him, then swung the creaking door open and led them out into the city.

Dusk was falling, transforming the alabaster city into a collage of deep shadow and glowing orange. Heat still radiated from surfaces in every direction, including the ground itself, yet Alyen was relieved to feel a hint of chill on the breeze that blew in from the sea that stretched before them. Conveniently, the shop's entrance had deposited them just at the edge of the docks, and Nah'dar was already making his way swiftly along the shore.

Alyen followed her sanhar, Aaron close by her side. She hoped desperately that Jah'dara's ship was nearby, and breathed a sigh of relief when Nah'dar turned down the third dock toward a ship bearing a standard depicting some sort of berry-laden branch on a red background and the name *Desert Star* painted on its prow. The ship was wide and heavy—a model typical to Sandamarian trading vessels providing ample room in the hold, but offering little in terms of speed or maneuverability. Dimly, Alyen knew that a faster, more agile ship would have been preferable, but she couldn't bring herself to care about any of that now, so long as it contained some small corner where she could sleep in peace and safety.

They reached the gangplank as the sun dipped low, throwing a ruddy glow over the ship and its crew. As if from a distance, Alyen heard Nah'dar's request to board, and a woman's voice, strong and commanding, replying her assent.

Alyen wasn't aware that she was swaying, but Aaron's arms were suddenly around her, helping her up the gangplank behind Nah'dar. She drew in deep gulps of the ocean air, willing her head to clear enough to make it to a bed before she collapsed.

Her feet hit the deck of the ship, and while the gentle swaying underfoot did nothing to help her sense of stability, the distance from the scorching earth combined with the cooler ocean breeze did momentarily revive her. With Aaron's steadying grip on her arm, Alyen looked up at the ship's captain standing before them, and her eyes widened. She supposed that she'd expected Nah'dar's twin to be a female version of Nah'dar himself, but Jah'dara was nothing of the sort. True, she radiated the same fierceness as her brother, but that was where the resemblance ended.

Jah'dara's skin was a dark and beautiful ebony, her hair a cascade of braids pulled back from her face. Silver tattoos gleamed as they swirled around her arms, and her posture bespoke a commanding strength that would rival any army general. Her black eyes, sharp and discerning, sized up Alyen in one burning glance, making her wish even more that she was not in such a weak and bedraggled state.

"This is your sanahara?" Jah'dara asked, her eyes still fixed on Alyen.

"Yes," Nah'dar answered.

Jah'dara seemed to come to a conclusion in her mind and gave a brief nod of her head. "Take her to my cabin. She will find rest and quiet most easily there."

Alyen mumbled her thanks, but Jah'dara had already turned away, shouting orders to her crew in Sandamarian to prepare the ship to sail. Nah'dar took Alyen's other arm to help lead her to the captain's cabin when she saw him pause, his muscles tensing as his eyes sharpened on the shore. Alyen turned to look where his gaze was fixed and saw a man clad in black striding alone toward the docks. He paused just before the shop that held the entrance to the assassins' tunnels, then he swiftly opened the shop's door and disappeared within.

A chill ran down Alyen's spine as she realized who the man must be, and how close they had come to crossing his path.

"Jah'dara," Nah'dar called to his sister. His voice was calm, but his sister's head turned sharply toward him as if she could hear the current of tension running beneath. "The palace will soon know. We have minutes before the alarm will sound."

Jah'dara held his gaze for only a second, then gave him a curt nod of her head. She resumed the shouted commands that Alyen couldn't understand, but she thought the captain's voice now held a new note of urgency, and her crew seemed to hasten in their duties.

By the time Alyen and her companions had reached the cabin door, the ship was sliding away from the dock, heading for the open sea. The sails unfurled, and the ship surged forward. It was heavy and awkward compared to the *Sea Sparrow*, and Alyen had to bite down on the impatience that rose in her throat. Seconds later, a bell began tolling somewhere in the heart of Lunalor. Alyen and her companions paused in the doorway, turning back to scan the retreating land with anxious eyes. On the shore, doors were thrown open and figures swarmed the docks, closing the port, and faint shouts could be heard as ships' captains protested the orders to remain anchored until further notice.

Alyen suddenly realized who must have ordered the alarm sounded, and who presumably had done it with the knowledge that an assassin had been sent to her palace. Her heart wrenched, and she glanced up at Nah'dar's face—a face devoid of emotion as he observed the activity on the docks.

"Your mother?" she asked quietly.

Nah'dar's head made a tiny jerk that may have been a nod. Then he lowered his eyes and turned away from the shore. "Come, sanahara," he said, his voice like an autumn leaf on the wind. "It's time you found rest."

Alyen wanted to say more. She wanted to be with her sanhar as he faced a world in which his own mother had conspired to have him killed. But suddenly exhaustion broke over her like a wave, and she knew it would have to wait. She had nothing left but to succumb to the healing void that awaited her.

Nah'dar and Aaron helped Alyen into the cabin and onto a soft bed that rocked gently with the swells of the sea. She barely had time to register her shoes being removed and a blanket laid gently about her shoulders before she sank at last into a deep and dreamless sleep.

18

THE MAELSTROM

In the dusky half-light of predawn, Lirianna lay on her cot, staring up at the planks that formed the underside of the *Belladonna*'s deck above her. She'd slept, but not much, and what she *had* managed was more of a restless doze than any kind of real slumber. Before that she'd spent hours poring over the parchment of Andair the Bard's ballad, applying herself in earnest for the first time to the task Captain Voros had set her. Her skin still crawled at the thought of bending to his will, but now that Tom was hurt and under threat of further injury, everything had changed. Rescue could not come soon enough, and Lirianna was terrified that she wouldn't be able to hold off the captain's ire long enough for it to arrive.

With these thoughts in mind, Lirianna reached for her hearing stone. *"Alyen? Aaron?"*

"Lirianna," Aaron's voice responded in her head. *"How are you?"*

188

Lirianna frowned. *"Where's Alyen? Is everything all right?"*

"She's fine. She's asleep. I …" The hesitation in his voice made Lirianna's belly clench. *"I did something stupid, and it exhausted her."*

A sinking sensation dragged Lirianna's heart into her stomach. Whatever had taken place, she was quite sure it wouldn't mean that rescue was imminent. *"What happened?"* she asked, trying to keep the dismay out of her thoughts.

For the next several minutes, Lirianna listened to Aaron's summary of their arrival in Tírann, the brief and disastrous voyage of the *Sea Sparrow*, their refuge in Sandamar, and their escape from Lunalor Oasis and Nah'dar's would-be assassin. She listened with growing consternation as it became clear that her friends were, in fact, *farther* away from intercepting the *Belladonna*, and that they seemed unlikely to catch up anytime soon. What had been a sinking in her stomach now turned into a ball of lead.

She knew Aaron wouldn't want to hear her news. She could already hear the guilt in his voice as he spoke, and, indeed, he ended his monologue with an apology.

"I'm sorry, Lirianna. I wanted to get to you faster. I thought we could with Alyen's magic. But I've made a mess of things, and if I'm being honest … the whole thing was probably just me trying to prove to Alyen that I didn't need her to be the one deciding everything. It's entirely my fault."

Lirianna heard the dejection in his tone, and she winced. *"It's all right, Aaron. It's completely understandable, given what you went through this spring. And … you're not the only one who's messed up."*

"Oh, Saints, Lirianna, what happened?"

Lirianna sighed and told him everything that had tran-spired the night before, from the session with the bards to the captain's discovery that she'd made no progress on the ballad, and Tom's subsequent punishment.

That is, she told him *almost* everything. When it came time to speak of the magic that had poured from her fingers and of the effect it had had on the *Belladonna*'s crew, the words suddenly stuck in her throat, and she found she couldn't say them. Instead, she made it sound like Captain Voros's fury stemmed from the fact that they hadn't been playing the ballad in the first place, then she hurried on to describe Tom's lashing, trying to ignore the burn of shame that rose in her cheeks.

"Lirianna," Aaron said, sounding aghast. *"I'm—is Tom all right?"*

"The wounds he already has will heal," Lirianna said. *"But I don't think he'll be able to take much more of it. And it's all my fault!"*

"It's not," Aaron was quick to reassure, and Lirianna was grateful that he'd said it. *"None of this is your doing. How could it be?"*

The gratitude vanished, and her heart constricted. Aaron had no idea—she'd never told him or Alyen about her magic at all, and certainly not that she'd used it at Faer Dinnán's behest to orchestrate their reunion. It was why she couldn't tell him about the bards last night, and why she couldn't admit to either of them that it was her actions and her magic that had led to this whole mess to begin with.

Because if she did, they might not understand. They would be furious with her, and rightfully so. If she told them, it might be the thing that finally broke the Trianid for good.

Luckily, Aaron didn't seem to read into her silence, and continued without waiting for her response. *"And what of the ballad? Do you have any idea what it could mean?"*

"Not yet," Lirianna admitted. *"But I haven't spent much time trying, either. I did come up with one idea last night, so I'll work on that today."*

"We'll look at it as well," Aaron promised. *"As soon as Alyen is up, we'll make a plan to reach you as fast as possible, and we can work on the ballad on the way."*

Lirianna managed a watery smile at the ceiling. *"Thank you, Aaron. But don't worry too much about it. Chances are it needs a musician to decipher it. Just ..."* She hesitated, unsure whether she should say the thing that was on her mind.

"What is it?"

"Maybe, just try to make things better with Alyen," Lirianna said, her thought small. *"We might all need to be strong together again before this is all over."*

Aaron hesitated only a second. *"I will. I mean to."*

"Thanks," Lirianna said, eager now to end the conversation before either of them felt any worse. *"I'll let you know if I find anything."*

"And we'll let you know when we're getting close," Aaron promised.

They dropped their hearing stones, and Lirianna's mind once more housed her voice alone.

It will all work out, she told herself, fighting for the optimism that had once come so much easier. *And if Alyen and Aaron can mend things, then it'll all have been worth it.*

Won't it?

With the memories of Tom's mutilated back fresh in her mind, it was becoming very hard to believe the words were true.

❧

At dawn, Tom reappeared, a bowl in one hand and the forgotten harp in the other.

"Tom," Lirianna said, rising quickly from her cot. "How are you feeling?"

"Fantastic," Tom said, nodding. "Really good."

Lirianna pursed her lips at his sarcasm. "How's your back?" she asked pointedly.

Tom gave a one-shouldered shrug, the movement still looking tentative. "It'll heal." He lowered the harp to the floor and fumbled with the key in the lock. When he entered her cell, Lirianna glanced at the bowl in his hand, noting that its contents seemed to resemble some sort of cold gray mash that managed to look both dry and slimy at the same time. She looked at Tom, one eyebrow raised. "My breakfast?"

Tom's face twisted apologetically. "Looks like you're on crew fare now."

"This is seriously what he's giving you all to eat?" Lirianna said, her opinion of her captor sinking even lower.

Tom wrinkled his nose. "I'll just leave it over here for you, shall I?" He placed the bowl to the side, then retrieved the harp and held it out to Lirianna.

Lirianna took the instrument and set it beside her, guilt for the events of the previous night flooding her once more. "I'll figure it out, Tom," she said, trying to sound more confident than she felt. "Really, I'll do my best."

"Well … thanks," Tom said, sobering. "I'm sure if anyone has a chance of figuring it out, it's you."

Lirianna didn't like the hopeless note in her friend's tone. She'd been so set on thwarting Captain Voros and ignoring the ballad's riddle, but the truth was that she had noticed one peculiarity as she'd learned the music—a peculiarity that had niggled at her, demanding attention. And now that the situation had changed—now that Tom was in real danger—she'd spent half the night mulling over the oddity she'd been so keen to neglect.

"I've started already," she said, hoping to reassure. "I did learn the ballad, and I have a few thoughts on where to begin. Do you … do you want to stay and help?"

Tom glanced toward the stairs to the deck, hesitating. "I don't think I should stay too long," he said. "But maybe just for a few minutes."

They settled themselves on the cot, Lirianna pulling out the parchment containing the ballad. "Look," she said. "It all follows standard ballad form with five stanzas in a repeating pattern. There's nothing really unusual about the melody, and the harmonic structure is pretty basic—until you get to this chord, here." She pointed to a spot in the fourth stanza where the word "cove" was scrawled beneath the music notation. "What would you say that harmonic marking is?"

Tom squinted at the parchment. "It looks like an 'A' to me."

"Exactly," Lirianna said with satisfaction. "But look at the same spot in all the other stanzas."

Tom studied the parchment, then looked up at Lirianna, one eyebrow raised. "All 'O's'? But 'O' isn't a note. Or a chord."

Lirianna shook her head. "No, but what do bards call the chord built off the root note of a song's home key?"

"The 'one' chord," Tom said, understanding flashing over his features.

Lirianna nodded, excited despite herself. "They're all 'one' chords except for this one, which is marked as an 'A.' And look: not only is this the only stanza that uses an 'A' chord in that spot—it's the only time that chord is used in the entire piece. There are several places where the harmony could have been more interesting if he'd used the 'A' more often, but it's almost like he was purposefully avoiding it. It's the only thing that doesn't repeat exactly aside from the lyrics, so at first I thought it might be a copying mistake … but maybe it's not. Maybe it's a clue."

"But what would it mean?"

Lirianna shook her head, wishing she had more to share. "I don't know. But at least it's a place to start."

Tom said nothing, and Lirianna couldn't tell what he was thinking with his head bowed over the parchment. "Lirianna …" Tom finally looked up at her, his eyes filled with uncertainty.

Lirianna frowned. "What is it?"

"That thing you did last night …"

Lirianna's heart dropped. "I shouldn't have done it, Tom. I didn't mean to."

"But what was it?"

Lirianna couldn't tell if Tom's expression held hope or fear. "I don't know exactly," she admitted. "I wasn't lying when I said I don't understand how it works. It's some sort of magic, and it's somehow related to the weaving magic I use as Seer. But …" Tom was silent, and Lirianna dropped her eyes as she continued, her voice low. "It does things, Tom. And I don't know how to control it. I don't know what it's for."

Tom regarded her for a moment. "You're afraid of it." It was a statement rather than a question.

Lirianna nodded, unsure why the motion made her want to cry.

"Do you think you can use it to help figure out the ballad?" Tom's voice was carefully neutral.

"I—I don't think so. I don't see how."

Tom nodded and looked away, but not before Lirianna caught the disappointment that flashed in his eyes.

"I'm sorry, Tom," she said quickly. "It's not that I wouldn't, I just don't know——"

"It's fine," Tom said, cutting her off. "It was just an idea." He rose from the cot, throwing a glance at the stairs. "I should probably get back up. The fourth stanza … it sounds like a good place to start." He attempted an encouraging smile, but Lirianna could sense the defeat in the line of his shoulders. He exited her cell, locking the door behind him, and climbed back above deck.

Lirianna sagged. She'd been hoping that her small discovery would give Tom some measure of hope, but it didn't seem that it had. And despite her own initial excitement, if she was completely honest with herself, she had no idea how to continue. The thought of Tom receiving ten lashes that evening over the raw wounds he already bore made her heart race and her throat constrict. She lifted the parchment once more, the markings swimming as she tried to view it through eyes half-filled with tears.

"He's not wrong, you know."

Lirianna jumped and almost dropped the parchment. Faer Dinnán was in her cell, leaning against the iron bars across from her.

"I really wish you would stop doing that," she said, barely concealing the irritation in her voice.

The faerie king ignored her comment and seemed to be waiting for her to continue. After a prolonged and awkward silence, Lirianna gave in, sighing in exasperation. "Not wrong about what?"

"About using your magic to solve the ballad," Faer Dinnán said, his tone suggesting that this should have been obvious. "I'm curious—why have you not attempted it yet?"

Lirianna didn't know whether to feel incredulous or confused. "Why would I? I don't know how my magic works, I can't control it, and bad things happen when I try. People get *hurt*."

"What ill has ever come from your magic? Was your young brother not saved from a tragic death? Was Aaron not given hope that Alyen's love for him still burned? Are the Keeper and the Slayer not traveling together once more?"

"Yes," Lirianna said, her voice betraying her waning patience. "But it also burned my weaving to ash, got me kidnapped by pirates, and last night Tom was beaten bloody after the crew nearly fell apart from weeping!"

Faer Dinnán's brows drew together and his eyes seemed to burn. "Do not take responsibility for the cruelty of others, Seer. Tom's wounds were not the result of your magic, but of a heart darkened by greed and a desperation for control. Remember: magic is a gift, and Béathan does not bestow gifts of evil."

"But that doesn't help!" Lirianna said, heat rising in her tone. "I'm the Seer of Strands! Weaving magic has always been given to the Seer, but never in a way that would actually *change* things. Purity of Sight is our highest law, but it's just supposed to ensure that we aren't biased when we interpret our visions—not to prevent us from actually *altering* the tapestry of the world. If every Seer could magically weave whatever future they wanted just because they were feeling strongly about it, it would be disastrous. So *why*—if Béathan made me to fill the role of Seer—*why* would I also be given magic that could be so very dangerous?"

Lirianna was nearly shouting by the end of her speech, her breath fast and her eyes stinging. Faer Dinnán studied her for a moment, his expression thoughtful and mildly confused. Finally, he straightened and moved to sit on the cell's small stool where he regarded Lirianna once more.

"Is it the fact that your magic is different than that of your predecessors that alarms you?"

Lirianna gave Faer Dinnán a hard stare. "This isn't how the Seer of Strands is meant to be."

"And how do you presume to know what is meant to be?"

Lirianna struggled not to glare at the faerie king, irritated at the question. "It's not how it's ever been. That has to mean something."

"Indeed, it does," Faer Dinnán agreed. "In fact, I believe it's the whole point. Your magic is different from every Seer's magic before you because the world is now different from the world of every Seer before you."

Lirianna's eyes narrowed. "What do you mean?"

Faer Dinnán raised one eyebrow. "Think of it, Seer. Aaron was given all he needed to fulfill his destiny as the Second Slayer because the world needed him to. Alyen was given her melding magic because she needed it to save our world from a darkness never before seen. Would it not be prudent to assume that Béathan possesses the wisdom to give you exactly the magic you need to aid the world you were born to serve as Seer? Perhaps, rather than spending your time fearing a departure from the traditions of times past, you should focus on discovering *how* your magic can be used for good in the world you find yourself in now."

Lirianna was silent, the faerie king's words echoing in her mind. She wanted them to be true. But Faer Dinnán wasn't a Seer. He wasn't even human. If she were to trust him and it ended up being a mistake … She didn't even want to think of what the consequences to the kingdom and to the Trianid could be. Suddenly weary, Lirianna looked back to Faer Dinnán.

"Even if that's all true," she said, "I don't see how my magic has anything to do with solving a decades-old riddle or finding buried treasure. I wouldn't even know how to *try* to use it for that."

The faerie king rose from the stool, his expression unreadable. "I see your mind is made," he said, then gave a slight shrug. "In that case, I wish you luck in your efforts to succeed where many others have already failed. But remember …" He paused, his gaze intent once more. "Tom's safety now depends on your progress. Are you truly so fearful of yourself that you are willing to endanger the life of your friend?"

Before Lirianna could protest that this statement was entirely unfair, the faerie king was gone, and she was left with his words burning in her chest like acid.

For the remainder of the morning, Lirianna threw her entire being at solving the riddle of the ballad. She stared at the parchment until she was sure her crossing eyes would burn a hole through it. She took the harp up on her lap and played through the music over and over until her fingers were sore.

She sang it until the words had been imprinted on her mind for all eternity, and she played through every other piece she'd ever learned by Andair the Bard, hoping beyond hope that perhaps something in one of his other creations would spark some insight into the workings of his final and most secret song. But no matter what she tried or how hard she thought, no revelation came.

By midday, panic was threatening to overtake her. She did her best to ignore it, knowing that it would do nothing to help her concentration, but as the day wore on with nothing to show for her hours of work, it was hard to keep the desperation at bay. When one of the other bards descended to leave a new bowl of some revolting concoction masquerading as stew, Lirianna felt only relief that it hadn't been Tom, so she wouldn't have to admit to her failure and see the despair in his gray eyes.

A few more hours slid by, and Lirianna had taken to pacing her cell, hands tugging on her hair as she wracked her brain for anything that might delay the fate she feared Tom was facing. Should she tell Captain Voros of her theory? Would it be enough to postpone his wrath and Tom's punishment? Somehow, she didn't think so.

Suddenly she noticed that the light was dimming, and her barely contained panic rose, sharp in her throat. Had so much time passed? Surely it couldn't be evening already? The ship was starting to rock beneath her feet as if the sea, too, shared her anxious thoughts. Lirianna's eyes flashed to the harp leaning against her cot. Fear tingled in her fingers, but time was running out. Perhaps the time for desperate action had come.

Lirianna sat on her cot and pulled the harp onto her lap.

She leaned it back against her shoulder, trying to let the familiar feel of wood against her skin calm her fluttering heartbeat. For a moment she paused, terrified that she was about to make another mistake—a mistake that could lead to consequences she couldn't even begin to predict. Then she steeled herself, drew in a breath, and closed her eyes, sinking into the space between that only Seers could find.

Immediately, music rose in her mind, but it wasn't the ballad. It was her music—the music that demanded to be heard and now leapt at its chance to emerge. But Lirianna pushed it firmly away, panic and irritation making the mental gesture seem like a slap. The music recoiled and silenced, and her mind was left empty, free to turn to the ballad, as she sank ever deeper into the space of the Balance.

Her fingers began to move over the strings of the harp, not unlike the way her hands moved over her loom as she wove. She played the ballad, now so familiar that she didn't even have to think about what her fingers were doing. As she played it, the words falling softly from her lips, a multitude of threading strands materialized before her mind's eye, all weaving together in an intricate tapestry of color and light.

But what were these strands? Usually when she wove, she saw the strands that formed the tapestry of the world, and the Balance itself would guide her to the ones that would show her what she needed to see. But those strands were always already there, ever present and waiting for her. This tapestry was being created before her eyes, the strands of warp and weft materializing even as she watched.

Slowly, it dawned on her that there was a pattern to the shimmering dance of the strands before her, a pattern that seemed to follow the one her fingers were making as she played. Yes, now that she'd noticed she could tell: those strands there were the melody, delicate and graceful. These thicker ones below were the low notes, ringing like bells. These here were the middle voices, playful and sweet, and all of them were interlocking and weaving together in a dance that created something magical and unique.

At once, she understood. Weaving, music—the world at large, really—it was all the same. Patterns manifesting and dissolving in the great cosmic dance of the universe.

Lirianna was so astonished by this revelation that she almost missed it. The flash that illuminated one strand in the pattern, just as her voice sang out the word "cove." Her heart skipped, and though her fingers continued to move over the strings of the harp, she reached out and grasped the glowing strand, pulling it toward her across the space between.

Images bloomed before her eyes. The parchment containing the ballad filled her vision, the word "cove" and its strange harmonic marking glowing and floating up off the page. They hovered before her, "cove" and "A," as if waiting for her to understand. *What is it?* Lirianna wondered, knowing that she was so close to the answer, yet still unable to grasp it. *Of all the words in the ballad, why would this one need an A instead of an O?*

The answer dropped so suddenly into her mind it startled her.

A cove with an "A" became a cave.

She knew she was right, felt the truth of it ringing in her bones. As if it could read her mind, the vision before her seemed to shimmer and glow in agreement. Lirianna's heart soared, triumph bubbling up, making her chest swell and her fingers dance faster across the harp strings.

Then suddenly, all was thrown into chaos. Lirianna was ripped from her vision as her body was hurled from the cot. The harp flew out of her hands, and she heard a jangling snap that made her heart lurch. But there was no time to investigate. The ship was tilting at an alarming angle, gravity pressing her against the bars of her cell. Lirianna whimpered in terror, still disoriented and confused, but cogent enough to realize that if the ship tipped much farther, it would capsize, and she would surely drown, trapped in her cage.

But Lirianna didn't even have time to scream before she was thrown across the cell once again, this time hitting her head hard against the *Belladonna*'s hull as the ship suddenly lurched and listed dangerously in the opposite direction. *What's happening?* Lirianna panicked as a moan of pain escaped her lips. Dimly, she could hear shouts from the deck, then the ship rocked violently and Lirianna was thrown a third time, flopping forward onto the floor as the ship righted itself. The *Belladonna* continued to buck and lurch, and Lirianna remained where she was, facedown on the floor, not trusting that she could keep the contents of her stomach down, let alone stand or walk, if she attempted to rise.

Gradually, she felt the ship steady, the sea growing calmer, though her breath remained fast and shallow. Suddenly there was a pounding of boots on the stairs and Tom's voice was shouting her name, fear making it sound rough and feral.

"Lirianna!"

Lirianna's eyelids fluttered as she tried and failed to lift her head. She heard the scramble of a key in the lock and the screech of iron, then Tom was there, his hands warm on her shivering skin.

"Lirianna," he repeated, terror choking the syllables. "Can you hear me? Can you move?"

It took Lirianna every ounce of strength she could muster to raise herself up, and still she failed, half-collapsing back to the floor. But upon seeing her conscious and moving, Tom let out a sob of relief, and his arms came around her, lifting her upright onto his lap. They huddled there on the floor of the *Belladonna*'s hold, Lirianna's clarity slowly returning while Tom held her, his hands stroking her hair as her cheek lay against the solid warmth of his chest.

"I'm sorry," Tom whispered into her hair. "I'm so sorry."

Lirianna attempted a pat on his arm. "It's all right. I'm all right."

"I thought ..." Tom's voice sounded thick. "Saints, when I saw you lying there, I thought ..." His voice broke, which should have made Lirianna sad, but somehow it made her feel warm and pleased instead. For some reason, the whole thing suddenly seemed quite funny, and a chuckle bubbled out of her throat, causing her shoulders to shake with mirth.

Tom pulled back to look at her, his face ashen and his eyes red. "Are you *laughing?*"

Lirianna nodded, his incredulity making her giggle all the more. Tom eased her off his lap, looking at her as if he wasn't sure whether to be relieved or irritated or concerned. He already looked a wreck, so for his sake, Lirianna forced her mirth to subside and lay a hand on his arm. "Really, Tom, I'm all right. What happened?"

"It was the maelstrom," Tom replied, relief winning out on his features, though his eyes still held a wary concern as they rested on her. "We passed it—but barely."

Lirianna nodded slowly in understanding. "The maelstrom from the ballad. We must be getting close to the island, then?"

"We'll reach it tomorrow," Tom confirmed. "But don't worry about that now. How do you feel? Should I help you to the cot?"

Lirianna shook her head. "No, I'm fine." She ventured a glance around the hold, and her eyes caught sight of the battered harp lying on the floor, three strings snapped and hanging at odd angles. Her brow knit together, heart constricting at the sight of the damaged instrument. Tom, misunderstanding, was quick to reassure.

"Don't worry about the harp. We'll think of something. Maybe I can convince the captain to let us work on the ballad together, or—"

But Lirianna shook her head, a quiet smile on her lips. "No need, Tom."

"No need?" Tom's face held confusion, then for the first time, hope. "You mean …?"

Lirianna nodded, and her smile widened. "I solved it. I know where to find the treasure."

Tom's grateful arms clasping tightly around her were like rays of summer sunshine warming her heart.

19

THE OPEN BOX

Alyen woke from a slumber that felt as though it had carried her oceans away. Ever so slowly, she let her mind crawl back toward reality, tentative and sluggish with sleep. She stayed as she was, nestled in the soft bed, long after her eyes had finally opened, taking in the cabin that had given her the peaceful rest she had so desperately needed. It was not grand, but tidy and well-appointed, its furnishings simple yet tasteful, accented in the cool colors typical of Sandamarian craftsmanship.

Presently, she noticed that a chair stood not far from her bed upon which were draped a set of garments made of silks and cut in the Sandamarian fashion. Resting on top was a slip of parchment that bore a scrawl of writing. Curiosity pulling at her, Alyen ventured to rise to a sitting position, gratified to find that her head did not spin as she thought it might. Indeed, she felt marvelously restored, and she wondered briefly how long she had been asleep. Daylight was filtering through the windows at the far end of the cabin, so she'd slept the night away at least.

Alyen swung her legs over the edge of the bed, her bare feet finding the rough wood of the floorboards beneath her. She rose and padded over to the chair, where she plucked up the parchment and read the tidy penmanship.

> *If you desire a change of clothing, you may borrow these. They should be roughly your size. And you may wash in the basin. The soap is new.*

Alyen looked around and her eyes found a basin and pitcher of water on a small table, with a cloth and a fresh bar of milky soap sitting at its side. She smiled at Jah'dara's kindness; indeed, now that she was up, her body itched to be rid of her sea-wrecked clothing and the salt that caked her skin.

She peeled off her garments, sighing with relief as the crusty fabric fell away from her body. She felt a moment of alarm when she realized that her hearing stone was missing from her neck; a quick glance around did not reveal it anywhere in the room. She calmed herself with the knowledge that she had definitely come aboard with it—she remembered fidgeting with it nervously as they watched Nah'dar's would-be assassin from the deck. Perhaps Aaron or Nah'dar had taken it? It would be like Aaron to do something like that if he thought she needed the rest badly enough. She tamped down the ache that rose in her chest at the thought, the intrusion on her peace unwelcome. She'd finish washing, then find the others, and with them, hopefully, her hearing stone.

Alyen took her time bathing. She carefully washed each part of her, moving from limb to limb, and ending with her hair. As she tended to herself, she kept her mind purposefully blank. There was more where that ache in her heart had come from—she could sense it pushing its way to the surface, demanding to be seen, heard, felt. Much had happened in the last few days, and she knew that she would have to address it, perhaps sooner than she'd like. But she knew that once she'd opened the lid of that box, she might not be able to control the things that came spilling out: the painful feelings, the chaotic thoughts … The quiet peace she'd woken with would vanish, and she wasn't ready to relinquish it just yet. So, she continued her ablutions, wishing she could wash away inner turmoil as easily as she did the grime from the sea.

When she felt clean once more, she moved to the chair to explore the garments Jah'dara had left for her. It took some experimenting to figure out how the clothing was to be worn, but once she'd figured it out, she found that she quite liked the look and feel of them, and she relished the whisper of silk against her skin once more. She ran her fingers through her damp hair, then tidied the bed and the evidence of her bathing. Feeling fresh and renewed, she allowed her mind to turn to the next thing she must do.

Nah'dar. Despite the lingering unease she felt without her hearing stone, the first thing she must do was to find her sanhar. She didn't know if he would welcome her presence right now; perhaps his sister would be a more welcome companion, given their shared history. But she had to find him, if only to see if he was all right. And if he wasn't, she could at least stand nearby, so he didn't face the darkness alone.

It didn't take long to locate him. He was standing at the rail of the deck, his eyes staring unseeing at the waves. He appeared somehow smaller than usual, and his eyes, usually so fierce, seemed to have lost their spark. It reminded Alyen forcibly of the way he'd looked after receiving the sphinx's riddle in Norhelm—the first time she'd caught a glimpse of the tragedy that was his past—but there was still something different now. For the first time that Alyen could remember, the warrior before her looked truly and utterly defeated.

What could she say? There were no words that would change his past or take away his pain, and no way she could pretend to truly understand. But something had to be said. Something to shake him out of the trappings of his own mind. Something to reignite his flame, even if it could only glimmer softly for a time. She moved to his side at the deck rail.

"Nah'dar."

The former assassin didn't acknowledge her, his eyes remaining downcast.

Alyen straightened. "Nah'dar!"

This time his eyes flicked upward, finding hers, though his expression did not change.

Alyen swallowed. "Nah'dar of Lunalor. You are the First Assassin of the Bahari, a true Son of the Desert. You are the kingdom of Dúramair's Captain of the Guard. You are protector and sanhar to the Trianid's Keeper of Scales, and you have trained the prophesied Second Slayer. You have fought and won many battles with honor. You are a noble warrior, and … and you are my friend. Nah'dar of Lunalor. It will not do to make yourself small."

For a long moment, Nah'dar said nothing, and Alyen did not let her gaze waver from his. Then, she saw it: a nearly imperceptible flash in the warrior's eyes, gone in the same instant it appeared. Yet, as Nah'dar straightened to face her directly, Alyen thought some of the deadness had gone out of them.

"Thank you, sanahara," Nah'dar said in a hushed voice.

Alyen lifted the corner of her mouth ruefully. "Everyone needs to be reminded of who they are sometimes. I'm merely returning the favor. Besides," she added, guilt raking through her stomach, "it's my fault you ended up in Sandamar again. I shouldn't have pushed myself so hard. I'm sorry."

"You are my sanahara," Nah'dar whispered. "You have nothing to be sorry for." His head bowed for a moment, then he drew in a breath, lifting his eyes to look out at the sea. "I am glad I came to Dúramair. At the time I wondered if it was foolish, but ..." His voice trailed off, then he turned and looked at Alyen once more. "I am glad," he finished simply.

"As am I," Alyen said, giving her sanhar a true smile this time, relieved to see his spirits lifting.

"Alyen?"

It was Aaron who'd come up behind her, his stance tentative, one hand clasped around something she couldn't see. He, too, was wearing new clothing in the Sandamarian fashion, and Alyen tried not to notice the way his tunic, designed to be cool in the desert heat, set his warrior-toned torso on display. "May I speak with you?"

Alyen looked back to Nah'dar, a question in her eyes. Her sanhar nodded and strode away toward the other end of the ship. Alyen turned to Aaron, her stomach suddenly squirming with nerves.

For a moment, Aaron's eyes traveled over her form, taking in her new attire. She recognized the way his eyes lingered and darkened, which only served to heighten the quivering in her gut. But he said nothing and instead held out his hand, revealing Alyen's hearing stone resting in his palm. "Here. I took it off so you could sleep uninterrupted in case Lirianna tried to reach us."

"Thank you," Alyen said, relief flooding her body. She took the stone from Aaron and clasped it once more around her neck. "Did she?"

Aaron nodded. "She's all right for now, but things aren't going well. The sooner we can reach her, the better."

Alyen nodded, and silence stretched between them. He was going to say something, she could tell. He was going to crack the lid off the box, and they would have to face whatever poured out from within.

"You look much better," he said at last, and Alyen knew he was asking if she felt well enough to have the conversation they both knew was coming.

"I feel much better," she said, opening the door for him to continue.

"Alyen …" he said, squinting at the sun on the waves. "I know … I saw everything. How it was for you. And I meant what I said in the tunnel. I want you to know that I truly am sorry."

Alyen nodded. "I know. I feel the same way, and I'm sorry for what I did, too."

"Then … if we both understand what we did, and we're both sorry …" Aaron looked at her, his face troubled. "Why doesn't it feel like this is fixed?"

Alyen took a moment before she answered. She hadn't thought through this part, not consciously, at least. But she felt the answer coming, and she knew before she spoke the words that they were true.

"Because it doesn't really fix anything. I'm still me and

you're still you, and that means that the next time something like this happens … we'll likely just hurt each other again."

Aaron was frowning. "What do you mean?"

"Think about it," Alyen said, irritation buzzing suddenly in her chest. "Even if we forgive each other this time, decide to reunite and move forward, you'll still want me to be someone who chooses love first every time. But I'll still be the person who has to prioritize my kingdom and my people. I'll want you to be someone who understands that, and I'll be angry and hurt every time you don't, because in the end …" She shook her head, not believing the words she was about to say, but knowing she had to say them. "In the end, Aaron, that's who I am. It's how I've always been, and if you can't love me that way, then … maybe you never really loved *me* at all."

Aaron looked as if she'd struck him, his face white. "How can you say that?"

"Well, it's possible, isn't it?" Alyen said, her voice quavering now. "Maybe we both made the same mistake. Maybe both of us were more in love with the *idea* of who we wanted each other to be than we were with the people we actually are. Maybe … maybe Rowenna and Morten were right. Maybe it's better for the Keeper and the Slayer to be alone." Alyen's voice cracked as she finished, silent tears running down her cheeks.

"Do you really believe that?" Aaron asked, his voice barely above a broken whisper. "Is that—is that what you really want?"

Alyen shook her head, a tiny sob escaping her lips. "I don't know," she said. "All I know is, I don't know how to make us work again."

Aaron closed his eyes and turned away, his knuckles white as they gripped the rail of the deck. Alyen wished he would say something—something that would fix things, something that would make her wrong. But she knew there was nothing he could say that would do that, so she just waited, letting her tears continue to fall.

When Aaron opened his eyes, they shone with wetness, but his cheeks remained dry. He looked at Alyen as if seeing her for the first time—as if searching for proof that he had loved the real her. He swallowed and nodded in a visible attempt to collect himself. "You should rest some more," he said, his voice gruffer than usual. "I'm sorry if my questions taxed you."

Before Alyen could reply, he turned and strode away, his boots echoing on the wooden deck as he left.

Alyen remained where she was, watching the way the dance of salamandar and undine changed as the sun rose higher in the sky. She thought her tears had finished when Nah'dar appeared at her side once more. He said nothing, but merely stood at the rail, watching the sea as she did, yet somehow the presence of her sanhar sent a fresh wave of wetness trailing down her face. Nah'dar made no mention of her tears, nor any indication that he even knew she was crying. But Alyen knew that he did, and that somehow he understood what she needed better than most.

When her weeping had finally stopped again, and a space of time had passed with no fresh tears, the warrior glanced her way. "Are you well, sanahara?"

Alyen shrugged, unable to say yes, yet knowing nothing could be done to make things any better if she said no.

Nah'dar nodded, his dark eyes knowing. "Some stories do not end the way we would like," was all he said.

Alyen made no reply, and they continued to watch the waves in silence as Alyen's breathing continued to steady.

After a time, Nah'dar straightened. "Come," he said. "It is time we made our plans for the Seer's rescue. Jah'dara is waiting with food in her cabin."

Alyen pressed her hands to her eyes and wiped the tear tracks from her cheeks. She took a breath, then nodded, giving Nah'dar her best attempt at a smile. The captain gave a small, approving nod of his head, then led Alyen back to Jah'dara's cabin and the riddle that awaited them.

20

THE BARGAIN

Jah'dara was sitting at the table in her cabin looking every bit a queen on a throne, awaiting her audience. A bowl of Sandamarian fruits had been set out, as well as plates, cups, and a steaming pot, presumably containing a hot beverage. From the sharp and earthy scent that reached her nostrils, Alyen realized it was likely khof—a traditional Sandamarian drink made from the dried berries of the khofa tree. Alyen had never acquired much of a taste for it, but suddenly the *Desert Star*'s standard depicting the berry-laden branch made sense. Jah'dara must be a khof merchant.

"Please," Jah'dara gestured to the other chairs at the table. She fixed an evaluating gaze on Alyen. "Are you well, sana-hara of my brother?"

"I am," Alyen replied as she took a chair, glad that her voice sounded much stronger than the last time she'd stood before Jah'dara. "Thank you for your hospitality and your aid. We are in your debt."

Jah'dara raised an eyebrow. "I am curious to hear the story that led to my brother being shipwrecked in Sandamar with two young Dúramairians. It is unlike him to travel in company."

The captain's words were casual enough, but Alyen thought she could detect a hint of suspicion in her tone, which made her wonder how welcome their presence actually was on the *Desert Star* despite the impeccable hospitality.

Nah'dar shifted forward in his seat. "There is much to tell, Jah'dara, and you will hear it all. But first, I must ask that the words spoken in this room will not pass beyond the door."

Jah'dara raised both eyebrows now. "You wish me to keep secrets from my crew, Nah'dar?"

"I understand, it is a weighty request."

"And whose secrets am I to keep?" Jah'dara asked, her dark eyes flicking to Alyen and Aaron before locking on her twin's. "Yours or theirs?"

"They are one and the same," Nah'dar said, his voice even. "You know, sister, that I would not ask for your oath if it were not of the greatest importance."

Jah'dara's eyes narrowed. "My oath?"

"I would have your oath on the matter," Nah'dar said.

Alyen could tell that these words did not sit well with Jah'-dara. Nah'dar had said that he trusted his sister implicitly, and Alyen didn't want to doubt his judgement—but the tension thickening the air suggested that trust didn't necessarily come without friction.

Jah'dara leaned back in her chair, the silver on her tattooed arms flashing as she crossed them in front of her chest. "Very well," she said at last. "You have my word." Though she didn't say it, her expression clearly stated that whatever secrets they were about to disclose had better be worth the demand of her oath.

Nah'dar nodded his gratitude. "The first thing you must know, sister, is that these are no ordinary Dúramairian youths."

Jah'dara's gaze cut to Alyen and Aaron once again, this time a spark of interest igniting in their depths. "You said the girl is your sanahara," she said.

"And she is. But she is also Alyen of Dúr, born crown princess of Dúramair, and the current Keeper of Scales of the kingdom's Trianid. Aaron of Doclann, likewise, is the Trianid's Slayer of Monsters, and the warrior foretold in Dúramair's most ancient legends."

Jah'dara's dark eyes were calculating. "The Trianid … the Dúramairian magicians?"

"It is not magic like that which we know in Sandamar," Nah'dar said. "But yes. They both carry powerful magic."

"And what brings two such esteemed Dúramairians to travel with you so far from their shore?"

Nah'dar shifted, and for a moment, Alyen thought her sanhar looked nervous. "The second thing you must know is that I am now Dúramair's Captain of the Guard."

Jah'dara's chin lowered an inch. "You serve their crown?"

"I do," Nah'dar said. "As to why we travel together …" With that, he launched into the tale of Lirianna's kidnapping and their quest to rescue her. Alyen did not miss the fact that his recitation cut off any further inquiry as to how or why he had become the Dúramairian Captain. But she was grateful to hear that Nah'dar omitted the original reason for their excursion to the south, nor did he make any mention of the strained relations between her and Aaron.

When Nah'dar finished, Jah'dara said nothing for a moment, then raised her chin. "I begin to see why you do not want my crew to know of your story."

"We do not wish for it to become common knowledge that the Trianid has been so compromised. There has been much unrest in Dúramair of late, and further instability will benefit no one. Furthermore ..." Nah'dar hesitated. "I do not relish the thought of my activities becoming common knowledge in Sandamar."

One of Jah'dara's eyebrows quirked upward again. "But surely this cannot be so secret. Word that Dúramair has a new Sandamarian Captain will reach our shore. It will not be difficult for connections to be made."

"True," Nah'dar conceded. "But to move against an agent of the Dúramairian crown on Dúramairian soil would be seen as an act of war, and likely more trouble than deemed worthwhile. However, it would be all too easy for an accident to happen on the open sea ... or anywhere else the arm of the crown cannot easily reach."

"I see," Jah'dara said, her tone not unkind. "And so, you must return to Dúramair as soon as possible."

"As soon as we have recovered the Seer," Nah'dar confirmed. "And this, sister, is where I must, once again, ask your assistance."

Alyen thought Jah'dara's expression looked suddenly wary. "You told me only that you wished to travel east. You said nothing of using my ship or my crew to fulfill a foreign rescue mission."

"Nor would I presume to place so great an obligation at your door," Nah'dar said with an incline of his head. "But I am hoping you will lend your knowledge as a seasoned captain of these seas to aid us in discovering the route we must take."

"Have you the coordinates? Or a map?"

Nah'dar cleared his throat. "What we have is a riddle. A treasure map of sorts. It comes in the form of a song."

For a long moment, Jah'dara stared at her twin. "This, I did not expect to hear," she said at last. "You surprise me, brother." But though her tone was dry, Alyen thought she saw a spark of intrigue ignite in the captain's eyes.

Nah'dar looked to Alyen, and she saw the barest shadow of a smile cross his features. "Sanahara, if you will please recite our treasure map for our host?"

"Of course," Alyen said. If she didn't know better, she'd guess that Nah'dar was trying to bait his sister's curiosity, rather than asking her for the use of her ship outright. Under Jah'dara's expectant stare, she recited.

"If you would find my greatest treasure,
Heed my words in equal measure.
I'll lead you to an island fair:
That which I lost is resting there.

Follow true the eastern mark
That rises only after dark,
And when you reach the Dragon's Mouth,
Choose your passage, north or south.

Beware the maelstrom and the snake,
But let them not your courage shake,
For one of these you must survive
If you're to reach the isle alive.

And when the shore is in your sight,
Wait for evening's gentle light.
There rests a cove 'neath seagulls' cries.
'Tis there my greatest treasure lies.

To you who seek, remember this:
Be grateful for the raindrop's kiss,
The sighing wind, and warming sun,
But most the arms of your loved one.

For tomorrow is guaranteed to none."

Jah'dara was silent for a moment after the ballad concluded. Alyen had watched the captain's face as she'd relayed the verse, and a few times she'd seen the woman's eyes flash with recognition—but also with something that may have been fear.

"These are the directions you set out to follow?" Jah'dara finally asked.

Nah'dar nodded. "We set sail following the Cradle of the Sun, assuming that it is the eastern mark to which the bard refers. But we have made no interpretations beyond that point. The Dragon's Mouth—we do not know what it is, but if it is perilous in nature, I wish to be prepared. Does it mean anything to you?"

Jah'dara drew in a breath, her lips thin. "You have nothing to fear from the Dragon's Mouth," she said. "If we continue to travel east, then later this day we will reach a rocky outcrop that rises out of the sea, so called as it resembles the head of a dragon. It is the following parts of your verse that should give you pause."

"The maelstrom and the snake?" Alyen asked. "You know what they are as well?"

Jah'dara shrugged. "If you are familiar with the seas in this region, the directions are quite straightforward. The Dragon's Mouth marks the boundary beyond which the sea becomes perilous. If you continue east north of the Dragon's Mouth, you will find a maelstrom—a whirlpool of such magnitude and strength that few ships can pass it unscathed. Sail east south of the Dragon's Mouth, and the waters are home to a vicious sea serpent that devours any ship that dares enter its abode. In short, choose the northern route and you risk probable death. Chose south and death is certain."

There was a pause as Jah'dara's unwelcome words registered, then Aaron spoke. "And what of the middle route? Couldn't a ship travel straight east behind the Dragon's Mouth?"

Jah'dara shook her head. "Impossible. The Dragon's Mouth is as its name indicates: the head of an entire dragon. The body of the dragon is formed by a long string of rocks stretching to the east for leagues, at times jutting out of the water, and often hiding just beneath the waves. There is no ship in the seas that could make passage along the dragon's back without its belly being ripped out by the spines."

"And what of sailing farther north or south, evading the maelstrom or the sea serpent, and then doubling back?" asked Alyen.

Jah'dara's mouth twisted with doubt. "It would be impractical at best. I know not the precise location of the isle you seek, but you would have to go so far off course in either direction that you would likely miss it completely. Not to mention that it would take far more time than you appear to have."

"But it *is* possible to reach it," Alyen said, frustrated. "Lirianna's captor has already been there once."

Jah'dara's eyes narrowed. "And what kind of ship does this captain sail?"

"We're not entirely sure," Aaron said. "But the captain was a prince of Lyndros and often poses as an eastern trader in port. It's fair to assume that his ship is an eastern model as well."

"Then that is why he has already been to the island," Jah'dara said with a shrug. "As I said, no ship can pass the sea serpent or the dragon's spine, but there are a few that may survive the maelstrom. No Sandamarian vessel could do it. I myself cannot even manage the rougher waters of the northern seas with this ship, though the trade for khof in Nethermair would increase my wealth tenfold. And, forgive me, but I doubt a Dúramairian ship could best the maelstrom either. A Nethermairian ship could, certainly, but they seldom sail these seas, preferring to reach the Eastern Kingdoms by the northern routes. The ships of the Eastern Kingdoms, however, are large and sturdy, well-balanced, and agile in the water. With some expertise and a bit of luck, an eastern ship might make it."

"So, you're saying that the only way we can reach Lirianna is to somehow get an eastern or Nethermairian ship to take us past the maelstrom?" Alyen asked, her heart sinking.

"And then on to the island to confront a pirate crew, yes," Jah'dara confirmed.

"Curses," Alyen whispered, running her hand over her brow.

"There may be another option."

It was Aaron who spoke, and the tentative note in his voice made Alyen look up quickly. "What do you mean?"

Aaron shifted in his seat, meeting Alyen's eyes with an expression she couldn't read. She thought she could still see traces of the rawness left by their earlier conversation in his face, but his gaze was steady. "I have an idea," he began. "If you don't like it, or if you think it's too dangerous or that it won't work, we won't do it, and I'll never mention it again. It's just that we don't seem to have many options."

"So, what is it?" Alyen asked, becoming both more wary and more curious by the moment.

"The undines," Aaron began, his expression still tentative. "They govern the water, but didn't you once say that they also tend to the creatures that live *in* the water?"

Alyen nodded. "That's what Rowenna told me the night I became her apprentice."

"So, that would mean," Aaron continued, "that they would also tend to the sea serpent, right?"

Alyen stared at Aaron, already feeling an objection rising in her throat. She held it back, if only for the sake of discussion. "Yes, I would imagine so."

"If that's true," Aaron continued, "then could it be possible for you to ask the elementals to stop the sea serpent from attacking our ship? Or even meld with the undines and keep it away yourself?"

Alyen frowned, deeply uncomfortable with what Aaron was suggesting, but unable to deny that it posed interesting possibilities. "I suppose it might be possible. But, Aaron, it would be terribly risky."

"I know," Aaron said quickly. "And you've barely recovered from my last failed idea. I don't want you to think that I'm asking you to fix everything with your magic alone, or that I don't know what it costs you to use it. But I *am* the Slayer of Monsters, and we have Nah'dar as well. Fighting beasts is what we're good at. Surely the two of us backing you up could best a sea serpent if things got out of hand." He paused, and in his eyes, Alyen saw how much he wanted her to believe in his proposition—and in him.

"That's quite a plan," Alyen said, hedging for time as her mind worked over the options.

Aaron's head dipped to the side in acknowledgement, his face clearly showing that he expected her to reject the idea all together. "I just thought that we're so far behind already, and the maelstrom route will delay us even more ..."

The inkling of an idea crept into Alyen's mind—an idea so absurd and dangerous that she briefly wondered at the state of her sanity. "What if ..." She hesitated, then decided to throw caution to the wind—at least for a moment. "What if we could use the sea serpent to make up for lost time?"

Now it was Aaron's turn to stare, his expression one of disbelief—and cautious hope. "What exactly do you have in mind?"

"Well," Alyen said, trying to decide if she had the courage to actually entertain the thought beyond theory. "A sea serpent should be able to swim faster than a ship can sail, right? If I work with the undines to let it get close enough without attacking, I thought maybe we could somehow harness it to the ship. Then if I can direct it to swim toward the island ..."

"It would give us safe passage and allow us to catch up with the pirates," Aaron finished, a gleam in his eye.

"Brother," Jah'dara now spoke, her tone pitched low with

warning. "Are your magicians truly proposing not only to sail willingly into the waters of the sea serpent, but then to purposefully attract and tame said serpent as if it were a wild horse?"

Nah'dar looked from Alyen to Aaron and back to his sister. "I believe they are," he replied.

Jah'dara looked as if she wanted to respond to what she clearly deemed her brother's egregious lack of objection, then turned instead to Alyen and Aaron. "As fascinating as this discussion may be, I must be clear. You will never execute the madness that is this plan with my ship."

Aaron's eyes broke from Alyen's. "I understand, this does sound like madness, but I can assure you, Alyen's magic is like nothing you've ever——"

"No," Jah'dara said, her voice like steel. "I have no use for magic, nor do I share your death wish."

"We could pay you——" Aaron began, but a sudden thought made Alyen cut him off short.

"What if we could promise you a ship?"

There was a silence and Jah'dara's eyes locked on Alyen's.

Alyen met and held the captain's gaze. "The pirate ship is an eastern trading vessel, surely capable of sailing to any port of trade you could wish. Once Lirianna is safe, the pirate captain must be brought to justice, and his ship and goods will be forfeit. As a member of Dúramair's royal family and the Trianid, I can promise you possession of the ship should you agree to aid us."

Jah'dara studied Alyen for a moment, and though her face remained stoic, she could see the hunger burning behind the captain's dark eyes. "And if the pirate should escape with his ship?"

"Then I will see that you are gifted a Dúramairian vessel of your choice," Alyen said. "As you've said, they aren't as robust as the eastern ships, but you'd still be able to expand your trade into Nethermair."

"And I would need to take your word on this?" Jah'dara asked.

"We can certainly draw up papers delineating the terms. But, as your brother's sanahara and one indebted to you, you do have my word."

Jah'dara held Alyen's gaze a moment longer, then looked away with a sniff. "I will admit, sanahara of my brother, that your offer is enticing, if reckless. But there remains the issue of my crew. I do not foresee how I can convince them to sail into the lair of the sea serpent without risking mutiny. In their place, I would do the same."

Nah'dar nodded, looking to Alyen. "It is true, sanahara. And even if they were willing to brave the serpent, they will not relish the thought of magic on board."

Alyen chewed on her lip, frustration pushing at her ribs. She was so close. There had to be some way, something they could offer the crew that would override their fear …

"This may not be my place," Aaron said, interrupting Alyen's thoughts. "But could you offer them partnership?"

Jah'dara's eyes narrowed. "How do you mean?"

"Well, you'll still have this ship," Aaron said, looking around. "Two ships is the beginning of a fleet, and that'll make you a shipmaster in need of someone to command your second vessel. You could offer a captaincy to the crew member who demonstrates the highest loyalty, leadership, and bravery."

Jah'dara's eyebrow rose. "That may work for one, but what of the others?"

"If your trade expands as much as you say with a second ship and access to Nethermair, offer them a cut," Aaron said. "I don't know much about trading myself, but there must be some amount of gold that would be both realistic for you to promise and enticing enough to inspire courage."

Alyen held her breath as she watched Jah'dara consider Aaron's words.

"An interesting proposition," the captain admitted at last. "But speculative at best. I am not sure the promise of potential future wealth will be enough to convince my crew in light of the very real and immediate risks."

"Then, what if it wasn't potential?" Alyen said, once again throwing caution to the wind. "What if the offer was backed by the Dúramairian crown?"

Jah'dara turned back to Alyen, black eyes locking on blue.

Alyen felt her skin tingle under the captain's steely gaze, but she kept her voice steady. "What if Dúramair would guarantee the sum to your crew in the event that something doesn't go as planned? We can add the terms to the papers, and Nah'dar can sign as witness."

Jah'dara considered Alyen a moment longer, but said nothing in response. Abruptly, she turned to Nah'dar. "Brother. I trust you above all others. Tell me, can I also trust your companions and the bargain they offer?"

Nah'dar did not hesitate. "You can, sister. I swear to you on my life."

There was a pause, then Jah'dara suddenly rose. "I accept your terms," she said. "I will speak to my crew and if they are agreeable, we will draw up the papers and ready the ship.

There is little time to waste. We will reach the Dragon's Mouth by high noon."

With that, she strode from the room, and in moments her shouts could be heard on the deck beyond the cabin door.

Alyen blew the air out of her mouth, feeling that she'd been half-holding her breath for the entire conversation. She'd been raised to rule and to negotiate with all manner of dignitaries, nobles, warriors, not to mention other rulers ... but there was something about Nah'dar's twin that was astonishingly formidable.

"Alyen."

Alyen looked up to see Aaron's eyes on her, his level gaze questioning.

"Are we really doing this?"

Alyen paused. She'd become so caught up in securing a deal with Jah'dara and convincing the captain of their plan that she'd nearly forgotten how insane the plan actually was.

Could she do it? Ask the undines to spare their ship, then tame and harness a deadly sea serpent? It seemed foolhardy at best, and she had never been one to opt for recklessness.

But what if it worked? It would solve everything—or at least a good bit of it. And, as a bonus, it would show Aaron that she was willing to listen to him and—at least sometimes—to follow his lead. Maybe they couldn't be together like they once had been. But at least she could show him that they could still work together. That their future together in the Trianid wouldn't be a terrible one.

Alyen swallowed, her head nodding faintly. "Yes. I think we are."

A glow lit in Aaron's eyes, and his mouth pulled up on one side in the closest thing she'd seen to a smile on his face since they'd met in Brann Dala. "Good. And don't worry. I'll be there, ready to fight the second you need me. We both will." He looked to Nah'dar for confirmation, and the warrior gave a nod of assurance.

Alyen gave a wan smile as reality settled over her, causing an anxious gnawing to twist in her stomach. "About that …" she said. "I know you're the Second Slayer, and you've bested morkshai and everything, but … You do know how to fight a sea serpent, right?"

Aaron's grin was slightly wicked in a way that did nothing to allay Alyen's fears. "I guess we're about to find out."

21

THE SEA SERPENT

It was more difficult to convince Jah'dara's crew of their plan than Alyen had hoped, but in the end it was done and the papers drawn and signed.

The *Desert Star* sat in the water, anchored before the rocky formation rising from the sea, nearly large enough to be considered a small island in its own right. It did, indeed, look like the gaping maw of a dragon about to devour any ship that passed, and for a moment Alyen shuddered, hoping it bore little resemblance to the sea serpent they would shortly encounter.

She squinted at the sea behind them, where she could still make out a small brown dot bobbing on the waves: one of the *Desert Star*'s shallops, containing the few members of Jah'dara's crew for whom no amount of money was worth risking the certain peril that awaited them at the jaws of the sea serpent. Alyen felt a pang of guilt at having lost the captain so many of her crew. Superstitious and mistrusting of the sea as

Sandamarians were, it couldn't be easy to find skilled and trustworthy sailors, and Alyen knew that, attractive as acquiring a new ship sounded, it was in good part Jah'dara's loyalty to her brother that directed her to tolerate their scheme. Alyen's mouth thinned as the shallop faded from view. She'd have to make sure Jah'dara's sacrifice hadn't been made in vain.

Alyen turned back to the Dragon's Mouth and drew in a fortifying breath. It wasn't lost on her that the success of their plan rested largely on her, though if she were honest, she very much doubted that they'd get through the ordeal without the aid of Aaron's battle skills. As if on cue, Aaron approached to join her at the prow, squinting up at the rocks that loomed above them.

"It's bigger than I thought it would be," he commented.

Alyen's mouth twisted wryly. "A sentiment I fervently hope I won't be saying about the sea serpent."

Aaron dropped his gaze to her face, hazel eyes tracing her features. "Are you absolutely certain?" he asked. "Given the way I acted the last time we were on a boat, I would under-stand if you feel like you have to agree with me, but really, you don't. I won't push if you object."

Alyen hesitated only a moment before she shook her head. "No. It's a dangerous plan—possibly an insane plan—but you're right. It's the only plan that gets us to Lirianna in time."

Aaron nodded, then reached out a tentative hand to grasp Alyen's arm. The southern midday sun was already blazing, yet she shivered at his touch, feeling the want and the sadness bleeding from his fingers into her skin. "We can do this," he said softly, his eyes gentler on hers than she'd seen in months. "We've always been able to do anything together."

Alyen returned his nod and dropped her eyes to the deck, unable to hold his gaze any longer. "Yes. That's true."

Aaron's hand lingered a moment longer, then he dropped it to his side, a gesture that seemed almost resigned, despite his optimistic words.

Alyen was almost glad when Jah'dara and Nah'dar appeared, saving them the need for further comment.

"Are you ready?" Jah'dara asked, her eyes steely with resolve. "If we are to cross these waters before dark, we must set sail now."

Alyen raised her eyes to Aaron's once more and saw the shadow of a smile pass over his face. "We're ready," she said.

Jah'dara gave a curt nod. "Then we embark. May fortune smile on you."

"And on you," Aaron replied.

Jah'dara turned and strode down the ship to take her place at the helm, shouting orders to her remaining crew as she went. Within seconds, Alyen could hear the rattle of a chain as the anchor was raised, and sailors scurried to haul on various ropes, filling the air with the hollow battering sounds of sails unfurling and billowing in the wind.

Nah'dar caught Alyen's eyes and gave her a nod of solidarity. "I shall stand nearby with my scimitar at the ready," he said. "May strength be with you."

"Keep yourself safe," Alyen replied with a tight smile. Nah'dar inclined his head, then moved away to his post.

Now it was only Aaron left at her side. As the *Desert Star* started to drift forward, he hesitated, then seemed to come to a decision. Swiftly, he closed the gap between them and wrapped his arms around Alyen's shoulders, crushing her against the warm solidity of his chest. "I believe in you," he whispered in her ear, then pulled back and took his place at the rail of the ship before Alyen could say anything in return.

Well, that's perfect. Getting me distracted and flustered right before I need to concentrate on not getting us all killed by a sea monster, Alyen thought dryly, though she couldn't deny that the tingling coursing through her body wasn't exactly unpleasant. She shook her head, forcing her mind back to their immediate situation, refusing to think about what Aaron's actions may or may not have meant in light of the conversation they'd just had earlier that morning.

The *Desert Star* slid past the Dragon's Mouth, gaining speed as her crew adjusted the sails according to Jah'dara's shouted commands. From the corner of her eye, Alyen saw Aaron checking his daggers, adjusting straps and shaking out his arms. As the *Desert Star* gathered speed and entered the open sea, Alyen drew in a breath and closed her eyes. The time was now.

She'd thought long and hard about the best way to go about taming the sea serpent. She could enlist the aid of the undines, or she could meld with them—both options had their advantages. Making a request of the undines might be less taxing, and it was certainly less flashy, which might make the whole affair more comfortable for Jah'dara's magic-averse crew. However, it would mean less control and therefore less certainty as to the success of their plan, and as failure meant a horrible demise for them all, crushed and devoured by a monster in the depths of the sea, success was something she was quite eager to ensure.

In the end, she'd decided that melding was the better

option. She'd never tried it, but she suspected that melding might allow her to sense the sea serpent before it arrived, giving more time to react and intervene. Even a few seconds of warning could be the difference between life and death, so she decided to trust in the bravery of Jah'dara's crew—and hope that her stamina held out long enough to accomplish what was needed.

Alyen turned her focus to the sea, to the undines that sculpted the swell of the waves and the dance of the tides. She filled her mind with memories of water until she could almost sense her body aching for transformation. Then she sent her whispered words out over the waves.

"Undines in the snowflakes twirling, spirits in the eddies swirling, meld your magic into mine, make of me the rain and brine."

She released and felt the now-familiar sensation of fracturing into an endless void, then pulling back together as the blue and silver sparks of the undines latched onto the pieces of her, embedding themselves in the fabric of her new and altered form. For a moment, she reveled in the sensation of possessing a body that now contained within it the enormity of the ocean, the surge and swell of the sea, the fragility of a snowflake, and the purity of the dew at dawn. Then, knowing she should not linger lest she lose herself to the pleasures of magical power and forget her purpose, she opened her eyes and pulled her attention to the world around her.

As always, her body had transformed, shimmering scales flashing across her limbs as rain and dew dripped from her webbed fingers, snowflakes frosting the waves of her hair. If Jah'dara or her crew reacted to her arresting appearance, she took no note, refusing to be distracted from the immediacy of her task. Instead, she trained her mind on the sea, sending her melded essence down into the depths, tendrils of magic searching for the serpent she knew dwelt somewhere in the vast world that rested beneath the waves.

The ocean was teeming with life. Immediately, Alyen felt a thousand sparks collide with the magic she'd sent into the deep, making her heart jolt with alarm. But after the initial shock wore off, she realized that none of these small twinges could herald the presence of something so massive as a monstrous sea serpent. As her panic subsided, she realized with a thrill of pleasure that she could sense what kind of being was creating each of the sparks. Most were fish of all different varieties, but she also detected eels, jellyfish, and the occasional sea turtle.

It didn't escape her notice that she encountered no animal larger than the turtles. No seals, no whales—not even very large fish. Alyen wasn't familiar enough with the ways of the sea to know what kind of ocean life was to be expected in this area of the world, but something told her that the absence of any sizable creature likely had much to do with the serpent she sought and the appetite it harbored.

The thought sent a temporary chill down her spine, but still, she was heartened to find that she could, indeed, sense the life below through her magic. When it did cross the serpent, she'd know, so she pushed her magic out even farther, hoping to give as much warning as possible when the time came.

The minutes slid by, and she sensed nothing of the sea serpent. Eventually, she began to wonder if it actually existed at all. Perhaps it had been a legend invented to discourage adventurers from reaching the island, much the way stories of being lost to the faerie world had been spread to keep people out of the Royal Wood. Or perhaps the serpent had existed, but had perished long ago, leaving only its memory to guard the waters it had once roamed. The minutes stretched into an hour and more, and Alyen was just about to ask how large the sea serpent's territory stretched when her magic collided with something so massive she felt it like a physical blow and almost lost her footing.

"Alyen?" It was Aaron's voice, sharp as he saw her stumble against the rail.

"It's coming!" Alyen confirmed, raising her voice to reach the helm. "It's not far off, and it knows we're here."

Shouts echoes behind her and feet pounded across the deck, but Alyen's mind was riveted on the bombardment of sensations the approaching beast was causing her to feel through her melded magic.

It was enormous. It was magnificent. Powerful.

And it had *emotion.*

Alyen didn't know what she'd thought it would be like, sensing the sea serpent with her magic, but it wasn't this. Everything the serpent was and felt, Alyen could feel as though it were a part of her. She felt the powerful, sinuous body cutting through water that was cool and clear, like liquid glass. She felt the hunger that ran through its veins, the rage that lit within as it detected something unknown and unwelcome in its territory, the eagerness of the hunt as it surged toward their ship. And laced through it all, Alyen felt what she realized the undines must feel for the serpent: adoration, tenderness, and love.

So mesmerized was Alyen by experiencing the serpent not as a monster or an enemy, but a marvel in its own right, that she nearly forgot that their lives would be imminently ended by said serpent if she didn't interfere. The waters in front of the *Desert Star* began to churn and froth, and suddenly the sea erupted, spray flying in all directions, as the sea serpent shot out of the waves in an explosion of horns, scales, and death.

The enormity of the serpent alone was enough to undo even the most seasoned of warriors, and from the sounds coming from Jah'dara's crew, Alyen surmised that was exactly what was happening. Knowing she had mere seconds before the ship was crushed by the thrashing worm, Alyen thrust her arms upward, hurling her melded undine magic forward, forming a shimmering barricade between the serpent and the *Desert Star*.

"Serpent, dweller of the sea, we do not come to threaten thee. I ask you halt in your attack, hold back, and let our ship go free."

Alyen didn't know if the singing speech would be an effective way to speak to a sea serpent, but as the language of the undines, it felt right, and it seemed to be working. The sea serpent reared its head, opening its fanged jaws wide, and unleashed a blood-curdling shriek to the sky. Alyen shivered as she sensed the frustration coursing through it, yet it did not advance toward the *Desert Star*. Alyen continued to send soothing thoughts through her magic toward the serpent, all the while ensuring that the barricade remained intact. Slowly, she felt the beast's ire subside as it gradually sank lower into the water until only its head remained above the surface, eyeing the ship with a baleful glare.

Alyen let them stay that way for a good space of time, wanting to be sure that the serpent was truly calmed before they tried anything further. When several minutes had passed without any signs of aggression, she ventured to lower her hands, though the barrier still shimmered between them and the horned serpent's head. Clearly, though it was no longer attacking, it had no intention of letting them out of its sight.

"Aaron," Alyen called, her eyes never leaving the serpent. She sensed Aaron move closer to her side, and though the serpent gave a small thrash at the sound of her voice, it remained in place. "Can you see the barrier between us and the serpent?"

"I see a faint shimmer," Aaron replied, his voice low and calm. "Is that what you mean?"

"Yes," Alyen confirmed. "I'm going to try to lower it. I don't think the serpent will attack, but be ready just in case."

Aaron nodded, and Alyen took a breath. Still keeping a steady calm flowing toward the serpent, she let the barrier drop.

For a moment she tensed, ready to fling her arms up once more at the slightest hint of movement, but the serpent remained still. Several more moments passed, and Alyen allowed herself a tentative sigh of relief.

"What do you think?" Alyen asked. "I don't think it's going to let us move unless I ask. Should we try to see if we can harness it, or shall I just ask it to let us pass?"

Aaron looked at Alyen, his face searching hers for signs of exhaustion. "How do you feel? You've been melded for a while already. We can do whatever will be easier for you."

His words lit a glow in Alyen's chest that was nearly as bolstering as rest would have been. "I'm all right for now. I think we could try to harness it, if you don't think it's too dangerous."

"Oh, it's definitely dangerous," Aaron chuckled. "But I'm ready if you are."

"All right," Alyen said. "But be careful, and just—don't hurt it. Not unless it's the very last resort."

"Sanctity of Life, I know. It's important for you."

"No, it's not that," Alyen said, unable to express in words what she was feeling. "It's just that … it's magnificent. And the sea loves it."

Aaron's eyes traced Alyen's face once more with an expression she couldn't read, then he nodded. "I promise." He looked back to the sea serpent and asked, "Do you think I should try to throw the rope to hook it, or would it be better to swim out and tie it on, myself?"

Saints, Alyen thought, marveling at the bravery it took to offer to swim toward an angry sea serpent and fix a rope to it by hand. *Of course, he's already hurled himself into the heart of a demon,* she reasoned, then shuddered at the memory. Aaron had nearly died that day, and the thought of it happening again sent a cold creeping through her belly.

"Try throwing it," she said, though her stomach squirmed uncomfortably, telling her that the sea serpent would not likely appreciate things being thrown in its direction. "But let me talk to it first." *If it keeps Aaron safer, then it's the better way to go,* she tried to convince herself, and pushed the squirming sensation aside.

Alyen turned once more to the sea serpent's head. Filling her tone with calming reassurance, she reached again for the singing speech. "We have a favor we must ask: your aid with an important task. Will you guide us through your seas, lend us your power and your speed?"

Alyen waited for some indication that the serpent had

heard or understood her plea, but it remained where it was, unmoving and vigilant.

"Should I throw it now?" Aaron asked, fingering a long rope with a loop at one end.

Alyen hesitated. "I suppose so," she said, uncertainty clawing at her chest.

Aaron stepped up to the rail and began to swing the looped rope over his head, taking careful aim at one of the sea serpent's long, pointed horns. Alyen saw the serpent's eyes flash red as they latched onto Aaron's form, tracking the motion of the swinging rope, and she felt its hunting instincts surge once more. She opened her mouth to stop Aaron, but before she could utter a sound, the rope flew from his hand, sailing through the air and smacking down not around the horn as intended, but onto the flat of the serpent's snout.

Immediately, the monster reared back, tail thrashing. It roared once again, shaking its head to hurl the rope from its snout, the water churning around it, causing the *Desert Star* to buck and rock. Alyen raised her hands, ready to draw up a barrier once more, but Aaron moved faster. Setting his jaw in a determined line, he grasped the rope and leapt into the roiling sea.

"Aaron!" Alyen shouted, horrified. She clutched at the rail with her webbed fingers, watching helplessly as Aaron retrieved the looped end of the rope and struck out with bold strokes toward the sea serpent, who had risen once more, still weaving in agitation as it loomed over the waves.

What should I do? Alyen agonized as Aaron drew closer to the serpent. She dared not raise the barrier now and risk trapping Aaron on the other side of it. Fortunately, the serpent's thrashing seemed to have distracted it, and it hadn't noticed

Aaron, a tiny figure in the turbulent water. She concentrated on sending more calming magic toward the beast, but it was much harder now with her heart racing in fear for Aaron's life. She drew long shaking breaths, trying to calm her frantic pulse, straining her mind to soothe both herself and the serpent.

For a moment, she thought it was working, the serpent sinking a few feet back into the water. But then Aaron reached the serpent and, looping the rope over his arm, he grasped onto the spines running down the creature's back, and hauled himself up, climbing onto the body of the beast.

The sea serpent felt the thing on its back and roared with rage. It thrashed violently, and Alyen was certain that Aaron would be hurled into the sea. Yet he clung to the spines, wedging himself between them, one hand working furiously at the rope. The serpent continued to scream and writhe, and Alyen realized with horror that Aaron had succeeded in strapping himself to the serpent's back. The serpent must have realized it as well, and, unable to dislodge the intruder, it suddenly recoiled and dove into the sea.

The *Desert Star* lurched forward, its prow angling downward, and Alyen was forced to grasp even more tightly to the rail to avoid being thrown overboard. Shouts from the sailors behind her echoed amidst the churning of water and her own blood pounding in her ears. "Aaron," she breathed, terror freezing her body and mind.

The waves began to settle and Alyen's throat constricted. How long had Aaron been underwater? Far too long by now, and he was strapped to the beast, perhaps unable to escape for air. He would drown any minute, and the thought of it sent a pain like fire searing through her veins.

Out of the corner of her eye, Alyen saw Nah'dar striding toward her, preparing to dive into the sea himself, but she knew he would be too late. In desperation, Alyen seized on the rope, heaving as hard as she could against the strength of the sea serpent, all rationality gone, and she sent one word screaming through her magic and into the sea.

Rise!

Rise!!

Then, just as her heart was about to shatter into mindless despair, and Nah'dar tensed to spring, the sea erupted once more and the *Desert Star* surged forward with a speed that pitched them both backward, slamming against the wood of the deck. Alyen scrambled to her feet, eyes desperately scanning the waters, and her heart leapt to her throat. Before the ship, the back of the sea serpent sliced through the crest of the waves, and astride its back, still tethered to its spines, sat Aaron, drenched and coughing, but very much alive.

Alyen nearly sobbed with relief as Aaron shook his head to regain his bearings. He seemed to suddenly realize that their plan was working, the ship cutting through the water on the sea serpent's power. His fists shot toward the sky and he let out a whoop of victory that brought a shaky grin to Alyen's face. Aaron twisted around as if to find Alyen, and she lifted an arm in a wave. He turned forward again, and suddenly Alyen's hearing stone was warm against her damp skin.

"Are you seeing this?" came Aaron's crow of triumph.

"I am!" Alyen replied, still weak with relief. *"Do you think you should come back to the ship now?"*

"Not a chance." Alyen could hear the grin in his thoughts. *"But what if it dives again?"*

In response, Aaron wriggled until his legs and waist were

free of the rope, leaving it firmly attached to the serpent's spines. *"There. If it dives, I'll swim free. But we did it, Alyen!"*

"We did," she replied, letting the glow in her chest fill the tone of her thoughts.

"Do you need to unmeld?" Aaron asked. *"Maybe you should rest and remeld if something comes up?"*

Alyen shook her head. *"I'd rather stay connected to the serpent. I can sense its feelings, and I'll know if something's about to change."*

"All right. But don't overdo it. We're going to make up plenty of time now." He paused a moment, then said, *"Do you want to come ride with me? You can climb down the rope; I'll catch you."*

Alyen tried to smile, but faltered. His words triggered memories of happier times—times they could never go back to with a love that hadn't been shattered, and she felt it like a weight on her soul. *"No,"* she said, trying not to let the sorrow enter her thoughts. *"I'll be able to conserve my energy better from here —and besides, I'm not dressed for it."*

"All right, then. But you're missing out." His reply came easily, but Alyen thought she heard a hint of disappointment in his thoughts and it made her heart twist.

For the remainder of the afternoon, the sea serpent sped the *Desert Star* through the sea, heading ever eastward. Alyen remained melded, finding that it wasn't nearly as taxing if she simply rested in her melded state without performing any magic. The sea serpent settled into a rhythm, its emotions soothed by the undulating of its powerful body through the waves.

At last the sun began to sink, and suddenly Alyen felt a shift in the creature's state; something wistful and sad, and without knowing how, Alyen found she knew what it meant. She reached for her hearing stone.

"Aaron, it's time to free the serpent. We're coming to the end of its territory, and it wants to go home."

In response, Aaron rose to a crouch on the serpent's back, fingers working to loosen the rope in the glow of the setting sun. The rope fell away, and Aaron used it to haul himself back to the deck of the *Desert Star*, his boots scraping wetly on the hull as he climbed up the side of the ship.

"Welcome back, Slayer," Alyen said, and Aaron returned a grin that mirrored the sadness that still lingered in her own.

She turned away as much to avoid his eyes as to attend to the courtesy required of her. She sent out her thoughts, finding the sea serpent as it sank gratefully back beneath the waves. "Thank you for your strength and speed; go now to the rest you need." A fondness spread through her chest as she felt it withdraw back into the depths, and for a moment she wished she could linger in the melding, not relishing the feeling of loneliness she knew was coming. But she'd already stayed melded longer than she ever had, so she whispered her thanks to the undines, and severed their connection.

She felt her body return to its usual form, sluggish this time, as if suddenly unaccustomed to its natural shape after so long with the undines. But at last, she stood on the deck, alone once more in her body and mind, a feeling that was at once both a relief and an ache.

But she wasn't entirely alone. Aaron and Nah'dar were both swiftly by her side, with Jah'dara standing nearby. Their concern as they inquired after her well-being was a welcome balm against the emptiness that followed the experience of being one with so many for so long. But it was also exhausting, and though this melding had been much less draining than many in the past, she was suddenly keenly aware of her need for solitude and sleep.

Jah'dara seemed to understand, and her eyes held a new respect as they leveled on Alyen's. "My cabin is yours once more, magician of Dúramair. Go now to your rest, and I'll have food brought to you."

Alyen nodded gratefully and, bidding her companions goodnight, headed for the cabin.

As she opened the cabin door, she saw Aaron move to follow her, and her heart involuntarily leapt, but he was stayed by Jah'dara's hand on his arm. She couldn't make out all the captain's words from her distance, but snippets of her voice reached Alyen's ears in the quieting evening air.

"... see how it is with you ... needs rest ... island tomorrow."

Alyen turned away before she could be caught eavesdropping and quickly entered the cabin, closing the door behind her. She breathed a sigh that was part exhaustion, part relief, part heartache. The truth was, half of her wished that Aaron *had* come to stay with her for a bit. But the other half knew that Jah'dara was right. She needed rest. And a visit from Aaron would just be asking for more turmoil.

Because in the end, she'd meant what she'd told him that morning. Much as they might want it to be different, the only future she could see with them together was one riddled with heartbreak and pain.

22

A Fragile Hope

The sun was sinking below the waves behind the *Belladonna*, coating the sails in pink and orange as the water danced a pattern of brilliant gold and deep shadows. Tom practically pulled Lirianna up the stairs to the deck, his hand warm and eager as it held hers.

"It will be all right," he whispered to her, noticing the tense lines of her face as they stopped at the door to the cabin. "Just tell him exactly what you told me."

"But what if it's not enough to satisfy him?" Lirianna asked, nerves quivering despite being convinced that she had, indeed, solved the mystery of the ballad.

"It will be," Tom assured her. "It's more than anyone else has ever figured out." His eyebrows raised, silently asking if she was ready. Lirianna nodded her consent, and Tom's fist rapped on the wooden door.

A voice bid them enter, and once more, Lirianna found herself standing before Captain Voros's desk in the luxurious quarters. A lavish meal was already set out on the table, and Lirianna tried to ignore the way her stomach churned at the scents that reached her nose after a day of being served food she wouldn't give to a pig she liked.

The captain raised one eyebrow, his fingers steepled before him. "Tom. And the harper witch. You remind me, it's time to reevaluate our situation. What shall it be? Good news to report, or another lashing for Tom?"

"Good news, sir," Tom said promptly. "Lirianna has solved the riddle."

"Indeed?" the captain said, his eyes flicking to Lirianna. She could tell he was unconvinced, and she swallowed at the dryness that scratched at her throat. "And all in one day, too. Tell me, what is it you've discovered?"

Lirianna pulled her spine upward to stand as straight as she could. She may fear the pirate captain of the *Belladonna*, but she wouldn't give him the satisfaction of seeing her cower. She gauged her words carefully, knowing that even if she did have the answer, she must also make him believe it was the right one. "On the island," she began, "are there any rocky areas? Cliffs or outcrops—mountains, even?"

The captain's eyes narrowed almost imperceptibly, but it was enough for Lirianna to know that she'd caught his interest. He studied her a moment before answering.

"Why do you ask?"

"Because I don't think the treasure is buried on the beach at all. I think what you're looking for is actually a cave."

Captain Voros stared at her for another long moment, his eyes practically snapping, though he remained motionless in his chair. "And what makes you think that?"

Lirianna stammered, unprepared for an explanation that

would avoid letting him know exactly how she had come to her discovery. "It has to do with the harmony, actually. And the notation. You see, most of the chords notated in one particular part of each stanza are marked as 'one' which indicates a chord—"

"Stop," Captain Voros interrupted, holding up a hand. "I care not a bit for musical technicalities. Summarize and be brief."

Lirianna drew a breath she wished was steadier. "It's the word 'cove,'" she said. "There's a clue in the notation that shows it should actually read 'cave.'"

Captain Voros leaned back in his chair, studying Lirianna for the longest interval yet. "Very well," he said at last. "For tonight, Tom is spared, and we shall soon see if your theory proves correct. We reach the island tomorrow. You are dismissed."

Captain Voros looked back to his ledgers, and Tom and Lirianna made for the door. Lirianna couldn't tell if the captain had believed her or not, but at least it had been enough to spare Tom a second lashing. As Tom reached for the handle of the door, Captain Voros's voice stopped him once more.

"And Tom, tell the cook that the harper is to be fed a plate of our finer fare this evening."

Lirianna glanced up at Tom's eyes and caught the shadow of a wink on her friend's face. "I will, sir," Tom replied, then ushered Lirianna out the door before the captain could change his mind.

⸎

Perhaps it was relief that he wasn't about to be beaten bloody again. Perhaps it was new hope sparking in his heart now that Lirianna had solved the riddle of the ballad. Or perhaps it was the fact that he got to eat some decent food when Lirianna's dinner was delivered to her cell, and she had insisted on sharing it. Whatever the reason, Tom seemed lighter than he had since she'd first seen him at the Gathering. So stark was the change, in fact, that Lirianna thought he seemed almost like the same boy she'd befriended at the music school years ago.

Almost.

There was still a sadness in his eyes, she thought. One that lingered when he looked at her, as they laughed together over shared memories of their barding days, both sitting cross-legged on the floor of her cell with her dinner plate between them. How many times had they sat like this as apprentices at the school, sometimes with Tris, usually with food (often pilfered from the kitchens), and always laughing over something one of the masters or apprentices had done? And now, she could almost pretend that nothing had changed, if not for the torment she knew still rested beneath the surface of Tom's gaze.

But I've changed, too, she thought, feeling the nostalgia that never used to be there rising to her throat, an ache for times long gone as people they would never be again. Still, it felt good to sit together, to share a meal and a laugh, holding to the hope that soon their trials would be resolved.

"I should get back," Tom said at last, regret tugging at his mouth.

"Must you?" Lirianna protested.

Tom nodded. "We're on Captain Voros's good side for

now. Let's try to keep it that way." He hesitated as if debating whether to say something, a strange look on his face as he studied Lirianna's. "There's something I want to tell you," he said at last. "But I don't want to make you angry with me again."

Lirianna put down her fork. "What is it?"

Tom looked down, chewing on his lip. "There's a chance … if everything goes well tomorrow and we find the treasure … I might be freed."

"Tom!" Lirianna gasped. "That's wonderful! Why would you think I'd be angry about that?"

"Because," Tom said slowly, "it was the deal Captain Voros made with me when he sent me to the Gathering. If I brought him the bard that could lead him to the treasure, my reward would be my freedom."

Lirianna's chin lifted with understanding. "You don't want me to think you kidnapped me for personal gain."

Tom's eyes were tortured as he raised them to Lirianna's again. "Honestly, Lirianna, I didn't want to take you. I didn't want to take *anyone*. And it's not like I could ever go back to Tiragel now after betraying the school and the guild. I'm probably the biggest scandal since Andair the Bard. But I thought, at least I could be free …"

Lirianna put her hand on Tom's arm. "I understand, Tom. I'm not angry. You deserve a second chance."

Tom looked down again before Lirianna could tell if his eyes looked wet. He nodded in thanks, then sniffed and lifted his head. "And now I really should go," he said.

They rose, and Lirianna handed Tom the empty plate. "Until tomorrow, then," she said. "Might be a big day."

"Might be," Tom agreed with a grin. He exited the cell

and twisted the key in the lock. As he turned to leave, Lirianna stopped him.

"What will you do?"

Tom turned. "What?"

"Tomorrow, if it all goes well and you regain your freedom. What will you do?"

Tom looked as though he had never actually considered it. Perhaps he hadn't let himself consider it. "I honestly don't know." He shrugged. "I'd love to go back to music, but there's no chance of that now."

"I'll vouch for you," Lirianna said firmly. "I'll go to Tiragel with you and get you accepted back into the guild. They'll have to at least listen to a member of the Trianid."

Tom stared at Lirianna for a moment, then took two swift strides to the bars of her cell. He grasped her hand from the iron and pressed his lips to her fingers, his mouth fierce and warm.

"Thank you," he said, his voice thick. "It's more than I deserve."

"Happiness is exactly what you deserve," Lirianna said, trying to control the tremble in her voice. "And it's what I want for you."

Tom didn't seem to know what to say to that, but his mouth pulled into something close to a smile as he reluctantly released Lirianna's hand. "Well. Goodnight, then," he said.

"Goodnight, Tom," Lirianna said, wishing desperately that the wanting in Tom's eyes was one she could fulfill.

❦

Lirianna lay on her cot, fervently hoping that it would be the last night she would do so. Despite her certainty that she'd interpreted the ballad correctly and the cautious optimism Tom seemed to harbor, she was still nervous about what the next day might bring. Any number of things could still go wrong, and Captain Voros had already proved unpredictable in his cruelty. If only Alyen and Aaron hadn't shipwrecked. If only they could have intercepted the *Belladonna* before reaching the island ... But it was no use wishing for things that couldn't be. Better to face reality and make the best plan possible.

With these thoughts in mind and sleep still far off, Lirianna reached for her hearing stone. She hesitated a moment, both Aaron's and Alyen's names posed at the edge of her thoughts—but she hadn't spoken to Alyen alone in a while. Perhaps it was her lingering nostalgia, but suddenly Lirianna longed for her dearest friend and one of their evening chats on the battlements of Monstar. Gently, she set thoughts of Aaron aside and trained her mind on one name alone.

"Alyen?"

"Lirianna! Are you all right? I have so much to tell you!"

Her friend's enthusiasm caught Lirianna off guard. Her first instinct was to be worried, but Alyen sounded excited, not alarmed. Lirianna allowed a cautious hope to flare in her chest. *"I'm well, but what about you? Aaron told me what happened."*

"Oh, I'm fine, it was just exhaustion again. But Lirianna, we made it past the sea serpent!"

Lirianna hardly dared to believe her friend's words as her heart leapt. *"Truly? How did you manage it? Did Aaron have to fight it?"*

"No, it's much better than that ..." And Lirianna listened as

Alyen conveyed their passage through the sea serpent's waters.

"*Alyen, that's incredible!*" Lirianna said when her friend had finished. "*If you're past the sea serpent and we're past the maelstrom, we can't be too far apart.*"

"*Wait, you're past the maelstrom?*"

"*Yes, and there's more. I've solved the ballad as well.*"

"*You didn't!*"

"*I did,*" Lirianna confirmed, and now it was her turn to relay the events of the past day.

"*But are you sure you're right?*" Alyen asked when Lirianna explained her theory about the location of the treasure. "*I mean, it's brilliant, but it's also a bit … technical. How can we be certain that's what Andair the Bard meant?*"

Lirianna hesitated, stomach squirming. Once again, she'd told her friend what she'd discovered, but omitted the fact that she'd used her magic in the process. And since it was her magic that led to her certainty, she didn't know how to convince Alyen of her theory without also exposing her secret.

"*I just … I have a feeling,*" she said, trying to gauge how close she could come to the truth. "*A bit like when I do a weaving, you know? It feels right. Can you just trust me on this one?*"

Alyen hesitated only a second. "*Of course I can. Far be it from me to doubt the Seer of Strands.*"

"*Thanks,*" Lirianna said with cautious relief. "*Though it's really starting to feel like ages since I did anything the Seer would usually be doing.*"

"*Well, don't worry,*" Alyen's reply came. "*We'll have you back at Monstar in no time, and you won't have to do anything but weave away to your heart's content.*"

Lirianna froze. The words were meant to be comforting. And they should have been.

But then, why did her heart suddenly feel as though it were sinking?

"Yes," she confirmed, absently. *"Yes, that will be wonderful."*

Moments later, with her hearing stone tucked back into her dress, Lirianna lay on her cot, sleepless eyes once again staring up at the deck in the darkness. A new terror was rising in her—one that had nothing to do with pirates or treasure or dangers at sea. One that came from her alone, so terrible that she didn't want to look at it or even admit it was there. In fact, she suspected she'd been avoiding it now for days.

She was terrified that she was no longer satisfied with a life spent as the Seer of Strands. And that, ultimately, it wouldn't be Alyen and Aaron, nor even Faer Dinnán, who broke the Trianid.

It would be her.

23

SAND AND MIST

The sun rose on the *Belladonna* in a splendor of yellow and gold. The sea, calm and clear, glittered in the morning light, stretching to the horizon as far as the eye could see in any direction. *It's like we're at the center of the world,* Lirianna thought, gazing out on the sparkling waters as the ship cut swiftly through the lapping waves toward the risen sun. *Or, perhaps we're approaching the end of it.*

Tom had been sent to fetch her above deck just as dawn was breaking. Apparently, Captain Voros wanted her near at hand as the island approached, and as nervous as that made her, she was grateful for the feel of the wind in her hair and the sun on her face after so many days in the dreary hold.

She spent the morning largely alone. Tom couldn't be seen loitering at her side, and the rest of the crew seemed content to ignore her presence. Captain Voros himself made no appearance, and Lirianna could only assume that he was

254

busying himself with preparations for the discovery of his last and greatest treasure trove.

But what if it's not there?

The thought flitted frequently through Lirianna's mind and, like always, she pushed it away. She knew she'd solved the ballad correctly—of that she was certain. But something was bothering her about it. Something that niggled at her mind, warning her that, despite her certainty, all was not as it seemed. Perhaps it was just her nerves or her conflicted emotions about aiding the captain, but something told her that the day would hold its own surprises. For some reason she didn't want to investigate too closely, the thought filled her with dread.

The sun had slid past noon when she saw it. A tiny dark spot on the eastern horizon, rising out of the endless sea.

"That'll be it, I suppose," Tom's voice spoke in her ear, making her jump. "Sorry," he amended. "I didn't mean to startle you."

Lirianna managed a tight grin. "Just a little on edge, I guess."

Tom's eyes searched hers. "It'll be all right," he said. "Like you said last night. We only have to get through this day, and then we'll be able to make our way home."

"Yes," Lirianna said, knowing Tom needed to hear the words as much as she. "It won't be long now."

Tom hovered for a moment, then gave her arm a gentle squeeze, and moved away to his duties.

Lirianna watched as the island grew. At this pace, they'd reach it by late afternoon. She wandered around her small section of the deck, surreptitiously scanning the sea for signs of a second ship, but she saw nothing. Perhaps she should check in with Alyen and Aaron, she thought, but dismissed the idea. It was too risky to take out her hearing stone in sight of the crew, and Captain Voros would likely emerge from his cabin at any minute now that the island was in sight.

Those were the reasons she told herself she was keeping her hearing stone tucked away. But she knew there were other, more troubling reasons she was avoiding her friends. The shame that had bloomed in her stomach the previous night as she realized her discontent with the Seer's life still burned, and the accompanying anxiety cast a cloud over the otherwise beautiful day. *One thing at a time,* Lirianna told herself. *Just focus on finding the treasure and getting out safely with Tom. The Trianid can wait.*

By late afternoon, they had reached the island. It was larger than Lirianna had expected, with a white sandy beach curving around a pristine blue cove. She saw immediately why her question about the rocks had sparked Captain Voros's interest. Starting not fifty feet from the shore, stone cliffs rose from the sand, growing gradually into mountainous terrain as they moved inland. From the tops of the cliffs, seagulls nested and swooped, their cries piercing the ocean air.

There was a shout, followed by a flurry of motion as the crew hastened to drop the anchor. The *Belladonna* gave a gentle lurch as the anchor hit the ocean floor, then Captain Voros's cabin door swung open and the pirate lord emerged at last. Lirianna's eyebrows rose as she took in the captain's appearance. Gone was the finery she'd seen him wear up until this moment, traded for plain boots and trousers with nothing to cover his bare chest. Strapped to his waist was a belt that held a sword on one side and a dagger on the other, and a leather strap around one arm held an additional knife that curved wickedly. Lirianna couldn't help but notice that the captain's torso and arms featured a number of angry scars—proof that his rise to power in these waters had not come easily nor without a price.

"Ready the shallop!" Captain Voros called, and several of his pirate bards hastened to maneuver a small boat into position, preparing to shuttle passengers to the shore. "Brutin, Tom, and you, harper," the captain continued. "You three will accompany me to the island. The rest of you, guard the ship and await my instruction."

With these orders, Captain Voros strode swiftly to board the shallop, Brutin following close behind. Tom and Lirianna followed suit, Lirianna not at all pleased to find herself in such close proximity to Brutin and worried about the captain's order to guard the ship. Surely, he couldn't be anticipating pursuit? Once more, her eyes scanned the horizon for signs of an approaching ship, but she saw nothing save for a white streak on the western horizon.

The landing party settled swiftly into the shallop, and it was lowered into the waters. The small boat bobbed in the waves, and Tom and Brutin took up oars and began rowing in the direction of the shore. Captain Voros, eyes fixed intently on their destination, could not see what Lirianna saw, facing as she was to the west: the white streak on the horizon was growing—no, it was approaching the *Belladonna*, advancing steadily over the blue of the sea.

A telltale tingle rose in Lirianna's limbs. A tingle she hadn't felt since leaving Castle Dúr months ago. *The Trianid,* she realized, feeling the familiar magic lacing the air, feeling her own magic rise in response. Whatever the whiteness was, it was coming from her friends. Alyen and Aaron were close.

At that moment, her hearing stone flared, its heat warming her skin through the folds of her dress. Lirianna struggled to keep her face neutral as her stomach squirmed with nerves. There was no way she could pull out the stone now, even if she did want to, and she shuddered to think of Captain Voros's reaction should he discover a working magical object in her possession. Aaron and Alyen would just have to wait, though now the stone was radiating so intensely she almost winced. She glanced at Tom and Brutin—both of them were facing the *Belladonna* and would be able to see her face along with the approaching band of white. But Brutin's gaze was down, focused only on his rowing, and though Tom's eyes held a question, he said nothing.

By the time they had reached the shore, the white mass had nearly reached them, and she could now make out what it was. A thick bank of fog had rolled in over the sea, enveloping the *Belladonna* and forming a thick wall of mist between the shallop and the waters beyond. *Of course. Alyen must be hiding their ship,* Lirianna realized, then lurched as the bottom of the shallop scraped against rocky sand.

Tom and Brutin leapt out to haul the shallop to dry ground, and Captain Voros sprang from his seat onto the sand. He turned, and for the first time noticed the fog bank. His eager expression tightened to ugly suspicion, and he whirled on Lirianna.

"Harper! What is this?"

Lirianna was caught off-guard, and from the corner of her eye, she could see Tom tense. "It—it's fog, sir."

The captain's eyes narrowed dangerously. "Do not play with me, witch," he growled, his hand wrenching his dagger from its sheath. "Fog does not appear over the sea at this time of day in these warm conditions. Whatever this *fog* is, it's unnatural, and you are the only witch among us."

"I didn't do it," Lirianna said, truthfully, allowing the fear to creep into her voice. "I wouldn't have the slightest idea how." She prayed that her face would not betray her secrecy.

Captain Voros studied her a moment, then scanned the bank of fog, searching for the threat he was certain it posed. "Tom," he said, finally. "Bind the witch's hands. In front where I can see them." Tom retrieved a length of rope from the shallop and tied Lirianna's hands before her, apology and fear flashing in his eyes as they briefly met hers.

His task completed, Tom moved to the side, then suddenly, Captain Voros lunged forward, his dagger held a hair's breadth from Lirianna's throat. She heard Tom's sharp inhale and willed him not to act, not with the dagger so close and rescue so near.

"Lift the fog," the captain ordered through clenched teeth, his voice deadly quiet.

"I can't. I don't know how," Lirianna whispered, tears standing in her eyes.

"Do it, or your life is forfeit."

One tear traced down Lirianna's cheek. She couldn't reach her hearing stone, she certainly couldn't lift the fog— could she somehow pretend to try and buy some time? She drew a shuddering breath, certain it could be her last, when she saw the captain's expression change and his dagger lowered.

Heart racing, Lirianna turned to face the sea and saw the fog swiftly evaporating. The *Belladonna* rested in the water as they had left it, alone in the vast stretch of blue. In moments, the air was clear once again, and there was no sign that anything out of the ordinary had occurred at all.

"Try one more move like that, and both you and Tom are dead," Captain Voros's voice spoke in her ear, and Lirianna felt the sharp tip of the captain's dagger scratch across the skin at the back of her neck, sending shivers down her spine.

The captain strode toward the rocky wall of the cliffs, then turned back to his companions. "So, harper. Where do we find the cave with the treasure?"

Lirianna, still shaking from the threat of the captain's knife, tried to focus her mind and steady her voice. "The ballad says to 'wait for evening's gentle light,'" she said. "There must be a clue that appears when the sun sets."

The captain glanced at the sun, already beginning to dip lower in the sky, then turned his cold eyes back on Lirianna. "In thirty minutes, the sky will start to turn. Your sign had better appear by then, witch."

Lirianna could think of no reply.

The party stood on the shore in tense silence, waiting for what, exactly, none of them knew. The minutes slid by as the sun lowered, its pace agonizingly slow. Lirianna's eyes roved over the wall of stone before them, searching for any sign of a cave or a crevasse—or directions telling which way to go to find one. But their shadows continued to lengthen, and the island kept its secrets close.

Time was running out, Lirianna could feel it. Captain Voros had removed the knife from its sheath on his arm and was sharpening it on a stone, his expression baleful. The scrape of the metal against the rock sent chills spreading through her body, and she shivered, though the air was warm. She felt a sudden movement on her hand and almost started, then realized it was Tom. He'd drifted to her side, and his hand against her palm was forming one of their signs from their school days.

Don't worry.

Lirianna threw him a grateful glance, then tensed as she saw Captain Voros look their way, his eyes narrowed dangerously. Clearly, he was done waiting.

Lirianna's eyes raked desperately over the cliffs one final time, wondering wildly if she and Tom should simply make a run for it, attempt to escape the pirates and hide themselves in the island wilderness until they could find Aaron and Alyen. Then, just as she was about to throw caution to the wind and drag Tom with her in a mad dash across the shore, she saw it. Her eyes widened, and her finger lifted, pointing to the cliff-wall before them. "Look!"

The others turned to follow the line of her gesture, and they saw it as well. The image of a golden harp set into the stone, undetectable in the daytime shadows of the cliff, but set to glowing by the slanting light of the setting sun. Captain Voros's face fell into a satisfied snarl, and he bounded over to the cliffs, examining the rock where the harp shone, his fingers tracing each crack and groove of the cliff.

"This stone can be moved!" he shouted. "Come help me pull it down!"

Tom and Brutin joined him at the wall, their fingers feeling for purchase along the barely visible edge of what was apparently a stone door. Lirianna stood to the side, excitement dancing in her stomach despite herself. Would they truly find gold or riches on the other side of this stone slab? The treasure that her ancestor, disgraced and grieving, had prized above all else and hidden so carefully before disappearing from the pages of history forever?

The three men were pulling at the stone now, their muscles straining against decades of abandonment to the sand, wind, and rain. At last, Lirianna could see the slab loosening, rocking only slightly at first, then more and more until, with a crackling rip, the stone fell forward, thudding onto the sand. The dust settled, and Lirianna saw a gaping black hole where the stone had once stood, a yawning mouth in the side of the cliff.

"A light!" Captain Voros shouted, his voice hoarse with the hunger Lirianna saw flashing in his eyes. Brutin quickly retrieved two lamps from the shallop, lighting them swiftly. He shoved one into Lirianna's bound hands and held the other out to his captain. Captain Voros practically snatched it from Brutin's grasp and strode into the cave, followed closely by the others.

The cave was small and clean, its limestone walls gleaming palely in the lamplight. Several things struck Lirianna at once, but one settled at the front of her mind, making her heart quicken with alarm.

The cave was empty.

Or nearly so. There was a large stone chest near the center of the room, and next to it stood what could only be the harp of Andair the Bard. Lirianna's breath caught as her eyes took in the beautiful curves of the legendary instrument, preserved from the elements for generations. *Is that his greatest treasure?* she wondered. *His harp?* It would make sense, but she had no time to consider further. Captain Voros was striding around the small room in agitation, his eyes cutting to every corner.

"Where is it?" he growled. He gave no second glance to

the instrument, rather his eyes landed on the stone chest. "It must be in here," he said tersely. "Help me move the lid."

The captain set down his lamp, and the others moved to aid him, but something was tugging at Lirianna's mind. Something that told her that all was not as it seemed, and that the chest should not be disturbed.

It was then that she noticed the walls. They were covered in beautiful paintings, each depicting scenes of what could only be her ancestor's life.

No, not his life. The life of the princess he'd loved. Of their brief life together.

Lirianna raised her lamp higher, moving down the walls one by one. Here, in this painting, Andair and Nerina were resting together in the gardens, a plate of fruit between them, and the harp sitting to one side. In this one, they danced together in a hall lit by a thousand candles. In this one, they walked together along the shore under the light of a full moon and a canopy of stars.

As Lirianna passed from image to image, her eyes were drawn not to the exotic scenery, nor the lavish lifestyle the artwork depicted, but to the expressions on the faces of the bard and the princess. The way their eyes turned to each other in adoration. The way their fingers gently touched. The way they seemed to relax into each other's arms as if they'd been formed to fit together just so.

Then suddenly, the last verse of the ballad rang in Lirianna's mind.

> *To you who seek, remember this:*
> *Be grateful for the raindrop's kiss,*
> *The sighing wind, and warming sun,*

But most the arms of your loved one.

For tomorrow is guaranteed to none.

Tomorrow is guaranteed to none, she thought, realization striking. "Stop!" she cried out to the others before they could remove the lid of the chest they'd gathered around, arms bracing to lift it from its resting place. "We can't open that."

"And why not?" Captain Voros almost spat the words, his eyes burning as they raised to Lirianna's.

"Because it doesn't hold what you think," Lirianna said, her words echoing off the stone walls. "This isn't a treasure trove. It's a tomb."

In the years to come, Lirianna would remember that it had taken only seconds for the world to change forever.

Upon hearing her declaration that his last and greatest search for riches had been in vain, Captain Voros's gaze swept over the room, seeing it now in a new light. As he took in the scenes painted across the stone walls, he let out a roar of fury, veins bulging from his arms and a face contorted with near-madness.

Tom darted swiftly to Lirianna's side as she dropped her lamp in shock, his own dagger cutting swiftly through the ropes that bound her hands. Then suddenly, the tomb blazed with the light of a thousand suns as three more people rushed into the enclosed space: Aaron and Nah'dar, weapons drawn, and Alyen—but a far different Alyen than Lirianna had ever seen. Her friend seemed to be made of fire, flames running over her body as lightning crackled from her fingers and hair.

Captain Voros's eyes widened as he took in the sight of Alyen and her accompanying warriors, and for a second, he looked like a cornered animal, feral and desperate. Then, before anyone could react, he let out another roar as his hand shot to the knife on his arm. The blade flashed as it sailed from his hand, hurtling straight for Lirianna's heart.

Tom shouted and lunged for Lirianna, and at the same moment, Aaron and Nah'dar moved in on Captain Voros, sending Brutin leaping forward, ready to defend.

But Tom's words held true. With the throw of his knife, Captain Voros' leg had shot out and to the side, where it now jutted directly into Brutin's path. Brutin tripped on his captain's leg and fell, crashing to the ground onto his own drawn blade, the steel sinking into his chest with terrible ease. Unbalanced as he already was, the force of his defender colliding with him sent Captain Voros hurtling backward, where the side of his head smashed into the corner of the stone sarcophagus with a sickening crunch.

Both pirates lay still on the floor of the tomb in pools of their own blood, a sight that should have signaled the end of danger and tragedy.

Instead, a wail filled the cavern, one that Lirianna barely registered as coming from her own mouth.

For she found herself kneeling on the cold stone floor, cradling Tom's limp form in her arms, the hilt of a pirate knife jutting from his chest.

24
THE SONG

The world had stopped, yet everything was spinning. Lirianna knew there was some sort of noise issuing from her mouth, but she couldn't tell whether it was a scream or a cry or if she was saying anything intelligible at all. All she could see was Tom, the way the light had faded from his eyes as he looked up at her and her hands, red with his blood as they clutched at his shirt and the wound in his chest.

Then Alyen was beside her—no longer the Alyen that burned with fire and lightning, but the friend she knew. The friend who was a healer. Lirianna's mind snapped into place.

"Heal him!" she rasped, her eyes wild and weeping as they locked onto Alyen's. "Quickly, Alyen, there's still time."

But Alyen's eyes were pooling with tears, and from her expression, Lirianna could tell what her friend was going to say before the terrible words could be spoken.

"No!" Lirianna shouted, angry now. "You can still heal

him! You can use the elementals! You have to do it now—heal him!"

"I'm so sorry, Lirianna," Alyen whispered, tears now tracing her cheeks. "But Tom's gone."

"Don't say that!" Lirianna shrieked. She yanked the knife from Tom's chest and hurled it to the side, where it clanged against the stone wall of the chamber. "Look, he's not even bleeding anymore. You need to heal him *now!*"

"What the Keeper says is true," spoke a new voice, heavy with sadness. Lirianna's head snapped up to see Faer Dinnán standing in the chamber, sorrow etching his features. Desperation flooded Lirianna's body.

"You," she said, her eyes latching onto Faer Dinnán's. "You owe me a debt. You can heal him. You healed Nah'dar, and you can heal Tom, too. Please," she begged, a sob ripping from her throat. *"Please."*

But the faerie king's head was shaking slowly. "I am sorry, Lirianna. Tom has already passed to the next world. It is a boundary not even I can cross."

A howl of misery erupted from her, echoing in the small cavern. Dimly, Lirianna was aware of Aaron kneeling on her other side, of both him and Alyen holding her tightly while grief threatened to rip her apart. How long they stayed there, she couldn't say, but eventually, her keening turned to words, words that gave shape to the chaos that stormed within her.

"It can't end like this. He was going to be free. He was going to be a bard. He deserved a happy ending. It wasn't supposed to end like this."

Faer Dinnán knelt down to regard Lirianna across Tom's still form. "Tom passed nobly, Lirianna. He died defending the woman he loved."

But his words sent rage burning through her. Rage that served to banish the panic that was also rising. The panic that whispered that the blame for Tom's death rested on her shoulders.

"This is your doing," Lirianna said. Her voice sounded ugly and unrecognizable, but she didn't care. Her eyes burned into the faerie king. "It's your fault Tom's dead. It's your fault that Alyen and Aaron are miserable. It's your fault that the Trianid is broken. And if you hadn't convinced me to use my magic to manipulate Destiny—to *trick* Alyen and Aaron into reuniting just to assuage your own guilt—Tom would still be alive."

"Wait, what?" Aaron said, his arms loosening from Lirianna as he looked up, steel edging his voice.

Alyen was looking incredulously at Faer Dinnán. "Is that true?" she demanded, already seeing on the faerie king's face that it was so. "How could you do that to us? To Lirianna?"

Aaron was standing now, and Faer Dinnán had risen as well. Jaw clenched in anger, Aaron drew his dagger. "Explain yourself," he said, his voice low and dangerous.

Faer Dinnán's gaze traveled over the Trianid, his face unreadable under the seething glares of the three before him. When he spoke, his voice was soft—and surprisingly vulnerable.

"It is true," he said, a helpless shrug falling from his shoulders like quiet snow. "It was my actions that led to all of this. Ever since Ylvain's magic poisoned me, I have either been fighting against the spread of her darkness within, or else trying to fix the damage I have done despite my efforts. Yet I find that every attempt to right what I have wronged has only made things worse. You told me, Lirianna, that I sounded almost human, and if that is true, then I find myself wondering how it is that humans can bear the chaos of their reality when the Balance within you, beautiful though it is, is also so very fragile."

Faer Dinnán paused, and for a moment, no one spoke. Then he turned his gaze on Lirianna, a plea standing in his fathomless eyes. "Seer of Strands," he said, his voice quiet. "Will you play for us?"

Lirianna looked at him blankly. "Play?" Her eyes flicked to the instrument standing next to the sarcophagus. "You mean the harp?"

"Yes," Faer Dinnán confirmed, his eyes beseeching. "I believe it is for this moment that you were brought to this place."

Lirianna's face twisted with disbelief. "You can't be serious. How—why would I want to play now? *Here?* After Tom …" Her throat choked on the words.

"Please, Lirianna," Faer Dinnán almost whispered. "Breathe deeply. Find your heart. And you will enchant us *all.*"

For a moment their eyes met, and suddenly Lirianna understood.

This journey wasn't—had never been—about reuniting Alyen and Aaron, at least not entirely. It wasn't even about the way the magic had faltered within the Trianid. This was about how the Trianid's trust in Faer Dinnán had been severed. The faerie king had felt it, had known that he'd lost his connection with the defenders of Dúramair's Balance, but he didn't know how to fix it on his own.

And somehow, he thought that Lirianna was the key.

Lirianna felt as if the pieces of some great puzzle were

falling into place in her mind, her understanding of the world and her place in it shifting as swiftly as if she were standing on a dune of dry sand. And yet, she also felt something else: a grounding taking hold within her like the roots of some great tree. Her mind stilled, and a certainty came over her, easing the storm that had threatened to consume.

Her eyes turned to the harp.

Feeling somehow both distant and keenly focused, Lirianna rose from Tom's side and moved toward the harp.

"Lirianna, you don't have to do this …" Aaron began.

"It's all right," she replied calmly, and something in her expression stopped her friends from protesting further.

The harp of Andair the Bard stood as if in waiting, a legend in itself, its curves of dark wood gleaming in the lamplight. There was a small stool behind it, and Lirianna lowered onto it, pulling the harp back to her shoulder. Her fingers rose to strings taught with anticipation, the song she knew she must play already rising to her hands. It was the one that had been coming to her more and more insistently over the course of her journey, the one that pushed at her fingertips, aching for the magic that would complete it. Only now, Lirianna understood how that magic was meant to work, and what the music that had been straining within her was meant to do.

It was time.

Fingers settling into position, Lirianna closed her eyes, and let herself sink into the world of the Balance. Her hands moved, testing the strings, allowing the ringing of the instrument to guide her deeper into the space between. In her mind's eye, the tapestry of the Balance bloomed before her vision.

As always, it was beautiful, shimmering strands weaving

together in a joyful pattern of color and magic. But it was not joy or harmony that she sought, and quickly her eyes found what she knew they would: holes in the pattern where strands had broken, their frayed edges floating loose as if longing for the parts that had ripped away.

There was Alyen's strand, shimmering green, and there was Aaron's, a vibrant gold. And there, in the place where the two should have intertwined, a hole where the magic of the tapestry dripped slowly away like blood from a wound.

She found Faer Dinnán's thread, strong and iridescent, flashing all the colors of the rainbow, sun, and storm. Yet, in the places where it should have woven together with Alyen's and Aaron's, the broken strands shrank from each other as the magic seeped away.

And there was one more strand. One that shimmered with the blue of Monstar and the Eastern Sea. It was her own strand, also broken from Faer Dinnán's, and fraying in the places she connected to the rest of the Trianid—damage inflicted by the secrets she'd kept and the way her magic had been used to control their fates. She saw how her strand, shining and beautiful, hung limp with loneliness, guilt—and grief for a strand that no longer wove through the tapestry at all.

Lirianna's heart swelled, filling with not only her own sorrow, but that of the other tattered strands as well, mixing with the music that ached to be free. Then, holding it all within a moment longer, she let the gathered magic flow, unreserved and uninhibited, into her fingers.

Lirianna played, her hands moving to a shape they somehow knew without being taught. As she played, she gathered the frayed and leaking strands to her and poured her music into them, letting the notes that carried her magic fuse the fibers back together, ever so gently, bit by bit. She played with the same intensity of desire that she had when she'd woven the magic that unshod Brother Hugh's horse, or saved her brother from an enraged bull, or set in motion the chain of events that had led them all to this small, island tomb. But this time, she wove her magic, not to alter or control Destiny, but to heal the broken places so that Destiny could weave its own magic unencumbered.

Her song had no words, yet the music spoke. It spoke of fate and choice, of love and heartbreak. It spoke of how joy and pain often shelter under the same roof, how so often they appear as two faces to the same coin. How maybe not all stories did end well, but that it was the middles that mattered: the small, quiet moments of laughter and tears shared with those who walked at your side. How each person was a beautiful chaos of storm and fire. That to stand near a fire meant to risk being burned, but that it was worth it for the chance to feel the warmth of its glow. How, in the end, every being was part of nature's dance—wild and brutal, but always beautiful. And it spoke of how no one escapes the accidental scattering of their own shadow, but that even in the deepest darkness, we hold within the greatest light.

In the years to come, Lirianna would never remember what, exactly, she played in that small island cavern. She remembered only that she eventually realized that the song was ending, that the tapestry stood once again whole before her, that her eyes were opening as her radiant hands stilled, and that the faces of all who stood in the tomb were wet with healing tears.

A FAERIE'S DEBT

Silence filled the cavern when Lirianna's music ended. Alyen, Aaron, and Faer Dinnán still stood around Tom's fallen body, but the hum of contention had dissipated from the air, Aaron's dagger resting once more in its sheath. Nah'dar, nearly forgotten, stood by the door, a silent guardian against the lengthening shadows beyond.

Aaron was the first to speak, his palms pressing the wetness away from his cheeks. "Lirianna … what did you just do?"

Lirianna let the harp rock back to the floor, away from her shoulder. Her hands were dimming now, though the faint glow of magic could still be seen winding around her fingers. "I used my magic—my full magic—to mend the bonds between us all."

"You made us magically forgive each other?" Alyen's brow wrinkled in uncertainty.

"No," Lirianna said, feeling a faint pang of guilt for her

past magical deeds. "I just mended the holes our strands made in the Balance so that we can decide how to move forward from a place of wholeness instead of pain."

"I thought the fireflies were the ones who mended tears in the Balance," Aaron commented, one hand absently massaging the place above his heart.

"Fireflies do mend the Balance, yes," Faer Dinnán confirmed, "from tears caused by misdeeds. But there are many ways in which the Balance can be compromised. When the bonds between people have been damaged, or when hearts have been broken, or hope lost—that calls for a different kind of healing. One, it seems, only the Seer's magic can provide."

Faer Dinnán drew himself up taller, looking for the first time in a long time like the faerie monarch Lirianna remembered. He regarded the Trianid, his face open and serious, holding no hint of guile. "Keeper of Scales, Slayer of Monsters, and Seer of Strands," he said. "I have caused great pain to each of you, and I find I must atone. Will you allow me an attempt to make amends?"

The three members of the Trianid glanced at each other, then nodded their consent. A flash of relief crossed the faerie king's face, then he turned his attention to the Second Slayer. "Aaron, will you step forward?"

If wariness flickered over Aaron's features, it was only for a moment, then he stepped in front of the faerie king. There was a sudden flash of steel, and Faer Dinnán extended his hands to offer the Slayer a gleaming sword. A familiar sword, bearing a ruby of dragon's blood in its hilt.

"Scala," Aaron breathed. He looked up at the faerie king. "But it was lost with Malscath."

"Anything the earth holds is within my reach," Faer Dinnán said. "It is rightly wielded by the Second Slayer of Dúramair, protector of the kingdom and the Trianid." The faerie king's voice dropped with regret. "I should not have altered your memory, and should not have asked Alyen to assent to it. I offer you my deepest apologies, Slayer, and if you would claim Scala once more, it is yours to take."

Aaron's gaze traveled over the blade, then he drew in a breath and released it. One hand reached out and grasped the hilt of the legendary sword imbued with dragon magic. His eyes met the faerie king's. "I accept your apology and your gift," he said. He extended his other arm, and Faer Dinnán grasped it, gratitude rising in his eyes.

Their hands unclasped, and Aaron moved aside.

"Alyen," Faer Dinnán said, and she stepped toward him. "I make the same apology to you as to Aaron. The things I asked of you were unwarranted and unfair, yet always you strove to make the decision that would be best for your kingdom and your people, at great cost to yourself and the person you loved.

"But I have also witnessed how you work with the Slayer when not compromised by my demands. You have shown me what true partnership should look like, and I find that in my partnership with Dúramair's Keepers, there has been an imbalance. Keeper of Scales, may I see your hand?"

Alyen's face was curious as she extended one hand to the faerie king. For a moment he held it, his fingers brushing over the place on her wrist that bore his leaf-shaped mark. Gently, he placed her hand over the same spot on his own wrist, and for a moment, his skin glowed under her palm. Then the glow faded, and Alyen's hand lifted away, revealing a new mark on Faer Dinnán's skin in the shape of a pestle and mortar.

"From this day forward, I shall bear your mark as you have born mine. You may use it to call upon me at your will, and I vow always to answer your summons. These marks shall stand as symbols of the equal partnership between the human and faerie realms, a tradition that will extend to every Keeper of Scales henceforth. I hope that this gesture will earn me your forgiveness, if not today, then one day to come."

Alyen's expression softened, and she stepped forward to embrace the faerie king. Faer Dinnán's eyes widened a moment, his hands tentative as they rested on her back. Then Alyen pulled away, and went to stand with Aaron, both their gazes turning to the third member of the Trianid.

"Lirianna," Faer Dinnán said. "Your magic is wondrous—a beautiful gift from Béathan. If there is any part of this ordeal of which I am glad, it's that it has led you to find your true power. However, I should not have placed pressure upon you to use it for my own purposes, especially not before you understood its full nature or how to wield it. You have correctly remembered that I am in your debt—three times now, to my count. Whatever wish you name, I will grant if it is in my power to do so."

Lirianna heard the words that came like something out of a faerie story. Who in their wildest dreams would ever expect to be granted a wish—any wish—from the faerie king himself? Yet, all Lirianna could feel was the sorrow rising once more to her throat. "All I want is for Tom to come back," she said. "And you can't give me that."

Faer Dinnán looked down for a moment, his expression troubled. Then he raised his eyes again to Lirianna's grief-stricken face. "It's true. I cannot return Tom to you. But perhaps I can do something else, something to honor his life and his passing?"

Lirianna's eyes were on Tom's body, sadness etching deep lines in her face. She seemed to come to a decision, and turned her gaze on the faerie king, her chin lifting a fraction. "Yes. I want Tom to be remembered—throughout Dúramair and throughout history. I want the world to remember him as he truly was, and I want you to promise me that he will never be named a traitor like Andair the Bard. I want you to ensure that the truth of his story lives on and that his memory is one of dignity and heroism. That is my wish."

Lirianna's eyes held fast to the faerie king's, and Faer Dinnán nodded. "In that case, Seer of Strands, let us move Tom to his resting place. His ending may not have been happy, but we will ensure that it is noble."

It was a solemn procession that left the island cavern. Faer Dinnán led the way, followed by Aaron and Nah'dar, who carried Tom's body between them. Alyen and Lirianna followed behind, Lirianna supported by her friend's arm around her waist. She felt odd—light and somewhat removed, yet also desperately heavy. She would have to sort it out later. Now it was time to honor Tom.

Faer Dinnán led them away from the cliffs and down a winding path through the inland swells of hills that emerged at last on a bluff that overlooked the sea. The sun was dipping low on the horizon, casting the cliffs in a ruddy glow and turning the long, dry grasses on the bluff to a shimmering carpet of gold. Faer Dinnán stopped, and Aaron and Nah'dar lowered Tom's body gently to the ground. The faerie king looked to Lirianna, his fathomless features unreadable.

"Would you care to say anything, Seer, before I proceed?"

Lirianna's brow furrowed as she looked at her friend's body on the ground. The sun was glinting off the pirate ring still hanging from his ear, and it sent a sudden surge of anger searing through her veins. Whatever Faer Dinnán was going to do, he wouldn't do it with Tom still bearing the mark of Captain Voros. Lirianna knelt down and removed the ring, balling it in her fist, then rose and strode a few paces toward the edge of the bluff. She reached backward and hurled the ring toward the sea, barely registering the shout of rage that issued from her mouth as the bit of metal left her hand. It arched through the air and flashed once, red in the light of the setting sun, then disappeared into the waves.

Lirianna returned to Tom's side, her breath coming heavy with rage and grief. She still didn't like how he looked, lying there as if he'd been left carelessly without even a cloak or a blanket to cover him. He should have something, but it was summer, and no one was wearing extra layers.

"Aaron," she said, her eyes still on Tom. "May I borrow your dagger?"

Wordlessly, Aaron handed Lirianna one of his daggers. Her fingers closed tightly around its hilt as her other hand grasped at her skirts. "Help me, Alyen?" she said, and Alyen knelt down to hold out the bottom of Lirianna's dress.

Lirianna placed the point of the dagger on her skirt, as high up as she dared, and pushed it into the finely woven threads. The blade bit through the fabric, and Lirianna continued to saw at it until the front of her dress was completely detached. When she'd reached as much as she could, Lirianna handed Alyen the dagger, and her friend continued in similar fashion around the back of her dress until the entire skirt fell away, leaving Lirianna's legs bare, the tattered remains of her dress fluttering around her thighs. The time it had taken to hack apart her dress had allowed her blood to cool, and without her anger keeping it at bay, she knew her grief would soon consume her. She took the severed skirt and knelt next to Tom. Gently, she tucked it around him, pleased to find his pipe still nestled in his pocket. Now, whatever Faer Dinnán was going to do—wherever Tom was going to go—his music and a part of her would go there with him.

Lirianna straightened and, finding herself unable to meet anyone's eyes, kept her gaze down on her friend's still form instead. She cleared her throat, praying that she could say what she must without succumbing to the sob that pushed at her throat.

"Tom of Tiragel was a gifted piper and the truest of friends. He had the makings of a great bard, but his deepest love was for the people he held close. He showed me kindness and friendship when few others would, and he would have given anything to ensure his loved ones were safe and happy. In the end, he gave his life ensuring just that.

"Tom had beautiful dreams. He dreamt of having a life filled with music and family and love. He deserved to have that, but ..." Lirianna's voice quivered and trailed off, and she paused, struggling for control. When she thought she could speak again, she took a shaking breath and continued.

"It would be all too easy for Tom to be remembered as a pirate and a traitor, but that's not who he was, and it's not the legacy he deserves. He should be remembered as he truly was:

loyal and brave, with a generous heart, and a beautiful song. He should be remembered with joy, and his death should be seen not as a tragic ending, but the beginning of something new and wondrous."

With these last words, she looked to Faer Dinnán, her leveled gaze demanding that he make her words a reality. The faerie king inclined his head, then he closed his eyes and lifted his face to the golden rays of the setting sun.

For a moment, all was still but for the sea breeze lifting the strands of hair away from Faer Dinnán's upturned face. Then, the faerie king lifted his hands, hovering them gently in the air above Tom's resting place. The world seemed to hold its breath for a heartbeat, then two.

Then Tom began to glow.

Lirianna felt her eyes widen as her friend's form shimmered, diamonds of sunlight radiating from every inch of his body. The glow intensified until Lirianna had to shield her eyes from its blaze, then suddenly it was changing. The light shifted, a column of dazzling brilliance rising up from the ground where Tom lay. It stretched upward, then branched out, sending shafts of light twining in all directions while below, the soil churned beneath their feet. The limbs of light continued to intertwine until they formed a canopy of woven sunlight above them, then suddenly the web seemed to explode, and a shower of sparks rained down around them, the droplets of sun-fire warm where they grazed their skin. The light dimmed, and Lirianna gazed at the thing that had taken the place of Tom's body.

It was a tree. But it wasn't like any tree Lirianna had seen before. A strong trunk rose from the golden grass, its bark a deep, rich brown. Yet, where the light of the setting sun hit it, she could see it was infused with a sheen of blue—the color of her dress, and the skirt she'd wrapped around Tom.

Her eyes trailed upward to the canopy of leaves and she saw that they, too, were unique. Each leaf curled around itself, spiraling downward from its branch. It seemed an odd choice, and she almost opened her mouth to ask about it—but then a breeze blew in from the sea, and she understood. As the air moved through the spiraling foliage, the tree began to sing, each leaf a different note, like so many pipes ringing in harmony to the tune of the wind. The sound was beautiful—gentle and soothing—and Lirianna instantly felt the ache in her heart ease. She looked to Faer Dinnán, tears standing in her eyes, lost for words.

The faerie king studied Lirianna, uncertainty and hope rippling across his face. "This tree," he said, "shall serve as a symbol for everything Tom stood for. It will lend its music freely to any who seek it out, and all who hear its tones will find comfort and contentment so long as they remain beneath its boughs. I thought it a fitting tribute to a loyal friend with the heart of a true bard."

Lirianna swallowed against the dryness in her throat and reached out a trembling hand to rest on the rough bark of the trunk. She could feel the life running through the wood, its pulse like a heartbeat, steady and strong.

Faer Dinnán spoke again, his voice almost tentative. "It is a new tree, the naming of which rightfully belongs to you, Seer."

Lirianna closed her eyes, letting the music of the leaves wash over her. After a moment, she opened them. "Piper's Song," she said. "It will be named Piper's Song. But who will ever see it? One tree on an island nearly impossible to reach …"

"Ah, but it's not simply one tree," Faer Dinnán said, and Lirianna thought she could detect a trace of pride in the faerie king's tone. "In honor of Tom's sacrifice, Piper's Song will spring up in Dúramair wherever an act of true selflessness has occurred. In this way, Tom of Tiragel will be known by his ballad, and remembered by his tree."

A line appeared between Lirianna's brows, and she turned her head to the faerie king. "His ballad?"

The shadow of a smile crossed Faer Dinnán's face. "Who better to set his legend to music than the harper he loved?"

The words were meant kindly, but Lirianna felt them like a knife in her heart. She was no bard, and the suggestion only served to remind her of her failure to the Trianid and her role in Tom's death. She turned back to the tree and felt the comfort of its sheltering arms wash over her once more. Her eyes found Faer Dinnán's. "Thank you," she said sincerely. "It's perfect."

Faer Dinnán's face flashed relief, then understanding. "Come," he said to the others. "Let us tend to the tomb and allow the Seer some time alone with Tom."

Lirianna saw the hesitation in Alyen's eyes, but she nodded her reassurance, feeling suddenly that solitude was exactly what she wanted. Alyen whispered a few words in the singing speech, and a trio of tiny lights ignited in the air before them.

"Salamandars," Alyen said. "For when the sun sets."

Lirianna gave her a small grateful smile, then her four companions turned and made their way back down to the shore.

Lirianna sank onto the roots of the Piper's Song and

wrapped her arms around its trunk, her cheek pressed against the warm bark. "Oh, Tom," she whispered. "I'm sorry. I'm so sorry."

The sky blazed with orange and gold, the sun sinking toward the beckoning sea, as Tom's tree sang, and Lirianna's tears traced rivulets down its trunk.

26

SECRETS SPOKEN

The bodies of Captain Voros and Brutin were unceremoniously removed from the tomb, and Faer Dinnán arranged for them to be swallowed by the sands, unmourned, in unmarked graves. The tomb itself was cleansed of the blood, and Nah'dar, Aaron, and Alyen lifted the stone slab back over the entrance, sealing it once more against weather and intruders alike. By the time they had finished, the sun had set and dusk had fallen, though the sky still glowed with the last vestiges of sunset.

And still, Lirianna had not returned from the bluff.

"We should go talk to her," Aaron said, worry in his voice. "It's not like her to shut herself off like this."

Alyen nodded, her brow furrowed. "It's not just today, either. Something's been bothering her for a while now—ever since we were on the road to Illya. Like she's been hiding something. Did you notice?"

"No," Aaron admitted. "I've been so caught up in … everything else. I always thought of her as the solid one."

Alyen shook her head. "Me too. But I shouldn't have let it go so long. I tried to ask about it once or twice, but she always brushed me off. I should have insisted."

Aaron's hand reached out to rest on her arm. "Don't be too hard on yourself. We're here for her now; let's go talk to her."

They retraced their steps back to Tom's resting place, this time led by a glowing contingent of salamandars. When they reached the top of the bluff, they found Lirianna resting against the trunk of the Piper's Song, staring out at the sea with eyes that seemed to gaze at something from a different place in a different time. Wordlessly, Alyen and Aaron lowered themselves to the ground beside her, one on each side, and for a time the three sat in silence, watching the last of the color fade into the darkness of the night sky.

When it became clear that Lirianna wasn't going to say anything, Alyen decided to break the silence. "Lirianna? How are you feeling?"

Lirianna didn't look at her friend, but her brows drew together for a moment at the question. "I …" One of her shoulders gave a small shrug, and she fell silent once more.

"We're a little worried about you," Alyen said gently.

Lirianna nodded slowly. "I know," she said, and Alyen was confused by the flash of fear she saw in her friend's eyes.

"You know you can talk to us, right?" Aaron added. "About … anything, really. We just want to help."

Lirianna's lip trembled, but still, she said nothing.

Alyen decided to be more direct. "How long have you known about your magic?" she asked, and this time, she was rewarded by a hasty glance that held guilt and, once again, a flash of fear.

"I didn't really understand it until today," Lirianna said, her voice almost a whisper. "But it started in the spring when everything was happening with Illya and the darklings, and— and with you two ..." Suddenly Lirianna's face crumpled and she buried it in her hands, shoulders shaking with sobs. "I'm sorry. I used it so many times before I knew what I was doing. And it did things, things I didn't know it would do, and it all started out as an accident, but then Faer Dinnán wanted me to use it on purpose, and I did. I used it to change Destiny. To make things happen the way *I* wanted them to. I've broken Purity of Sight so many times ... I shouldn't even be allowed to be the Seer anymore. And that's not even the worst of it."

Lirianna paused until Aaron ventured to ask the obvious. "What's the worst of it?"

"The worst of it," Lirianna whispered, hands still covering her face, "is that I don't even know if I want to be the Seer anymore."

There was a stunned silence after these words, and Alyen and Aaron exchanged an alarmed glance.

"You don't know if you want to be in the Trianid anymore?" Alyen asked tentatively, trying to ignore the stab of panic the words sent through her stomach. "Have you been unhappy at Monstar?"

Lirianna raised her wet face to the sea again, wiping away the strands of hair that stuck to her cheeks. She shook her head. "Not exactly. I love Monstar, and I love the weaving—or at least I thought I did. But it's not easy being the only one always left behind, never getting to do anything or go anywhere or fix anything. And then this magic appeared.

Magic that let me feel like I could actually do something more than just warn people. Magic that made me feel powerful and in control again. I tried not to use it. I tried to ignore it, really I did ..." Lirianna looked to her friends, her eyes beseeching them to believe her. "But it just got stronger. And then I went to Tiragel and remembered the life I left and how much I loved music. I didn't realize how much I missed it, and then Tom ..." Her voice faltered at Tom's name, and her tears started to flow anew.

Alyen put her arm around Lirianna. "Faer Dinnán said he died defending the woman he loved. Did you love him, too? Are you wishing you'd stayed with him?"

Lirianna shook her head. "No," she said, her voice thick. "I never loved him like he loved me. It's awful, but it's true. I didn't even know how he felt until a few days ago. I never dreamed of a future with marriage and children and all the rest. Not like the others did. And when Mother Brenwyn came to Tiragel and found me ... it just felt right. It seemed like such a good fit. But I've ruined it all. Tom's dead because of me, and I couldn't even return his love. I've betrayed the Trianid. I've betrayed you both. And when I think of going back to how it was ... I just don't think I can, and I'm sorry!"

Aaron seemed at a loss for words, and Alyen waited until the fresh wave of tears was ebbing before she spoke. "I wish you'd told us about all this sooner, Lirianna. I could have helped you so much more."

"How could you possibly have helped?" Lirianna choked out, meeting her friend's eyes.

Alyen looked at her frankly. "Lirianna. Of all the people in the world who might understand what it's like to have new, confusing, powerful magic that has unintended, sometimes terrible consequences that make you feel like you've failed in your life's purpose and destroyed any hope of redemption … don't you think I'm the one who would understand that the most?"

Lirianna stilled as the words sank in. She held Alyen's gaze, her expression unreadable, but for a moment, something like hope flashed in her eyes, and Alyen thought she could see the lines of her friend's shoulders ease, if only a fraction.

"I've broken the Keeper's law, too," Alyen continued, encouraged to see her words finding their mark. "And it takes a lot of time and a lot of work to heal from that. I know. But I'm still here. I'm still trying. I still belong. And I think you do, too."

Aaron reached out to grasp one of Lirianna's hands in his. "Alyen's right," he said. "You're the Seer of Strands—not just because it's what you chose or what you do, but because it's who you are. The Trianid doesn't need just the part of you that fits the mold of all the Seers that came before you. It needs you. All of you. The real you. It needs your magic, however it comes and however it works. What you did tonight …" He broke off a moment and looked at Alyen, and her breath caught as she realized it was the first time in months she'd seen his eyes free of pain or anger or sorrow as they met hers. "It was incredible," he continued. "A true gift. The people of Dúramair need healing right now, and not in a way Alyen or I or anyone else can provide. They need their Seer. They need your music. They need *you*."

"Then," Lirianna said, her voice quivering, "you're not angry with me?"

Alyen pulled back, incredulous. "Angry? How could we be angry? You're allowed to be happy, Lirianna, and what Aaron says is true. Personally, I don't see why you can't be the Seer and a harper at the same time. In fact, with your magic, I think it's necessary. No one said you had to weave all day every day, did they?"

Lirianna managed half a smile. "I suppose not."

Aaron gave Lirianna a playful nudge with his shoulder. "You know, you're not the only one who doesn't want the Trianid to be the only thing in their life. I have something I love, something important to me, that has nothing to do with being the Slayer."

"What's that?" Alyen asked, curious.

"Quivers," Aaron replied, his face completely serious.

Lirianna snorted.

Alyen raised one brow. "Quivers? The tavern game?"

"Yes," Aaron said, his expression confused as the girls giggled.

"Aaron, be serious," Alyen chuckled. "Lirianna is really upset."

"I am serious!" Aaron protested. "I love playing quivers, and I'm extremely good at it. When I'm traveling around, I look forward all day to evening when I can go back to the inn and spend the night playing a few rounds. And if I'm being honest, sometimes I've taken a day here or there just to rest at the inn, talking with the innkeeper and the guests and practicing quivers. It makes me happy."

Both girls were laughing outright now, and Aaron looked indignant, save for the sparkle in his eye. "The point is," he said, more seriously, "we can't uphold the Balance if we don't maintain it in ourselves first. Like Alyen said, we deserve to be happy, too." He caught Alyen's eye again, and she saw from his gaze that there was another important conversation she was going to have that night.

Lirianna let out a shuddering sigh, and Alyen was relieved to see something like peace settle on her friend's features. The Seer pulled her friends into a three-way embrace, her head resting on Alyen's shoulder and Aaron's arms around them. "Thank you," she said. "I love you both."

It was full dark now, and the salamandars cast an orange glow over the Trianid as a full moon rose to mingle with the stars over the sea. After a few moments, Aaron and Alyen pulled back from Lirianna. "Are you ready to go yet?" Aaron asked. "We should probably be getting back to the ships if we don't want to spend the night on the sand."

"You two go ahead," Lirianna said, then smiled reassuringly when she saw Alyen's brow constrict. "I won't be long. I just want a few minutes alone to say goodbye to Tom."

"Of course," Alyen said, giving Lirianna's arm a squeeze. "I'll ask some of the salamandars to stay with you. We'll meet you back on the shore."

Then Alyen and Aaron rose and quietly left the bluff, leaving Lirianna to her small circle of salamandar light and the soft harmonies of the Piper's Song.

They were silent for the short journey back to the beach. The land sloped gently downward, and it wasn't long before the earth beneath Alyen's feet loosened back to shifting sand. When they both stood once more on the shore, Alyen felt Aaron's hand slip into hers, halting her in her steps. Gently, he turned her around to face him.

"I think we should talk as well," he said, and the look on his face in the salamandars' glow took Alyen's breath away.

She nodded, collecting her thoughts. "We probably should. I—"

"Do you mind if I start?" Aaron cut her off. "Sorry, but there's something I really need to say, and I want to get it right."

"All right," Alyen said, surprised at his insistence. She looked into his face expectantly, but was further surprised when, instead of speaking, he reached for her other hand. He took both her palms and rested them against the warmth of his chest, and Alyen felt the drum of his heartbeat pulse beneath her fingers. Her eyes closed for a moment as she remembered lying against that steady beat in the Keeper's cottage, the way it had lulled her to sleep, the way it had grounded her in Illya when she was melded to the darklings, the way it had comforted her in the darkness and brought joy to her days. She opened her eyes once more and felt tears prick at their corners, though not a word had yet been spoken.

"Alyen," Aaron began. "You told me on the *Desert Star* that you didn't know if I had ever really loved you—the real you. And you were right about a lot of it. It's true that I was angry with your choices. It's true that I didn't accept your priorities. And it's true that if I really knew you, I shouldn't have expected you to act any differently. But you were wrong about one thing. You were wrong that I never loved you."

Alyen swallowed as Aaron reached out a hand to the side of her face, his fingers brushing back the strands of hair that hung loose there, just as he'd done in the tunnel at Monstar.

"I love everything about you, Alyen," his voice came almost as a whisper. "I love how much you love your kingdom and your people. I love the way you fight for their happiness. I love that you have the heart of a ruler and the soul of a healer. I love that you're brave even when you're scared, and that you never shy away from hard choices or impossible tasks. I love that even in your darkest moments, you always find a way back out, and instead of trying to escape your pain, you use it to help others find their own healing."

Alyen was crying in earnest now, but Aaron wasn't finished. "I love your magic, I love your memories, I love the way you laugh and the way you cry. I love the way you snore when you sleep."

Alyen's eyes flew wide. "I do *not*—"

"You do, and it's adorable. But anyway ..." Aaron's voice trailed off, and in the light of the salamandars' glow, Alyen saw that his eyes also glistened with unshed tears. "It's not just an idea I love. It's you. And I don't think it's better for us to be alone. We've tried that these past few months, and I can honestly say they were some of the most miserable months of my life. I want us back together, even if we can't see exactly how it will all work out, and even if it means we'll get hurt again. Because it's worth it. You're worth it."

Alyen bit her lip, aching to say yes, but knowing that there were other words she needed to say first. "Aaron, I want to be with you too, but there's a lot I can't promise you. I can't promise that you won't get hurt again. I can't promise that there won't be a time when I have to make sacrifices for the kingdom again. I can't promise that I'll always be able to put us first. But I *can* promise you that I'll never keep secrets again. I'll never betray you again. And I'll never lie to you again."

"And I promise *you* that I'll never force you to make the hard choices on your own again. I'll never leave you again,"

Aaron said. "Whatever comes, and whatever we do, we do together."

Alyen grasped onto Aaron's hands and nodded, a smile pushing through her tears that Aaron slowly mirrored. "All right," she said. "Let's try again."

"Are you sure?" he asked, as if he couldn't quite believe it. "You're truly certain?"

In response, Alyen reached her hands around his neck and pulled his mouth down to hers.

In a second, Aaron's hands were on her back, pressing her against him, as he returned her kiss with lips that tasted of salt and sunlight. Alyen felt as though she were gulping water after days in the desert, and if the way Aaron's fingers knotted themselves into her hair as if he never meant to stop was any indication, she knew he felt the same.

27

NEW BEGINNINGS

Lanterns were glowing on the deck of the *Desert Star* when the shallop returned, glints of orange reflecting off the inky waters around them. Alyen heard Jah'-dara's voice shout a command, followed by the muffled clatter of a rope ladder being thrown against the side of the ship for them to ascend.

Jah'dara was waiting for them on deck, the silver of her tattoos gleaming in the lantern light. Alyen and Aaron had told Lirianna who Jah'dara was, and warned that Nah'dar's twin could be intimidating. Nevertheless, Lirianna still felt herself fighting the urge to squirm as the *Desert Star*'s captain swept her gaze over them, her eyes homing in on Lirianna.

"You have been successful, it seems," Jah'dara observed. "And the pirates?"

"The captain and his first mate perished," Nah'dar reported.

Jah'dara's gaze moved to Alyen. "And his ship?"

"Waiting in the cove, and yours as promised," Alyen confirmed.

Jah'dara's expression didn't change, but Alyen thought she saw a flare of triumph in her eyes. She looked to Lirianna. "Seer. You have spent time on their ship. Do you know its name?"

"It's the *Belladonna*," Lirianna said. "They called it the *Red Falcon* when they want to pose as a trading ship, but its real name is the *Belladonna*."

"And its crew?" Jah'dara asked. "Are they loyal to their captain? Should I expect opposition if I claim the ship?"

Lirianna frowned and shook her head, remembering the fleeting hints of thoughts and emotions she'd gleaned from the crew when they'd played together the night Tom was lashed. "I don't think so. The only one truly loyal was Brutin, and he's dead. The rest are all bards, and prisoners at that. Some of them have learned to love the sea, but I think most just want to go home."

A look of satisfaction crossed Jah'dara's face, and she shouted out an order to her crew who scurried to ready the ship to sail.

"In that case, we shall not delay in delivering the good news," she said.

The *Desert Star* slid over the black water, silent but for the splashes of the oars hitting the waves. As soon as they rounded the corner of the island, they saw the *Belladonna*, anchored in the cove and illuminated by its own lamps. As they drew alongside it, Alyen saw the crew of the *Belladonna* lined up along the deck rail, their faces registering a mix of wariness, fear, and tentative hope.

At a command from Jah'dara, the anchor was lowered and

the captain of the *Desert Star* stood at the rail to address the crew of the *Belladonna*. "Permission to board?" she called over the narrow span of water between the ships.

The pirate crew glanced nervously at each other, then one spoke up. "Where is our captain and our fellow crew members?"

Lirianna stepped forward before Jah'dara could answer. "There was no treasure to be found on the island. Captain Voros and Brutin were killed. And Tom—" Her voice hitched, but she steadied herself. "We lost Tom as well."

At these last words, there was a stirring amongst the crew, and a few bowed their heads. Several turned to fetch a gang-plank, while others threw ropes over to the *Desert Star* to aid in securing the ships together.

Jah'dara crossed over to the *Belladonna* first, her steps on the gangplank that straddled the water between her ships steady and confident. Alyen went next, followed by Aaron and Lirianna, and finally Nah'dar. Jah'dara waited until they had all safely crossed before addressing the pirate crew, who were once again eyeing the captain with caution. Her voice rang out over the stillness of the sea.

"I am Captain Jah'dara of the trade ship *Desert Star*. The *Belladonna* has no captain, and according to the laws of the open sea and a treaty backed by the Dúramairian crown, I claim ownership of this vessel and assume command of its crew. However, I harbor no love for piracy and have no use for a crew enslaved."

The gathered bards glanced at one another, as if unsure whether Jah'dara's words might allude to their imminent demise, and Alyen saw a few hands stray to the hilts of daggers. But Jah'dara's next words stopped them cold.

"As of this moment, you are once again free men," she said. "You may throw your earrings to the sea, and they will not be replaced. For those of you who wish to return to your previous lives, or begin anew on land, I grant you safe passage to Dúramair, where you may disembark at the first port. If, however, you wish to remain at sea, I offer you employment aboard my ships. I run an honest trade, and my terms and wages are fair. I will give you all until the turn of the morning's tide when we set sail to make your decisions. Now, are there any who oppose my claim?"

No one stepped forward, and in moments the air was filled with joyful shouts as a dozen gold rings sank to the ocean floor.

The hold of the *Belladonna* was dark, and Lirianna could see only what passed beneath the glow of her small lantern. It seemed quieter, somehow. Quieter and also lonely, as if waiting for something that would never come.

Lirianna paused as her lantern light illuminated the bars of her former prison. The cage, too, seemed smaller. Now that she was free, she'd thought that seeing it might evoke feelings of fear or anger—but that wasn't at all what arose in her mind. Instead, she stared at the floor of the cell, remembering how she and Tom had shared a meal there. Or how she'd tended his wounds on the cot. How he'd pressed her fingers to his lips when she'd offered to advocate for him with the barding guild. How his eyes had regained their spark when he thought that freedom and music were once again within his reach. Lirianna sighed, the shadows of the hold seeming suddenly heavy around her.

"Is this where they kept you?"

It was Alyen's voice behind her, soft yet horrified.

"It wasn't as bad as it looks," Lirianna said, turning to her friend. "Tom made it bearable."

Alyen's face remained unconvinced. "We were wondering where you'd gone. I didn't expect to find you down here. Are you all right?"

"I think so," Lirianna said, remembering why she'd come to the hold in the first place. "I wanted to get this." She entered the cell, and her light fell across the harp, still leaning against the hull of the ship. Lirianna picked it up and exited the cell with it cradled against her hip.

Alyen eyed the instrument, still dented and missing strings after passing the maelstrom. "It doesn't look like it's in very good shape," she observed.

"It's seen better days," Lirianna agreed. "But I need something to play, and it'll do for now."

Alyen's eyes searched hers, and Lirianna could see that her friend was still concerned, though hesitant to say it. Lirianna felt a sudden rush of fondness, and her face relaxed into a smile. "You don't need to worry about me, Alyen," she said, realizing as she spoke that the words were true. Something was changing in her—had been changing ever since she'd played in the island tomb. It wasn't done yet, but she could feel the rightness of it, and the way her power was anchoring itself in her being. "I've finally found my magic. With weaving and music together, my life is more complete than it's ever been."

Alyen returned her smile, and some of the worry drained from her face. "And you're sure it's what you really want?"

Lirianna didn't hesitate. "Absolutely. Dúramair needs new music, and I know how to write it. It was the final missing piece, and now we're the Trianid we were always meant to be."

Alyen reached out and wrapped her arms tightly around Lirianna. "You will write beautiful music. Ballads that will be played for generations to come."

Lirianna sniffed against her friend's shoulder, not bothering to fight the prick in her eyes. "I hope so," she said. "And I'll start with 'The Ballad of Tom the Bard.'"

Alyen took the lantern from Lirianna and grasped her hand. "Come," she said. "You'll find more inspiration in the starlight than you will down here."

Lirianna followed Alyen up to the deck, where they found Aaron waiting. He saw the harp in Lirianna's arm and grinned in understanding. "I take it you'll be staying up?"

Lirianna nodded. "For a little while, at least."

"We'll be nearby if you need anything," he said.

They all bid each other goodnight, and while her friends went in search of spare cots in the cabins, Lirianna found a space out of the way to sit alone with her harp.

Alyen had been right. It was soothing to sit beneath the stars and the moon as the ship gently rocked beneath her. For a moment, she closed her eyes, letting the cool sea air caress her face. She sensed her magic shift, a feeling that was joy and sorrow and purpose flooding through her limbs and into her fingertips. Without opening her eyes, she let herself sink into her magic, into the realm of the Balance, where floating strands were waiting for her to weave them in a tapestry of sound and light. The corners of her mouth lifted.

Her fingers rose to the harp strings, and she began to play.

EPILOGUE

Upon a rugged cliff on the highest peak of the Mountains of Geal, the faerie king sat, watching the sun sink, yet again, into the Western Sea.

From this spot, he could see the whole of Dúramair, and from here Faer Dinnán had watched as light and darkness ebbed and flowed in their eternal dance throughout the centuries.

His gaze fell to the cliffs far below. Lirianna's crystal blue magic was rising above the towers of Monstar, weaving together in new and intricate patterns with her music. A satisfied smile tugged at his mouth as he felt the web of the Balance growing stronger and ever more beautiful as her notes and harmonies danced throughout the tapestry of the world. The time had come for new songs and new beginnings, and Lirianna would be the one to usher in the new era.

He turned then to the trees of Sheanen Crann, knowing already what he would see. He found their magic quickly—

Alyen's deep green and Aaron's vibrant gold—shimmering strands twining together in the dusky sky above the Keeper's cottage. His fingers traced the new mark on his arm, and he felt a momentary pang of regret as he thought for the last time of a world with Alyen as the faerie queen and of the immortal life he could have offered her. Such magic as hers was wondrous and precious—enthralling even to him, who had seen so much for so long.

But no. Alyen desired a love eternal. She deserved to live with that wish fulfilled, and even the strongest faerie love would not last so long as eternity. Eventually, Faer Dinnán would find a new interest; it was his nature after all. But Aaron would love her to the end of their days, and she him. Better to leave them to their human love in their human lives, even if their forever lasted only as long as the flicker of a candle flame.

The call of an owl pulled him away from his thoughts and back to the lengthening shadows. The faerie king drew in the night air, savoring the tingle of evening magic in the gathering darkness. He stood, banishing the melancholy from his mind. Darkness would one day rise again, and a new Trianid would rise in turn to meet it. It was always so. But tonight was for laughter, for dancing, for rest, and for frolic beneath the trees with his faeries around him.

He sent his magic spinning outward, weaving throughout the web of the Balance that connected each strand to all the others. Calling his elementals to him, he melted into the fading light until all that remained on the rugged cliff was a rustling breeze that carried the hint of early autumn, and the lingering scent of forest green.

ACKNOWLEDGMENTS

In her wonderful book on creativity, *Big Magic*, Elizabeth Gilbert speaks of creative ideas as self-aware entities that present themselves to the artists they feel will best aid them in their worldly manifestation. If the artist accepts, a beautiful partnership blossoms, filled with inspiration and ultimately creation. If, however, the artist does not act swiftly enough, the idea will withdraw and seek out a new artist more immediately amenable to its cause.

I hope this is true. The concept closely aligns with how creativity has always felt to me, and it smacks of something almost magical, which I love. But if it *is* correct, that leaves me faced with one truth I cannot escape: the idea that became The Trianid is unfailingly patient.

I am a slow writer. The first hints of what would become *Keeper of Scales* came to me over two decades ago—far longer than any idea could reasonably be expected to stick around. So, as I prepare to close out this final chapter of a tale that has been my joy and my privilege to usher into the world, my first note of thanks must be to the story itself. Thank you for choosing me. Thank you for sticking with me. Thank you for allowing me to be your artist.

And now for the beautiful humans who aided me along the way.

To my husband: thank you for choosing me. Thank you for sticking with me. Thank you for being my rock, my support, and my biggest fan. You mean the world to me.

To my children: thank you for making my life full of magic. A special thanks to Elitsa for your dedicated assistance with the mapmaking. You did a fantastic job, and your work is deeply appreciated.

To my editor, Rebecca Heyman: your brilliant insights and steadfast honesty have been indispensable in making this trilogy the best it can be. Here's to many more collaborations to come!

To my proofreader, Lucia Ferrara: once again, you've kept me consistent, clear, and made sure that every sentence sparkles. I am so grateful for your detailed attention to my work.

To Damonza.com: I love each cover more than the last. Thank you for creating the finery my story dons as it ventures into the world.

To my readers: thank you so much for taking this journey with me! It means so much that you chose to spend your precious time in my story. I hope that in its pages you found what you were looking for, and that you enjoyed your stay in my world as much as I enjoyed preparing it for you.

A special thanks to my Kickstarter backers: you were the first to champion this book, and I am eternally grateful to you for it!

And to my many music teachers: thank you for showing me the joy of the musical path, and for teaching me the skills to enjoy it fully. If music isn't magic, I don't know what is, so thank you for making me a magician.

ABOUT THE AUTHOR

Anne Mollova is an author and musician living with her family in Pittsburgh, PA. Aside from writing, she loves being in nature, making music, eating chocolate, drinking tea, and creating things out of yarn and needles.

"Thank you for reading! Please consider leaving a brief review of *Seer of Strands* on the site of your choice. Even a very brief one helps to ensure I can keep writing books for you. Please accept my gratitude in advance!"
—Anne Mollova

Connect with Anne
For books and updates visit: www.annemollova.com

Subscribe to Anne's newsletter at
www.annemollova.com/newsletter
and receive a free bonus scene.

goodreads.com/Anne_Mollova
bookbub.com/authors/anne-mollova

www.ingramcontent.com/pod-product-compliance
Lightning Source LLC
Chambersburg PA
CBHW011149310726
48973CB00010B/2835